Praise for
Cheer Up, Mr. Widdicombe

"It's a comedy of Northwest manners, as if *Where'd You Go, Bernadette?* had been written after a long alcoholic weekend, an exquisite corpse cobbled together by a raucous, sophisticated group of writing instructors. . . . As the members of the Family Widdicombe spin off in their own directions, the people around them are spinning toward one another in different combinations. Their machinations are the point of this debut novel, as frothy and bitter as a pot of freshly brewed dark-roast coffee, the kind that's always available on the Widdicombes' sideboard. And the dialogue, oh how it singes and sears! . . . James is a writer to watch, one with a fresh take on American flaws and virtues that nevertheless feels old-school screwball."

—Bethanne Patrick, *Washington Post*

"James's debut novel—a comedy of manners about the banes of upper-middle-class characters—bubbles with self-realizations, love in the patois of addiction speak, incipient love that could bridge oceans and a self-help expo keynote address imploring the freeing of our inherent wildness."

—*The New York Times Book Review*

"I can't think of a writer better equipped to write a contemporary comedy of manners."

—Literary Hub

"Oh look, it's the perfect book. . . . It's LOL levels of funny, each sentence is quote-worthy, and it's also pretty heartwarming. The only bad news is that it goes by way too fast."

—*Cosmopolitan*

"*Cheer Up, Mr. Widdicombe* is rather like a P. G. Wodehouse novel, updated with sex and profanity: throw a bunch of wealthy, eccentric people in a country house for a period of time and see what happens. In this, his first novel, Evan James expertly unfolds hopes, dreams, and neuroses, managing to gently skewer his characters' foibles while revealing their humanity. . . . The book is a deliciously funny personality stew, and James deftly guides us from one character's head to another as they maneuver their way through a madcap summer—one that you, dear reader, should definitely share."

—Eileen Zimmerman Nicol, Bookreporter.com

"Funny and beautifully written, this family saga set on Bainbridge Island in the Pacific Northwest is an escape to end all escapes. There's tennis, there's novel-writing, there's the wild outdoors, and there's much-discussed decorating indoors. The Widdicombe family has much to discuss in general—they are a mass of contradictions and contrasting agendas that intersect in brilliant ways—and the dialogue is just so good. It's one of those books you hoard time with, and you float around in its atmosphere even when you're not reading it. I hate that it ended—I loved being in it so much!"

—Jean Godfrey-June,
executive beauty director at goop

"Spend a head-spinning summer with the Widdicombes and their entourage in James's gleefully over-the-top satiric debut."

—*Kirkus Reviews*

"An absurd and hilarious satire full of unlikely characters who are all wildly introspective, dysfunctional, and prone to New Age philosophizing."

—*Library Journal*

"James's debut blends saucy wit with a fresh voice. . . . The dynamic characters will satisfy many tastes, and it's with a writerly sleight-of-hand that the peculiar humor and quirky truths of family, friendship, and love are revealed."

—*Publishers Weekly*

Cheer Up, Mr. Widdicombe

Evan James

WASHINGTON
SQUARE PRESS

ATRIA

NEW YORK   LONDON   TORONTO   SYDNEY   NEW DELHI

WASHINGTON SQUARE PRESS

ATRIA

An Imprint of Simon & Schuster, Inc.
1230 Avenue of the Americas
New York, NY 10020

First Washington Square Press/Atria Paperback edition January 2020

WASHINGTON SQUARE PRESS / **ATRIA** PAPERBACK and colophon are trademarks of Simon & Schuster, Inc.

For information about special discounts for bulk purchases, please contact Simon & Schuster Special Sales at 1-866-506-1949 or business@simonandschuster.com.

The Simon & Schuster Speakers Bureau can bring authors to your live event. For more information, or to book an event, contact the Simon & Schuster Speakers Bureau at 1-866-248-3049 or visit our website at www.simonspeakers.com.

Interior design by Kyoko Watanabe

Manufactured in the United States of America

10 9 8 7 6 5 4 3 2 1

ISBN 978-1-5011-9961-5
ISBN 978-1-5011-9962-2 (pbk)
ISBN 978-1-5011-9963-9 (ebook)

PART I

G et that God-forsaken creature off the net," Frank Widdicombe called from the baseline. The tennis ball he had just tossed into the air plummeted to the green hard court, then bounced unattended as he stepped forward with a frown. He fixed upon a black-capped chickadee that sat, preening, atop the net; it looked as though it thought that slack rail of white plastic a private beach, and the court a stretch of sea on the shore of which it could take its avian leisure as it pleased. The nerve, the nerve!

Just beyond this shameless display of animal privilege, at the other end of the court, stood Bradford Dearborne, his sunned, sweaty face tense with concern. He waved his arms, hoping the winged innocent would scoot away before exciting the full brunt of Frank's wrath. Yet while we may open on this little drama as though on the brink of some meaningful, murderous turn in a tragic play, it was not the first time that Bradford had waved his arms in such a way—to no avail—only to find that the wrath in question, as much as he had feared it, amounted, in the end, to nothing very noteworthy.

The bird cocked its head to and fro. It hopped along the line of its new perch. It whistled a simple, three-note song, one that sounded to Frank like "*Hey, sweetie!*" All in all, he found that a bit too impudent for a bird intent on delaying his tennis victory.

"Shoo!" cried Bradford. "Shoo!"

"Son of a bitch," said Frank. Bradford moved to chase the bird off, but his opponent proved swifter: Frank charged ahead, his racquet raised above him like the battle-axe of some Viking berserker; the bird, suddenly hip to the barbarian siege taking place, darted over to the doubles alley with what its attacker took to be an air of outrage. Outraged in turn, Frank chopped the top of the net with his racquet repeatedly, glaring. "Get lost, freeloader!"

"Christ, Frank," said Bradford. "It's only a cute little thing." He watched the chickadee caper down the sidelines. Having popped a Klonopin that morning to quell his anxiety over playing tennis with Frank—whose flawless strokes and foot-work still crackled with the white-hot fire of the private tennis club where Bradford's father had taken lessons with the man years before—he felt a certain drowsy sympathy for this bird and crouched down on his haunches in the closest thing to an expression of solidarity he could manage. In the end, it was this loving interspecies gesture that drove the chickadee to fly from the court once and for all, the dark of it slicing through the air and into the nearby woods.

"Good work, champ," said Frank. "You killed him with kindness. Now—we ready?" He took a new ball from his pocket and bounced it, walking back to the baseline. "Forty-love." He noted Bradford's defensive position, vaguely appreciative that, even in retirement, he could still intimidate a young adversary. "Match point."

Bradford followed the drift of the ball tossed skyward, Frank's hand frozen in the motion of its release; at the ball's sus-pended peak, Frank's body, coiled and crouched like a loaded spring, launched into action—propelled from the ground, he torqued his trunk, snapped his wrist, and grunted loudly, seeming not to give a thought to any of this as he served an ace in one fluid, merciless motion.

"*Yes!*" Frank cried, pumping his fist and bounding up to the net. Bradford strolled forward to shake his hand. "Good game," said Frank. "Maybe tomorrow we can work on those lazy feet of yours."

"They're my Achilles' heel," said Bradford.

Frank stretched his arms above his head, gripping his racquet at both ends. Darkness gathered at the armpits and chest of his shirt; rivulets of sweat ran from his greying temples. "Well, you should be happy you have legs at all, Bradford," he said. "I remember this one time, courtside, I was going on and on, griping about how god-awful I had played in the first round of a club tournament, and this friend of mine, Mark, who was temporarily in a wheelchair at the time—your dad knows him; Irish guy; did you know that people in wheelchairs play tennis? It's true, they have their own league—just smiled as I stood there talking about myself, and when I was done, he looked me up and down and said, 'Well, at least you can use your legs, you whiny fucking cunt.' Can you believe that?"

Bradford rooted around in his tennis bag. "I'd be curious to see wheelchair tennis."

"It's interesting," said Frank. "You roll around. The ball can bounce twice. But listen—there's a lesson here, Bradford. Mark was trying to tell me that even when this and that isn't going well, you have to take joy in the . . . fucking . . . *little* things. Little things, you know, like legs. The basics—food, shelter, legs. You're *alive*, Bradford! That you can feel anything at all is a fucking miracle!"

"I suppose so," said Bradford. "Unless, well." He paused,

thinking to himself, "Is there no word for the opposite of a miracle?"

"Anyway, can you guess what happened then?"

Bradford said he could not. Perhaps he *could* have, but he felt that by guessing he might somehow implicate himself in the *what* that had *happened then*, which was sure to have been something altogether offensive.

"I looked at him and said, 'You know what, you asshole? You're right,' and then I started skipping and jumping off the court, hooting and hollering like a Looney Tune."

Frank laughed heartily and scratched his prim little mustache. Seeing that Bradford's mouth hung open in horror, he said, "Oh, come on. He practically *asked* me to. We had that funny kind of relationship. You know, *talking shit*. He cursed me out with a vengeance after that—words I'd never even heard before. We're still in touch. And he got me back later by introducing me to Carol."

"Well, *that's* funny," said Bradford. He finally managed to fish the translucent orange cylinder of a prescription bottle out of his bag. He shook one tablet into his palm and swallowed it with a swig of water. Now, with the mention of Carol Widdicombe, his thoughts turned to her able assistant, Michelle. "Do you think everyone's up and about by now?"

"I try not to think about things like that," said Frank. He crouched down on the concrete and kicked his legs out behind him, getting into push-up position. "Only fools think, Bradford. Wise men reflect." He lowered himself to the ground and, holding himself there, added, "And at this point, if I'm not a fucking wise man, I don't know who is!"

Bradford chuckled at this, feeling it to be in better taste, at least, than the mark anecdote. He then began the short walk back to the house, his legs—though he was glad to have them—sore and shaky from defeat.

———

Although the invigorating aroma of coffee greeted Bradford as he passed through the hall, it was with trembling hands that our would-be Casanova entered the breakfast nook of Willowbrook, the brick-red house with white trim recently purchased by Mrs. Carol Widdicombe of San Francisco. Bradford had showered, his face was shaved clean, and he was dressed in an elegant ensemble from his preferred purveyor of preppy threads, Chamberlain & Sons. His compulsive thirst for beverages with invigorating aromas presently took a backseat to the all-consuming dread he felt at having to ask his father for a large sum of money later that day. His father the coffee mogul, the coffee *king*, with all his money earned selling the very brew Bradford was about to sit down and sip. While the Klonopin worked to calm his mind like maids making the beds in a recently trashed hotel room, dread refused to budge, settling in among the mess of tennis humiliations, requests for cash, and—oh, yes!—thoughts of Michelle Briggs, object of his as-yet unrequited, heavily medicated affection.

Frank came storming by just then. He punched Bradford in the arm and shouted, "I've still got it, Dearborne! I've still got it!"

"That you do," said Bradford.

"Fuck if I'm not a wise old man." He skipped up the stairs to go shower.

Bradford sidled up to the sideboard in search of a snack to calm himself. A Danish Bodum of frothing black coffee stood next to a large ring of pastry topped with slivered almonds and stuffed with apricots, and some summer figs arranged on blue-

and-white plates. Mrs. Widdicombe herself sat across the room, perched on the edge of an Edwardian Louis Quinze–style chair that had been reupholstered in hot-pink moiré. Her slender, disheveled son, Christopher, home for the summer after a year studying abroad in Italy (a period during which he had apparently shunned Old World tourism in favor of documenting that country's fragrant garbage crisis in watercolors, and had suffered some kind of heartbreak at the hands of a "withered Albanian bellhop—ah, my Kreshnik!"), curled up on an antique sofa, meeting the lovely landscape outside the window with a heavy-lidded stare; he noticed Bradford and raised his eyebrows in silent greeting. "Heya," said Bradford, and then he smiled at Michelle, who, in her capacity as the Widdicombes' personal assistant, was far too busy scribbling her instructions for the day into an agenda to notice him. A hired hand stood on a stepladder trying to position an abstract painting created by Carol's dear friend Gracie Sloane.

Carol was addressing all those present, a flurry of talk.

"It's still crooked—look at the *sconces*, dear, and just tilt it slightly. Christopher needs to be dropped off at the library by noon. Christopher, I assume you'll be home for dinner—we're having salmon. Good morning, Bradford—you look nice. Speaking of which, stop by the auto shop and see what's taking them so long with the car—it was only a small accident. Nobody *died*, for heaven's sake."

"A part of me died," said Christopher. He covered his face with his hands. "My sense of enchantment died. What little left of it there was!"

"Disenchantment builds character," Carol snapped.

"You want me to do that? Go to the auto shop?" said Bradford, serving himself two pieces of pastry.

"No, no, Michelle can take care of it, you're just here to *relax*, Bradford, and to write your movie thing—that's perfect, you can go now—thank God that's taken care of; Gracie arrives tonight, and I had forgotten completely to hang up her wonderfully creative painting. Don't you just love gifts? Although I quite like it hanging there now, with that owl perched on that . . . totem pole, or whatever that's supposed to be. Enjoy a krangle, Bradford—Michelle made it. It's delicious. That is what you call it, right?"

Michelle waggled her pen. "Kringle. It's a Danish specialty."

"Well, great," said Carol. She paused to take a long breath through her nose. Bradford took advantage of the lull in conversation to look at Michelle as she made competent notes in her little book. Could she be writing: *2 p.m: Fall in love with fascinating houseguest?* She kept her blond and wavy hair in a simple, shoulder-length style that he liked. Presently she tucked a strand of it behind her ear, the lobe of which was tightly attached rather than free-hanging and, to Bradford, all the more alluring for its compact efficiency. She wore a summery orange dress and a necklace of gleaming, oversized amber beads. Oh, to be that heavy rope of beads, hanging sloth-like from her neck! He was a burdensome sloth, she a swan, yet somehow they would find love. The fact that he was working on a frightening screenplay went some way, he felt, toward persuading her to pay attention to him. Yes, he would one day soon touch the pale skin that seemed to radiate with a halo that might either be something sacred or a pharmaceutical side effect.

He realized that she had been speaking to him.

"Are you still with us, Bradford?"

"Oh," he said. "Sorry—having a little daydream."

"How perfectly daydreamy." Michelle smiled, a twinkle

in her eye. "You look super put-together, as usual. What's the occasion?"

"Money," said Bradford, thinking of his father. "And it won't come easy." He bit into a piece of kringle. "This is delicious. Really good."

"Thank you. A friend in Denmark gave me the recipe."

Bradford chewed and stared at her. As he turned the shadowy fragment "a friend in Denmark" this way and that in his head, he felt his jaw stiffen with jealousy.

Carol, who had evidently recovered from the strain of her earlier directorial monologue, turned to him as though recalling an urgent matter and said, "How was Frank today?"

"Good, good." Bradford shifted in his seat, reckoning with a wave of nausea. His tongue weighed heavy as he spoke, and his mouth watered. "I mean, he wouldn't let me get a single point in. He approached the net a lot." He decided not to tell them about the chickadee incident, as Carol loved birds. "He's *still got it*, as he says."

"I think she means his mood, Bradford," said Michelle.

"His 'state of mind,'" added Christopher, making air quotes. He spoke these words as though to have a mind at all constituted an ironic state of affairs.

"Oh, right," said Bradford. He swayed; his queasiness, he feared, was growing more conspicuous to the rest of them by the second. "Right. He's still got that, too."

"Yes, his mood," said Carol. She lowered her voice to a conspiratorial whisper. "You know, he's been very upset since his trip got canceled. God knows we would have been happy to get him out of *our* hair for a while."

"Mm, right," said Bradford. "France."

Carol frowned. "Yes, that's it. *France*. Only, that's *not* it, if you catch my drift." She paused to adjust the position of a John Singer Sargent book sitting on a side table—the rippled dust jacket showed a dark-haired darling tucked into a floral teacup of a chair, her gauzy dress giftwrapped at the waist by a long, pale pink bow—and then, sighing, she added, "Frank is *depressed.*"

Michelle scoffed. Her hands flew to her hips, and the bronze bangles around her wrists clinked together softly. "What? Not Frank. He can't be. He's too fit to be depressed. All that exercise! It seems, well, chemically impossible. All those *endorphins,* Carol."

Carol shook her head. "But he *is,*" she said. "I'm sure of it."

Christopher turned away from his pained windowpane reverie, adding, "Well, I can't say I blame him. This country, this empire, this era—it's hopeless." He sank deeper into his corner of the couch with a pout. "And what's worse: this island! The very thought of it . . . oh, now *I'm* depressed. This island—this island, Mother! Why? It's beautiful, yes, but—oh, God. It's like living in a Thomas Kinkade painting!" The question of the island—why?—was rhetorical. Christopher threw an arm over his forehead as though dying of a fever; he began to mutter to himself in Italian.

"Is that how they teach you to talk about your mother country at RISD?" said Carol. Christopher merely snorted and cried, "I hate all countries, Mother!"

"Well, okay," said Bradford, trying, in his drugged muddle, to reason out the mood of the elder Widdicombe. "Maybe he's a bit bummed out about his *vaycay.* They go every year, don't they? He wanted to see his friends and everything, drink wine in the country . . . you know, in the *country* and everything . . . that's understandable. I would be sad, too. So sad . . ." For a second, he wondered if he was, in fact, sad. He couldn't tell, although he was beginning to feel a bit dizzy.

"No, Bradford," said Carol. "No." His answer had failed to acknowledge what she felt to be the true gravity of the situation. She looked around the room, afraid her husband might pop up unannounced. "Not just *sad*, Bradford—Frank doesn't know it yet, but he's *clinically* depressed." She was speaking in a hush now, and she was twisting her wedding band. "I did some research, and he shows all of the signs."

"What signs?" said Michelle.

"*Psychomotor agitation*." Carol pronounced these words in triumphant staccato, as though revealing a great discovery to a panel of scientific colleagues. "And he wakes up too early. He's unpredictable and sad, and it's affecting all of us."

Before Bradford or Michelle could protest further, they heard Frank himself descending the stairs. He was whistling a merry, three-note tune somewhat similar to the call of that chickadee.

"I'm not fooled by a little cheerful whistling," Carol whispered, leaning back into her chair. "Not one bit."

Frank's birdsong stopped short as, stepping into the nook, he stubbed his toe against the leg of a tasseled ottoman. "Motherfucker!" he shouted. "God damn it. *Ow!* I'm tired of these fancy footrests—lying around all over the place! Christ!"

"Frank!" cried Carol. "Please, we have *guests*. And maybe that will teach you to walk around without house shoes or even slippers, like some feral animal."

Frank limped into the room, his owlish, salt-and-pepper eyebrows pulled together in anger. He surveyed the present company. "Guests? Michelle works for us. Hardly a day goes by she doesn't hear me say *fuck* a hundred times. Bradford did his fair share of swearing on the tennis courts this morning as I was serving his ass to him on a silver salver, and Widdicombe *fils* over there, he can't even hear me 'cause he's staring out the window and dreaming of some old dwarf in Italy."

Christopher whipped around to glare at his father. "I'd like to hear you say that to Kreshnik's face!"

"You won't be bringing that old Albanian around *here*," said Mr. Widdicombe. "You're going to marry a nice American boy."

"God, I hate Americans!" said Christopher. "I'm going to join a terrorist cell."

"I think that's just your thirst for adventure speaking," said Mrs. Widdicombe. "Why don't you marry someone with EU citizenship?"

"I'll start my own terrorism cell," said Christopher. "With my own kind of terrorism."

"Well, fuck, I'm all for entrepreneurship," said Frank, leaning over to kiss his wife on the cheek. "That's the most American idea of all!" Carol gave him an impatient look as he retreated to the breakfast spread. She had hoped that her husband's problem with foul language would disappear over time, retreating along with his hairline, but it seemed to have reemerged with a vengeance the last couple of weeks. What's more, he had started dressing down—he wore, now, a raggedy red tee-shirt and a pair of ripped jeans from the cuffs of which poked his short, bare feet. Yes, she had always loved his smooth, toylike feet, but even still, she had hoped that the influence of the young and dashing Bradford, who made up for his carefree loafing with his charm and wardrobe, might rub off on him. ("Isn't that Bradford a snappy dresser?" she sometimes hinted. "I remember when *you* used to dress that way.") Yet last week they had convinced him to wear a dinner jacket and tie for a night out at the Osprey Lounge in Seattle, and he had resembled nothing so much as a convict gussied up for an important court date. The Honorable Judge Mrs. Widdicombe had, ultimately, deemed his inability to "look right" in a suit further evidence of his failure to repent for the crime of a mounting—and very serious—midlife depression, a fate for which she held him entirely responsible. He simply refused to cheer up, she thought, when it was well within his power to do so. That reminded her: "Frank, have you finished reading the book I gave you?"

"Book?" said Frank, taking his coffee standing up, curling and uncurling his toes against an intricately patterned crimson rug from Isfahan. To his family he seemed to be a man more and more on the go these days, unable to sit still, often distracted. Carol made a mental note to do some internet research into adult attention deficit disorder; she secretly relished the possibility of a compound diagnosis. "Oh, Gracie's book. I skimmed through it. Something about the child-self and snapping yourself with a rubber band until you feel happy."

Carol groaned as though physically wounded, clutching at Michelle's knee with her bony hand. "You must not've read very closely," she said. "Because it is much more *profound* than that. Oh, well. I just thought it might be nice if you did, so that you could tell Gracie how much you liked it."

"I don't have to read it to do that," said Frank. "And what makes you think I would like it in the first place?" The work in question was called *The Golden Road* and had been authored by their latest incoming houseguest, that wild-haired maven of New Age self-help, Gracie Sloane. Carol had met her years earlier at a seminar held in San Francisco about recognizing and dismantling negative thought patterns. A "remedial creativity specialist with twenty years of experience," she appeared on the back cover of the book (the front cover being dominated by a brass-toned landscape painting with a road winding through what could only be described as amber waves of grain) wearing a look of lynx-eyed concern for the reader, her fiery locks tousled and mad, as though the effort of becoming enlightened in the particular pop-psychological fashion of the time had left her disheveled, almost postcoital. She looked as though she had not only been improved by creative, positive thinking, but ravished by it.

The book did include a repetitious, hypnotic chapter about something Gracie Sloane called "void-states," titled "When I'm in the Void." The line that Frank remembered best from this read:

When I'm in the void, I feel clarity of purpose.

He had found unnerving the suggestion that a clear sense of purpose eluded those outside the void—it seemed very counterintuitive—and had dealt with the subsequent gnaw of anxiety by getting out of bed to weep before the television in the middle of the night, watching a long on-screen tennis rally through a blurry scrim of tears. By morning he decided he must keep such meltdown-provoking literature as far from his person as possible and had thrown *The Golden Road* in the garbage.

"Clearly, Mr. Widdicombe is in one of his *difficult* moods today," said Carol, turning to Michelle and then to Bradford, to all appearances expecting them to do something about it.

"What's difficult is for me to catch a break around here," said Frank.

"Oh, cheer up, Frank," said Carol. "We're surrounded by wonderful people and beautiful things."

"Pardon me a moment," said Bradford, who had fallen silent

in observation of the crude, *Rite of Spring*–like dance being performed in his stomach by two Klonopin, two pieces of kringle, some coffee, and a handful of figs. Overcome with nausea, he exited the nook with a polite smile and a nod. He could then be heard lurching irregularly, bumping into things as he attempted to hurry down the hall.

"What's *his* problem?" said Christopher.

"Drugs," said Frank with a grunt. He sat down and flapped open a copy of *The Bainbridge Review*, the local island newspaper. The paper bent in the middle of the page, and he spent a moment wrestling with it noisily. The others watched him, anticipating a violent fit of profanity. When he managed to fold the thin piece of newsprint to his liking, he punctuated this achievement with a victorious nasal blast of air. One long hair, which stuck out from his left nostril, quivered as he did so; it caught the eye of Michelle, who, both fascinated by the Widdicombes and slightly bored, began to consider how and when she might extract it. She reminded herself to do something about it later and then excused herself, eager to check in on Bradford.

She found him leaning against a china cabinet in the hall, his head lolling.

"Brad!" she said, seizing his arm. "Are you all right?"

Bradford looked into her eyes, which he found to be a radiant, otherworldly blue, and said, "Your eyes!"

"What about them?" Michelle looked around for a mirror. Then Bradford, at once troubled by stomach pain and unable to contain his passion any longer, said, "Listen—how would you like to go over to Lynwood Theater tonight and see a movie with me?"

Michelle, flattered and not a little bit giddy at the prospect— she had suffered one pleasant distraction from her mystifying role as house-helper after another since Bradford had arrived a week ago; there he would be, sauntering in from a tennis match, white shorts showing off the athletic curve of his hamstring; and then there he would be again, nearly bumping into her as he rounded a corner, hurriedly apologizing and lifting one side of his mouth in helpless, crooked flirtation—made a show of reviewing her schedule, so as not to appear too eager. It was just this firm, practical streak, she knew, that endeared her to most everyone in the house. Truth be told, it endeared her to herself. How admirably *grounded* she was. "Hmm, you know, I do have a *lot* going on today. Carol is starting a major decorating overhaul, and stressing out about Gracie showing up in the middle of it—"

"Oh, dear."

"—but there *is* that documentary that just came out, about that town in Japan where they kill and eat all the dolphins. I've been wanting to see that. If we catch an evening show—"

"Oh, God." Bradford held his hand up to Michelle and swayed. His face paled. "I'm sorry, can you . . . oh, I think I'm going to be sick."

"Come here," said Michelle. She grabbed his arm, put her hand on the small of his back, and rushed him into the nearest bathroom.

"Easy," said Bradford. He steadied himself against the sink. The tiled granite floor gleamed under light shafts cutting through the shuttered windows. He knelt before the Japanese toilet, saw the reflection of his own handsome face waver in the water of the bowl, and said, quickly, "My tie—Michelle, hold back my tie."

Michelle reached around and, grabbing the strip of polka-dotted navy silk in question, lifted it up behind his neck. The position struck her as strange and punitive, bullying even, and for a moment she grappled with the surprising temptation to pull the tie back even harder and choke him. She remembered her mother once saying to her, "When you meet a man who every now and then you feel like killing for no reason—well, honey, that's when you'll know you're in love."

"Shouldn't you loosen it?" Michelle asked Bradford.

"I just bought it," said Bradford, who then proceeded to be sick.

Michelle turned away. "Poor thing," she said, rubbing her free hand over his back. "It wasn't the kringle, was it? God, I hope it's only you that gets sick. No offense."

Bradford enjoyed the feeling of Michelle's hand on his back. He lingered there perhaps a few moments longer than strictly necessary, spitting into the toilet a few times, then moved over to the sink, rinsing out his mouth with water and mouthwash. "It wasn't that," he concluded. "That was delicious, really. I'm just nervous about my father later. We don't quite see eye-to-eye, you know. So it's all just . . . psychosomatic? Psycho-so-*matic*, Michelle."

He splashed water on his face. Then, after patting himself dry with a fluffy towel, he noticed her amused attentiveness, her folded arms. Perhaps she thought this entire episode had been some strange and elaborate courtship ritual he had trotted out for her sake. "But you still want to see the dolphin movie, right?" she said.

"Oh, yes," he said, straightening his tie with a grin. "Most *dolphinately*."

———

Back in the nook, Frank had started pulling down his upper lip in such a way as to seize individual mustache hairs with his teeth. Having done so, he would pluck them out one at a time, wincing, and then spit them quietly from the side of his mouth as he scanned the newspaper. He had neglected to trim his mustache since the day he was supposed to have boarded a flight to Paris two weeks earlier, and somehow this habit helped alleviate the sense of injustice he felt at the cancellation of his annual trip to France, which, he would be the first to admit, was having a disproportionate effect on his will to live.

"Did you see this?" he said, slapping the paper with the back of his hand. "A local farmer reports—I kid you not—that one of his chickens laid an egg that had another egg inside of it. A fucking egg within an egg. There's even a diagram here." Then, after a short burst of laughter, he shook his head and added, in an almost hysterical warble, "What does that even *mean*?" He gave the newspaper a violent shake, as though by doing so he might force an answer from it. "Well, I guess that's just what passes for news in this town. Never mind war, famine, politics—my goddamn chicken laid an egg in an egg! Alert the press, call the—"

"Oh! Frank!" interrupted Carol, leaning on the edge of her chair, seized by what appeared to be a fit of inspiration. "Chickens! Wouldn't that be great?"

Frank lowered his paper. "Wouldn't what be great?"

"*You* know," said Carol, her hands flying to the sides of her temples as though a mystical vision now possessed her. She spoke quickly, her eyes closed: "A few chickens running around in the backyard, pecking at things and clucking away like little darlings. We could even eat their eggs." Carol envisioned their new island home as a rustic country retreat. She had "set an intention" to keep the house open to visitors all summer and hoped to cultivate an atmosphere of unencumbered pastoral innocence on the property. "A sense of community," she liked to say. "Yes, yes—*that's* what we need. *That's* what we should be creating." Chickens and vegetable gardens fit into this vision nicely (as did a visit from Leanne Pendergast, whom she hoped would, after feasting her eyes on Carol's *coup de décor*, be inspired to photograph her home for *Inside Places*, her favorite interiors magazine), but clinical depression, pharmaceutical nausea, and adult attention deficit disorder did not. People were not supposed to show signs of urban or even suburban psychological disorders at the country estate. Carol hoped, in fact, that the introduction of certain elements like hens clucking around the grounds and wild strawberry plants growing along the edge of the patio, would, for the most part, negate the more troubling aspects of the human psyche—most of all her husband's.

"Chickens," she concluded.

"Chickens," muttered Frank. Though the man challenged his wife on many fronts, he knew better than to attempt to interfere with the creation of her own henpecked corner of Pacific Northwestern paradise. He understood all too well that no matter what he said, he would come home one day soon to find a flock of hens mincing around their backyard, clucking away like little darlings.

"Just make sure you get a rooster, too," he said. "I hear they're wild about each other."

Christopher, who had been sitting in gloomy silence, wondering when he might sneak off somewhere to smoke a cigarette—a habit he had picked up abroad, unbeknownst to his parents—cleared his throat, sat up straight, and held an index finger aloft.

"Chickens are filthy creatures," he said. Frank and Carol exchanged looks, both of them noting a familiar tone in their son's voice—a tone that alerted them to yet another strong and developed opinion on a subject of unexpected expertise. When, they both wondered, had he found the time to research and draw conclusions about chickens? But it had always been this way with Christopher. As a young boy, he had been morbidly obsessed with disease, coercing playmates to spend the day dying with him (of scarlet fever, of tuberculosis, of leprosy— how he had loved to play "leper colony"!), begging his father to make "Quarantine" signs for him as he rattled off symptoms, timetables, and possible treatments. They had looked upon this virtuosity with hopefulness, imagining that he might eventually go into medicine, only to have their dreams of doctor parentage dashed when an adolescent curiosity about the word *homogenized* on the side of a jug of a milk prompted him to spend an entire year struggling, with the help of many library books, to understand the relatively simple process of homogenization "on an intimate level" (and, lest they hold out any hope for a strictly scientific aptitude, he put this particular interest to bed by producing a series of abstract, white-on-white watercolors "about milk, memory, and knowledge"). Countless other laser-fine obsessions had followed as his teenage years unfolded, his bedroom filling with the evidence of God-knew-what new *idée fixe*: intricately marked-up maps of foreign cities like Mexico City and Prague, printouts about waste management in Iceland, criminological surveys of urban Brazil. In high school he had baffled the entire teaching staff and administration by neglecting all other subjects in favor of highly specialized readings in high school administration; at one conference with the Widdicombes, a concerned teacher complained that while Christopher appeared to know enough about the way schools worked to manage the entire operation, he showed no actual interest in his own grades. Neither it seemed did the Rhode Island School of Design, which enthusiastically accepted him on the basis of a series of watercolors "inspired by the seven members of the San Francisco Unified School District's Board of Education." And so, while he still occasionally mystified his parents, they had also grown used to being mystified by him—even delighted by it—and had more or less come to accept that their only son would one day be remembered as a homosexual watercolorist who happened to know everything about the history of airports. Now, on the subject of chickens, he added, "They'll eat anything—including one another's own excrement."

"Thank you for sharing," said Frank, nodding to his son.

"Oh, what do you know about chickens?" protested Carol.

Christopher looked at her, stunned. "Everything."

"I mean *really* know," she said.

"I do know I couldn't stand to even be near one," said Christopher. "They're vile, just *vile*. Their dirty feathers, their filthy talons—yuck! I feel sick simply thinking about them."

"Well, all right then, Einstein," said Carol. "You're entitled to your opinion, but if you ask me, chickens are gentle, and intelligent, and affordable. Chickens wouldn't harm a fly."

"They're also complete sex maniacs," said Christopher.

"Language, please, Christopher," said Carol.

"But it's true," he said. "On some farms there are, like, ten to twenty females for every male."

"That's called polygamous," said Frank. "Like the Mormons. And it's wrong."

Christopher shrugged. "Right or wrong, I'll bet the roosters like it," he said.

Frank allowed himself a laugh.

"Well," said Carol, exasperated, "I hardly think it's fair to judge chickens by our own inexorable moral standards. I just think it would be fun to have them around. This family, I've decided, needs start having more *fun*. Isn't that what life's all about?"

Christopher sighed. "I hate talking about fun," he said. "And I hate the very idea of fun. Talking about fun, and the idea of fun, are no fun at all."

"From what I've come to understand," continued Carol, "we've all been put on this planet to have as much fun as possible."

"Sounds like you've been reading too much Gracie Sloane," said Christopher. "Where is she, anyway?"

"She's in the void," said Frank. "Having fun there, too, I'll bet."

"Very funny, Frank," said Carol. "She'll be here tonight. She's flying in from Boston."

A far-off look came into Christopher's eyes. "I wonder what terminal her flight left from."

"I don't know about that," said Carol. "But we should all be very nice to her, because she's in town to work on her new book and has an important speaking engagement, too. Apparently, there's a big sort of New Age expo coming to town."

"I love expositions," said Christopher.

Frank gripped his newspaper, looking alarmed. Before he could flee the room, his wife, as he had feared, said, "We should all go! You know, you could all learn a thing or two from Gracie. She's very enlightened."

This dangerous idea, "enlightenment," loomed, threatening, like the ghost of an unpleasant event shared by the family, something nobody wanted to think about or discuss. Judging from the effect this utterance had, enlightenment might have been a family member who had died too young and whose memory was still too painful to talk about; the male Widdicombes began to stir, to rise from their antique seats in a round, murmuring pleasantries about how they had better go get ready for the day, as though the day were a kind of military attack for which they needed to prepare. And was that so far off the mark? After all, time's numberless army stood at the all-too-pregnable gates of their lives ready to maraud, to burn down the ramshackle structures of order they had erected to protect themselves from its onslaught. Only movement, mental and physical, could fortify these fragile outposts of routine: Christopher headed for his room, saying, "I bet she flew United. I bet it was Terminal B . . ." Frank said, "What is *wrong* with that boy?" and then walked off grumbling something about chickens in the void. It was at this moment that Michelle returned to the breakfast nook to collect her agenda. She found Carol relaxing, for a moment only, against the hot-pink moiré of her treasured chair.

"Do you see what I mean?" Carol shook her head at Michelle. "Frank is most definitely depressed!"

Michelle nodded, penciling her movie date with Bradford into her little book. "You might be right. Maybe Gracie can help?"

"That's part of the plan, dear," said Carol, her voice a near-whisper. She took a theatrical sip of coffee from her china demitasse. "But you know what they say . . ."

" 'Life is suffering?' " said Michelle.

Carol clutched the arm of her chair. "For heaven's sake, Michelle, *no*," she said. "Who would say such a thing?"

"I think Buddhists."

"How *morbid*," said Carol. "No, no. They say, 'It takes a village,' or something nice like that."

"Oh, that's right," said Michelle. She snapped shut her agenda and smiled. "That does sound a little better."

———

Frank sat in his office behind a wide, uncluttered oak desk, squeezing a blue rubber stress ball. His coiled forearm muscles pulsed as he did so, sinewy and cord-like from decades of vigorous sport.

"Motherfucker," he muttered, swiveling in an expensive ergonomic chair. Outside his window, the crescent of Douglas firs that secluded their luxurious home swayed in the summer breeze; the water of the bay sparkled with light. Frank extracted a few mustache hairs with his teeth, letting the play of sunshine on that watery body soothe him into a state of deep reflection.

Semiretirement had been a fucking nightmare so far, he thought. It had not suited him at all: he had always been a body in motion that tended to stay in motion, an achiever achieving if not to the highest degree then at least to an upper-middle one. For decades he had devoted his efforts to sweaty self-improvement, guiding multiple generations of San Francisco glitterati toward socially strategic tennis competency. Such a surfeit of good old-fashioned fighting energy had he that in Christopher's eerie toddler years, he had juggled not only work at the club, enthused fatherhood, and a stretch of husbandly duty marked by both buoyant libido and domestic attentiveness, but the earning of an advanced degree in sports psychology. Even with all of that, he had remained almost disturbingly (to Carol) energized and impetuous. Like his blessed Pops Widdicombe before him, Frank hummed with such an irrepressible vigor as to make any idleness not only cause for alarm, but more or less impossible—sickness, for instance, was almost unheard of in a Widdicombe, and when the occasional bug did come around to fell some male of that warrior clan, the fighter inevitably saw his forced convalescence not as an opportunity to rest, but to review and update his ten-year, five-year, and one-year plans. Part and parcel of their able-bodied appeal, this burning life force was also a family curse: a Widdicombe stopped to rest only in death, as Frank's father had—and his father's father before that—when visited by a massive heart attack in his still quite lively eighties.

And now *he*, Frank Widdicombe, was expected to potter around their mansion like a mellow old patriarch, to be cheerful, interested in chickens and "fun." To make matters worse, he was beginning to think his wife had invited Gracie Sloane to their house in the hope that she would call upon her punishing New Age worldview to hang a wreath on this hell of inactivity—to persuade him to "chill out" (how often he had heard that ridiculous demand!), to deck the halls of this forced holiday with whatever boughs of childish nonsense she came bearing.

Well, Frank Widdicombe had already had an annual heart-attack-preventing holiday in place, and it had been canceled for the first time in a long time. He looked back at the screen of his laptop and read over the email he was composing to his old buddy Channing Goodman:

Dear Mr. Goodman, Faggot-at-Large,

I'm writing to wish your she-cow of a niece and her idiot husband all the best on their nuptials. Why, why? Why did you have to offer up the Auvergne house for the honeymoon? Couldn't they have honeymooned in a cow pasture somewhere, among their own kind? We should all be getting pleasantly buzzed thousands of miles

away from our families right now. Speaking of which,
I'm copying your partner on this email. In light of this
unprecedented act of assassination between intimates,
I hereby hope that every state in the Union outlaws gay
marriage for all of time. Hope you're having a nice time on
the Cape.

He stopped, and, having blown off a little steam, saved the
email as a draft. He and Channing Goodman had known one
another since their Stanford days; they enjoyed a kind of free
and easygoing conversational trade that allowed Frank to call
his old friend a faggot on occasion and for his old friend to call
him, in return, a "bedroom community breeder." All in good
fun. However, Frank had long since learned, after reading a
biography of Abraham Lincoln, that the wisest men of courage
and leadership slept on any letter composed in extreme emotion, often finding it to lack a certain stoic, presidential quality
the morning after.

They had been making the trip every year for nearly a decade: a small group of college friends (majors in psychology
mostly, many of them gone on to take various positions in that
prestigious, head-shrinking field), they would come together
to spend several weeks at Channing and his partner's country
home in Auvergne, France. There, the men of psychology
drank cognac produced in the department of Charente, fine
wines from all over the damn place, and herbaceous green li-
queurs mixed up by industrious monastics in French mountain
ranges. They drank and complained about their wives (and
their "life partners," their "lovers," their "husbands"), about
their children, about how so-called success had failed to bring
them the unshakable happiness they had longed for as students

of the mind, body, and spirit. Since many of them were publishing in order not to perish (academic papers, popular articles,
books; Frank, for his part, had put out a relatively well-regarded
pop psychological volume on leadership and self-actualization
called *Zoning Out*), they discussed and debated at great length
whatever aspects of the human experience happened to be consuming their interest at the time.

They laughed and sometimes drank too much, said cruel-
kind things to one another, and indulged themselves in necessary mental and emotional breakdowns. Some of these ended
in physical altercations. It was just how they relaxed. In Mr.
Widdicombe's case, he had, one evening in the year 2006, guzzled red wine until, drunk enough to finally find expression for
his grief, he had wandered out of the house and into the night,
shouting obscenities over the loss of his father and his "stupid,
fucking stupid heart attack!" After he had punched the trunk of
an oak and allowed tears to stream down his face for an hour,
he had passed out in a nearby field, the stars in the sky above
him a nauseating merry-go-round. He had come to around
sunrise, exhausted, curled into a ball against the hard ground,
his mouth filled with a sour taste, his knuckles covered in dried
blood, his teeth—could he have seen them at the time—stained
a faint crimson. With his tongue he had felt a gap where one of
his incisors had been the night before. A sheep that had strayed
from its tribe was standing two yards away, staring at him.
Frank had laughed to see it, and the sheep had, in response,
turned and strutted away, presumably to find its friends and tell
a tale at the man's expense.

In any case, Frank had come to see this annual trip as necessary to his mental well-being. It cheered him up. Oh, he had
seen plenty of therapists; not one of their programs of so-called

mental health could achieve the full release of drinking too much with his friends at least once a year, of allowing his deepest insecurities to dissipate in a slurred, Dionysian outpouring before a panel of grizzled peers.

This year Channing had agreed to lend his home for the purpose of his niece's honeymoon. The freshly minted couple wanted to spend their summer living among the shrubbed hills and crabby country people, sitting on picnic blankets and devouring soft French cheeses, cooing softly and delighting in one another's charming tics and neuroses. All of the men of psychology had been warned about this unceremonious takeover well in advance, and while Frank had expressed good-natured disappointment at the time ("May your niece sit on poison oak in a mustard field. Love, Frank"), he had never expected it to trouble his spirit so thoroughly. Now that he had been denied the pleasure of prolonged retreat and found himself at the center of an estate bound for strange, utopia-seeking summer visitors, he felt increasingly agitated by every responsibility to his family. They only served to further emphasize the fact that Frank was not in Auvergne like he ought to be. And while he was hard-pressed to think of an alternative that would be as stress-relieving as this canceled trip, which required a minimum of planning and execution on his part, he had been left with the overwhelming compulsion to refresh his senses, to get away from his family lest he wind up tying them all to beautiful chairs and setting fire to Willowbrook.

———

Michelle had her tasks for the day. This in itself felt like an achievement, since the Widdicombes often operated in a way that she might charitably describe as "nonlinear." Taking refuge in Carol's office to collect her thoughts, she sat at the cluttered desk with her laptop and notebook open so that she would look busy if anyone happened to walk past the door. True, it scarcely mattered to them how busy she looked, but it mattered to *her*—she was never quite sure what to make of her work for this peculiar family, and it centered her to keep various professional-looking apparatus at hand. Pens, notebook, laptop, smartphone. Some days she ended up putting these things to good use; other days, she had come to accept, more or less consisted of her showing up in order to serve as witness to the Widdicombes' minidramas and well-heeled existential crises. This had confused her at first, for it didn't seem to her like "work" as she understood it. The size of her paychecks, however, persuaded her otherwise, and she came to embrace her double role as assistant and audience.

She did worry a little that their all-around eccentricity had started to rub off on her. She could even see it in the way she had written down her to-do list that day. Her normally no-nonsense style had started to give way to something that looked more like the inside of a Widdicombe mind:

(*live!*) chicken inquiry—Bay Hay and Feed
follow-up mechanic wreck
IMPORTANT: online research: *paintings of mandrills*
   (a kind of monkey)
wash hybrid
tennis balls, "and not some off-brand kind"
"victuals" (?!) / sundries—see next page

There was something about the way they talked, she thought. Sometimes it seemed as though they spoke their own private family language. Then it would suddenly sound to her like each *individual* Widdicombe had his or her own private language. Listening to this clash of tongues, to say nothing of trying to maintain a part in it, could lead to giddy laughter and a pleasant kind of delirium, as well as to the distinct feeling that none of the world's problems would ever be solved.

On top of this, the question of time. The Widdicombes swung between languid relaxation, crazed urgency, and a number of other difficult-to-categorize attitudes toward time in an unpredictable fashion. She recalled a day when Christopher—with whom she felt she was beginning to forge something like a friendship—fell into an inconsolable despair because he missed a matinee screening of what looked like a very bad summer blockbuster called *Department of Shadows*, even though it was playing every two hours and he appeared to have nothing else to do. "I wanted to see it at three! *Three!*" More often, though, the whole family proceeded with an elastic attitude toward time, regularly losing track of it, showing up late for appointments or not at all, and drawing her into long conversations—quite a few of which were, as might be guessed, "conversations"—that seemed to unfold endlessly without any particular regard for whether or not *she* had someplace to be, or something else to do, or an all-too-human need to eat or drink something after hours of talk about the greatest contemporary decorators of the Western world, the majority of whom were apparently Carol's personal friends.

It was the way some people who had grown used to having money treated time. That was her theory. She remembered beginning to think this as a teenager, when friendships formed through middle and high school activities (French, yearbook, track and field) brought her into contact with families of a higher socioeconomic class than her own. Their children—her friends, for a time—struck her as curiously unbothered by the passage of time, as though the days were mere dollars in an impossibly ample inheritance. Why, she wondered, was she drawn to such people? Why did she so often find herself taking care of people who never deigned to count their hours?

The arrival in the driveway outside of someone in an old yellow truck interrupted her reflections. She wasn't expecting any workers that day. Carol and Frank sometimes scheduled things without her knowledge, though, and then forgot about them. In one of the back pages of her notebook where she jotted down private observations, she wrote:

What does it mean to forget?

———

Frank heard a polite knock. He turned his head toward the door; there stood Michelle. Of all the people around him, Frank minded Michelle perhaps the least, though lately it seemed that her presence in his doorway augured bad news. So it seemed today.

"Frank," she said, "I'm just on my way out, but there's a man in overalls here to see you."

Frank said nothing. Narrowing his eyes gave adequate expression to his displeasure.

"I think it's the person Carol hired to do the garden."

"Fuck. Why does he want to see *me*, then?"

"Well, he asked for Carol, but she's gone out with her bird-watching group."

At the mention of bird-watching, Mr. Widdicombe grumbled, tightening his grip on the stress ball. He hated Carol's bird-watching group, although *that*, at least, stemmed from an irrational feeling about bird-watching in general. To his mind, bird-watching was one step removed from senility and impotence—an erection-threatening pastime—and though his wife had suggested he might enjoy spending some time with her growing circle of island friends and learning about the local wildlife, he told her he would be damned before he picked up a pair of binoculars to try and catch sight of a fucking red-breasted robin in flight. "All birds can go to hell," he remembered adding. His wife had seemed hurt, as though she herself identified with the birds. Frank made a mental note to tell her that she identified with other things too readily.

"Fine," he said to Michelle. "I'll show him to the plot."

Michelle thought he looked very restless standing there at the window and glowering at the beautiful panoramic view. Though it was hardly her place to inquire into her employer's emotional state—or wasn't it?—she felt sorry for Frank. She also still wanted to do something about the rogue nose hair sticking out of his left nostril. She needed to buy herself time, to cultivate an intimate atmosphere.

"Is everything okay, Frank?" she said. Frank looked at her with surprise.

"I don't know," he said. "Probably not."

"That's great," said Michelle, distracted by her hair-related mission.

"It is?" said Frank. "Well, that's nice to hear for once. You're the only one who seems to think so in this house. When did it become such a crime to be in a bad mood?"

"You're telling me."

Frank softened, feeling his assistant's gaze shine on him with something like admiration, or at the very least a youthful intensity that could be mistaken for it. He felt compelled to be honest. "Let me just say, Michelle, for your own sake—because I like you, you're a wonderful assistant—that if I seem angry lately it's because I should be in France right now, having an entire bottle of wine with lunch."

Michelle sighed. "Oh, gosh," she said. "I heard about that. I'm so sorry. I know how you feel—I just love Europe. And Scandinavia. Denmark, especially. If I didn't love living here so much I would certainly live there."

Frank looked at her curiously. "Yes, well, best not to dwell on it," he said. Heading toward the door, he added, with a note of fake glee, "I'd better not keep that green thumb waiting!"

"Right," said Michelle, clapping her hands together and following him out. The two made their way down the hall, arriving at the racks and pegs in the foyer where they put their shoes and umbrellas and coats. She could not restrain herself any longer.

"Mr. Widdicombe," she said, her voice stern.

"Yes?"

"I feel it's my duty as your assistant to inform you of a large nose hair sticking out of your nostril."

"Oh," said Mr. Widdicombe. "Really? I'd better find a mirror . . ."

"Just—hold still." In a moment she would later regret as too impetuous—a moment, we shall come to see, that would also set into motion a series of unpleasant late-night reflections for Frank that we cannot even begin at present to fathom—Michelle reached for his nose, her eyes locked in concentration; Frank flinched as though she meant to strike him; she took hold of the rogue nose hair in one swift movement and, with her index finger and thumb, plucked the offending strand from his nostril. Frank cried out.

"I'm sorry," she said. She held the white hair up for his inspection, frowning at it as though it represented a gross flaw in the design of civilized life. "I had to."

"Miss Briggs," he said, dumbfounded. He brought a hand to his smarting nostril. "Please give me some warning in the future. I have a sensitive nose."

Michelle laughed, then realized by the grave furrow of his brow that he meant it. "Oh, relax," she said. "It was just a little nose hair. You look much better now."

Frank, disoriented by the exchange, touched his nose as they made their way out the front door, pulling his hand away and looking at it as though he expected to see globs of blood or a dribble of brain fluid there. Michelle, meanwhile, walked with her chin high, exalted by a sense of accomplishment. She hurried out to the driveway, leaving Frank to greet the gardener as she got into the Widdicombes' new hybrid car. It sat next to a dented, mustard-colored Toyota pickup truck that evidently belonged to the hired hand.

The man standing before Frank appeared to be in his mid-forties. A head taller than him and possessed of a broad, brawny frame, he had a touch of hard-bitten slackness to his face—a certain mild sag about the cheeks, across one of which stretched a long scar; a pucker of aggrieved defeat between his dark, angled eyebrows—that gave his trim beard the look of holding the rest of his features in place, as though they might droop more considerably were he to shave. He adjusted the brim of a worn grey baseball cap as he greeted Frank, who took note of the colorful tattoos peeking from the cuffs of the man's long-sleeved shirt. "You must be the gardener," said Frank, thinking that there was something about this guy's expression that reminded him of a fox who had just snatched and swallowed an egg from the nest of a pink-footed goose.

"That I am," said the man, extending a rough, calloused mitt. "Marvelous Matthews."

Frank shook his hand. "I'm sorry, did you say Marvelous?"

"Right," said the gardener. "That's my, uh, company name. Marvelous Matthews's Community Gardens. But all my clients have started calling me Marvelous Matthews. Now my friends do, too. It just kind of stuck."

"What can *I* call you?" said Frank.

At that moment Michelle, who had started the car but had not yet driven away, began laying on the horn; the sound grated on Frank—he hated blaring sounds, alarms—and he glared at her. Marvelous laughed anxiously, craning around to look as Michelle climbed out of the car and started calling, "Chris! Christopher!" over the hum of the engine. Frank felt a hand on his back as his son almost ran into him on his way out the door.

"Pardon you," Frank said.

Christopher dismissed his father's comment with a wave, and then, catching sight of Marvelous, stopped in his tracks. He cradled his chin in his hand and cocked his head, assessing the gardener with a cool, painterly eye. "Well," he said, "hello."

"I'm Marvelous," said the gardener, extending his rough paw once again.

"I'll be the judge of that," said Christopher.

"Move along, Renoir," said Frank. Feeling a headache coming on, he started rubbing his temples. He despaired at the thought of his son being moved to set up his easel in sight of the bearish new gardener with the weird name and embarking on another baffling series of portraits. Why couldn't he paint pictures of the harbor? It was one thing to be gay, thought Frank—why did his son have to be an unmarketable watercolorist as well?

"I'm sorry, Marvelous. That was my son," said Frank. "Or should I say *is*. He's in art school."

"Must be nice," said Marvelous. Were his voice not so thick and potholed by what Mr. Widdicombe could only assume to be many miles of rough road, it might have betrayed a guarded longing for artistic endeavor. As it was, Mr. Widdicombe felt no need to comment upon whether his son's ambitions were nice or not; he gazed once again at the gardener's scar.

"Rake accident." Marvelous lifted his shoulders. "It's okay, it's hard not to notice it."

"I see. So you stepped on a rake, it popped up and hit you, that kind of thing? Like a cartoon."

"Not exactly," said Marvelous, his words fringed with shame. "My ex-girlfriend hit me with it."

"Really?" Frank eyed him with a suddenly more admiring variety of suspicion. "Fuck." The profanity issuing from his lips put him in mind of his wife's ongoing insistence that he make an effort to exercise more tact, and so he decided not to pry, and added, with a sniff, "Well, it suits you. This way, please."

Frank guided Marvelous along a rock path that led through the landscaped side yard, where spindly Japanese maples, a flowering dogwood, and pale pink rhododendrons presented a colorful scene.

"You have a beautiful place," said Marvelous. Then, turning to Frank, he startled at the sight of blood trickling from the man's left nostril.

"Pretty spiffy," said Frank, surveying the lavish landscape and sniffling. "It was all here when we bought the place. Lord knows I don't know the first fucking thing about these things. I should learn."

"Your nose is bleeding."

Frank touched his nose, drew his hand away, and scoffed at

the bright, watery stuff leaking out. Though never one to quail at the sight of a little blood, something about the sight of his own red life force leaking out filled him with dread. A brief spell of dizziness and panic passed through him. He steadied himself, uttering a soft "Ah, shit."

"Please, take this, I insist," said Marvelous. He pulled a dark blue handkerchief from his overalls. Frank, in a concession to male fellow-feeling, accepted the proffered rag. "Could be allergies," said Marvelous. "It's a sea of pollen out here. New to the neighborhood?"

"To the island, yes." Frank stanched his bloody nose. "To the area, too. Came up from California." At the mention of that state, the gardener stiffened a little. Frank knew well enough that the locals had seen their fair share of transplants arrive after making their fortunes in California, and that this gave rise to a waspish regional pride. Like they were about to give the land back to the fucking Suquamish people or something, he thought. A few birds lit out from the brush around them, chattering, chirping, slicing the air. Just then, Frank felt a quiver in his right calf; though he had stretched after his tennis match, a cramp seized him now, shooting down to curl his foot, and he stopped, making a pained face and sucking air through his teeth. "Fuck, fuck, fuck," he said. As if adding insult to sports injury, a black-capped chickadee resembling the one he had reckoned with on the court that morning alighted upon a dogwood branch right in front of him. "You again!" he barked. "These birds think they're *sooooo* cute. Just a cramp," he added, shaking his leg out as it started to untense.

"Ah, women's troubles," said Marvelous. Apparently tickled by his own impertinence, he laughed. Frank gave him a look that at once spoke to the poor quality of the joke and the appreciable risk the gardener had taken in uttering it, and then swatted the chickadee-bearing branch of the dogwood. The bird darted across the way, alighting on another tree.

"Birds like that," said Frank, "are not a problem in Auvergne."

"What's Oh-Vern?" said Marvelous.

Frank sighed. "*Auvergne* is a region in France. Smack dab in the middle of goddamn France. A few of my friends and I meet there every summer—except *this* summer—and have a grand old time. Just a bunch of psychological types drinking their cares away. It seems I overestimated their reverence for tradition."

At the mention of drink, the gardener went quiet. After a pause, Marvelous said, "You're a psychologist?"

"I have a master's degree in sports psychology."

"I see," said Marvelous.

"I've written a book."

They arrived at a modest garden plot filled with rich, dark soil and boarded in by weathered-looking wood. It stood out as a piece of makeshift inelegance a few yards from their prissy patio. Mr. Widdicombe had built it himself—Carol had wanted to add a touch of rustic charm to their backyard in the form of a small vegetable garden. ("Carrots and cabbages and such," in her own words.) He had liked that idea and had been happy to let this project distract him for a couple of days.

"Oh, that's it, then," said Marvelous, a hint of disappointment in his voice.

"I built it myself."

"Easy to take care of, anyway. Great exposure." Marvelous knelt by the planter box and, running his hands through the soil, started in on a spiel. "Well, I think it's great that you've decided to do this. I think you'll really appreciate what a difference organic vegetables can make in your quality of life." His ragged voice delivered this line in such a way that not even he seemed convinced of its truth.

"Uh-huh," said Frank, glancing over at the edge of the woods bordering their property. His ears had perked up at some distant voices, some rustling in the trees. He pressed Marvelous's handkerchief hard against his nose, then removed it. His nosebleed had stopped.

"And of course," added Marvelous. "I think the community will truly appreciate what you're bringing to the table."

Confused—and, he felt, potentially enraged—Mr. Widdicombe squinted at this overgrown garden gnome of a man that he had, up until that moment, thought might prove friend and ally in a strange land. "What's that now?" he said. "What community?"

"*The* community," said Marvelous, pronouncing the word *the* as though it were a heavy stone he had been carrying a long time, looking for a place to lay it down. "Part of my program includes community-building and helping my clients to cultivate social capital. There's an incredible, welcoming community on this island—it exists, if only people would open their eyes and look for it."

"Oh, fucking hell."

"One fucking hell of a community."

"Will you stop saying that? I thought this was just about vegetables. Carrots and cabbages and such."

"This goes beyond cabbage," said Marvelous, seeming to search his mind for lines he had not quite memorized. "This isn't just about the, uh, production of vegetables, but the production of a public who cares about them. And your wife sounded so excited about hosting the Midsummer Feast this year."

"Dear fucking God."

"Hey, man," said Marvelous, holding up both gloved hands in a gesture that might have appeared defensive were it not for a gleam of impatience in the gardener's eye. "I'm just trying to provide a service."

Marvelous stood to his full height—which, given the heated tone of the moment, struck Frank as not inconsiderable—and removed his gardening gloves. If the patriarch of Willowbrook could have seen into his gardener's mind at that moment, he would have perceived a struggle taking place; Marvelous, grasping at one of the techniques he had learned to modulate his flights of fury (in the face of this insult to his fledgling business—a scrappy venture that represented to him a sincere act of contrition, an effort to do good in the world—all that threatened to fly out the window), was doing everything in his power not to do something that might provoke his new client; he longed to spit on the garden plot, to say to this pompous Californian, "What's the matter? Can't handle a problem on your own? Can't even grow your own fucking heirloom lettuces?" Taking a deep, ragged breath through his nose and counting to twelve, Marvelous Matthews managed to ride out the storm for the moment. Finding his most reasonable tone, he said, "It's just a little party. Nothing too crazy."

Now, a Widdicombe, be he strapping young cadet or middle-aged man sliding unconvinced into his so-called golden years, can turn the other cheek at many an insignificant slight: accusations of a) prickliness, b) foul-mouthed insensitivity, even c) a certain degree of intellectual ineptitude (the men of the Widdicombe clan, after all, were men of action). However, to snub a Widdicombe's courage—his vital, fighting spirit in the face of life and its endless, fearsome obstacles—was to slander his essence and his worth in the world. No doubt Marvelous had, on some impishly fraternal, animal level, perceived this in regard to Frank Widdicombe—so Frank thought, anyway—and was restraining himself while he carried on drawing conclusions about Frank that he imagined *cast aspersions.* Presumptuous, this man; what did he know about the Widdicombes and what they had been through? Nothing. In this way the self-restraint of one provoked the self-restraint of the other, and it was only by the slightest intercession of reason—Frank had a history of imagining slights where there were none, and he knew it—that the man of the house resorted to his preferred cure-all, food and drink, and invited Marvelous to take a seat on the patio while he grabbed some refreshments.

Amid these delicate negotiations the sound of voices and thrashing in the nearby woods grew louder and clearer. Carol soon stepped from the shadows wiping a few brambles and pine needles from her sun dress as she spoke to a small group of people behind her. She brandished a pair of black plastic binoculars. The whole group was in a twittering ecstasy.

"Did you ever *see* so many birds?" Carol was saying.

"Such a fowl-rich property," said the tall and sturdy Judith Harrison, a waddle of loose skin working beneath her chin.

"I still think that cormorant was a Pelagic, not a Brandt," said the balding, pink-faced Jack Pinder, looking at a bird identification book—*Birds of Washington*—through his glasses. "You can tell a Pelagic from the white rump patch. You see, here, it says 'the Pelagic, possessed of a white rump patch, is easy to distinguish from the Brandt cormorant, with its whiskery white filoplumes.' I suppose that was its breeding plumage we saw."

"Breeding plumage!" said Don Jacobs in disbelief, scratching his beard. "How exciting. Birds on the make, eh?"

"Frank! Yoo-hoo!" Carol called to her husband, leading her party across the lawn. "Yoo-hoo!"

"There she is," said Frank, stepping through the door onto the patio. In one hand he held two bottles of beer by their necks, in the other a tray of olives, cheeses, and cured meats.

"Mrs. Widdicombe, I presume?" said Marvelous. Having slouched into one of the patio chairs, he now straightened up. He raised a refusing hand at the proffered bottle. "No thanks," he said. "I'm sober."

"Not for long," said Frank.

Marvelous clarified, gravely, that his sobriety was to remain a permanent state. Frank did his best to make little of the revelation, pausing and giving his new acquaintance what he felt to be an excusably short look of disbelief. Uncertain respect rushed in forthwith to tidy his expression, and he returned with a can of soda. "Much obliged," said Marvelous.

"Anything for the community," said Frank.

Carol and her group soon broke in on this tenuous peacetime. She walked up to her husband, squeezing his arm and pressing herself against his body. She was making every effort lately to act cheerier than usual, Frank thought—more enthusiastic, more high-energy. There was something in it that made him want to lay her down and mount her, animal-like, as though her enthusiasm was a mating call, a pent-up excess of primal energy.

"We just witnessed the most darling little goldfinch," said Carol, excited.

Jack Pinder nodded, still gripping his binoculars with both hands. "Wonderful coloring!" he said.

"We were just getting to know each other," said Frank. He tipped his beer at the gardener, who had stood from his chair upon the group's arrival. "This is Marvelous."

"Well! I'm glad to hear your attitude's improving, even if your nose is all red and puffy," said Carol, tickling Frank's chin. She peeled away from her husband and extended her hand. "I'm Carol. And you are?"

"Marvelous, ma'am. Marvelous Matthews. That's my business name, but—"

"Oh, God! I forgot you were coming today." She shook his large, dirty hand. "I'm *so* sorry. I hope my husband has shown you every hospitality." She noticed the scar on his cheek, the blades of grass that had somehow gotten into his beard hair. She cast a quick look of inquiry at her husband, then said, "Everybody, this is Marvelous, our new gardener. He's come to plant some plants and build a community."

Marvelous smiled and tipped his hat. Nodding at Carol's dirtied hand, he said, "Sorry about—"

"Oh, nonsense," said Carol. "Do I look like someone who's afraid of a little dirt?" She winked at the gardener and laughed. "I've spent the whole morning traipsing through the forest!"

Frank scrutinized this exchange and guzzled cool beer. Marvelous, he noted, seemed nervous and apologetic around his wife. Frank still wanted to know what he had meant by the horrible-sounding words *social capital*, and what happened at a Midsummer Feast. There was something about the latter that sounded a bit pagan to Frank, like he might come home one day to find other garden gnomes and maybe elves or even sylphs prancing through the house in their birthday suits, raiding his wine cellar and rolling around in an orgiastic heap on the lawn. That was the kind of thing one did with friends while in a foreign country, thought Frank, and definitely not with strangers in the town of one's residence. Now, however, he set these concerns aside; all of a sudden, a light dawned on him as to the versatile uses of social capital. He stood to address the birders. "You all must be thirsty," he said. "Would anyone like anything?"

The birders turned their heads back and forth, murmuring softly and nodding, indicating a sporting willingness to drink some water.

"I think that sounds lovely, Frank," said Carol as though daring him. The fact that he had managed to both be a good host and avoid swearing in a single sentence buoyed her spirits, but she still had her doubts. "Just lovely," she added. "I, for one, am absolutely parched."

"You got it," said Frank. He went into the kitchen.

The birders, meanwhile, gathered around the garden plot. They stared with great interest at the fertile soil.

"Mr. Matthews runs the most innovative program," said Carol, smiling sympathetically at the new gardener; had he fallen prey to one of her depressed husband's unpredictable outbursts? "He hires out his services to people who have space for a garden but don't have the time or the notion to take care of it themselves. He'll set up a garden at your house, and come by every so often to check on the vegetables and things—is that right?"

"Exactly," said Marvelous. "Just because you don't want to take care of a garden yourself is no reason not to have one."

"That sounds great," said Judith Harrison.

"Isn't it just fabulous?" said Carol, reaching out and touching her friend's arm.

"It's a smart idea," said Jack Pinder.

"I think it's just so innovative," said Carol.

"Thanks," said Marvelous, who in the wake of his tense moment with Frank was beginning to feel the dark shadow of shame hanging over him. He had lost his temper again, and by throwing open that floodgate had also ushered in the thought that maybe one drink wouldn't kill him. Anxiety ate at him; he needed to call his sponsor. "I'm just glad to put my God-given green thumb to use," he said. "I don't see why the community shouldn't benefit from my skills, as long as they're willing to let me sneak around their yards a few days a week."

Carol and the birders all laughed. The sound of irritated grunts coming through the patio doors, however, cut their laughter short.

"Something's wrong with the fucking sink," said Frank, carrying out a tray with four glasses on it. "It won't run cold. So I had to give you warm water with ice cubes."

The birders smiled politely, their eyes darting around the yard.

"That's okay," said Don Jacobs, taking a glass. "Water's water—am I right?"

"The ice will cool it down," said Judith, as though this were a possible outcome which only she, in her helpfulness, could imagine.

"Frank," said Carol, "your nose is bleeding." She walked over to him with her own glass and, grabbing Marvelous's bandana from the table, dipped it in water and began to dab at his nostrils and mustache. He sat down in one of their wrought-iron chairs. "What on earth have you been doing?"

"It's all this talk of birds," he said. He twisted away from her ministrations. "They give me a stress headache."

"*You* give *me* a stress headache," said Carol.

"Michelle ripped out one of my nose hairs earlier." He snatched the bandana out of her hand.

"What was Michelle doing anywhere *near* your nose hair?"

"My body hair is my business, Carol."

"I wish to God that were true."

Don Jacobs, who had driven the other birders over in his Jeep, said, "Well, we really ought to be going." He looked up at the cloudless sky. "Connie needs the car later."

The other birders, given an out, set aside their empty glasses, struggling as a group to take the Widdicombes' bizarre bickering in stride. They all fidgeted, murmuring and moving to air-kiss Carol, who distributed proper good-byes with perfect grace. Frank gave them a curt wave as he leaned forward, pinching his nose above the nostrils.

"Good to see you all," he said. "You're welcome back to watch the birds at any time, as long as you don't mind your giving me a nosebleed." The birders laughed at what was, after all, a good-humored tension-breaking on Frank's part. Carol bid them final farewell with a look that said, "You know how marriage can be—like one long nosebleed that comes out of nowhere."

———

Though the streets of downtown Winslow on Bainbridge Island hardly lent themselves to rambling *flânerie* in the way, say, Florence did, Christopher Widdicombe felt uninhibited by received notions of suitable purpose. Wherefore, after all, suitability? He had spent the morning in the public library leafing through an oversized book on the American realist painter Thomas Eakins, admiring at first that uncompromising document of surgical theater, *The Gross Clinic*, but finding himself turning back, again and again, to the mesmerizing *Self-portrait*, until gradually the appeal of the image revealed itself: the force and directness of Thomas Eakins's gaze impaled him; he felt pierced, discovered, at the Philadelphian master's mercy, called upon to respond in some immediate way. And because Christopher had not felt the touch of another man since saying so long to Kreshnik, the private stirring felt by our dear watercolorist had found itself addressed manually, behind the walls of the public library's bathroom stall, the severe bedroom eyes of Mr. Eakins coming to life in the young man's eager imagination. He had kicked off the afternoon, then, by taking the unsuitable in hand. It was only natural that he should want to smoke a cigarette and go for a stroll.

A filthy habit, smoking. Neither mother nor father would approve. But then, not so many years ago, before he had shipped off to Rhode Island, his father had pulled him aside, and in one of his spontaneous, almost frantic deliveries of elder wisdom, told him that one of the secrets to life was to take joy in the little things—"the foam on a latte, the way the light comes through the window." Bourgie little things were those, to be sure—it was, too, the best his father could do with a young man who didn't fit the time-honored sporting Widdicombe mold—but it was in this spirit that he smoked and walked, and watched himself smoking and walking, watched himself watching himself smoke and walk, thinking that as the ember at the end of his cigarette brightened, it burned away, too, at the family tie.

This tie seemed furthermore to fray as he strolled, feeling self-satisfied, down a long, relatively busy street through the town and toward what he presumed would be the harbor. (Something in him vibrated like a dowsing rod: when he walked, he drifted unthinking to the water's edge always, be

it a fountain or a bay. He had heard it said that the sight of
the sea was a home for those who felt they didn't have one.) A
cute town, he thought, noting the modest apartment buildings
and dentistry offices in a variety of architectural styles, each
structure a hopeful certainty made less absolute by its neighbor.
Sun-warmed conifers stood dark green between them; new
cars gleamed, gliding up and down the street. He dropped his
cigarette butt down a rain gutter and took a breath of the clean
island air.

He had not gone to Europe, like some of the fetishistic
tourists with whom he had crossed paths, to grovel before old
beauty. Anyone looking at a photograph of him and Kreshnik
sunbathing at one of Florence's grim, residential public swim-
ming pools could have told you that old beauty had barely
crossed his mind. Short and mole-rich and with hawk-like
facial features that promised to wizen one day into one hell of
a haggard mug, Kreshnik may have been more attractive in his
bellhop uniform than he was out of it. Christopher had been
enchanted, anyway. He did not need people to appear triumphant over life to feel attracted to them. There was something
to be said for a little wear and tear.

Though the likelihood that he would ever see Kreshnik
again was slim, Christopher took pains not only to impress
upon his parents the threat that he may come to stay with
them, but to reminisce about their affair in detail: the romantic
day trip to Cinque Terre, that charmed compound of villages
on the Riviera where they had planned to sleep together on the
beach until an unexpected summer storm drove them to spend
the night cowering beneath the awning of some storefront; the
nights spent dancing, fucking around in Florentine gay bars
with pitch-black back rooms. Christopher alluded to all of

this, eager to court disapproval from his family. To his unending frustration, he found them to be not only supportive but proud, perhaps even envious of his freewheeling tomfoolery abroad. Was it so hard, in this day and age, for a young homosexual watercolorist to be disowned by his family? "I wish you were Mormons!" he had yelled after one of these unsuccessful episodes of provocation, storming from the room.

While he freely referenced those spheres of activity which might court castigation, he remained secretive on other, crucial counts. His parents knew nothing about the upstart (but *known*) gallery in New York that had been representing his work for going on two years now, and which was currently showing his series of paintings about the garbage crisis in Naples. Likewise, that growing number of art aficionados knew nothing of his tolerant family background—how could they, when he had embellished his artist's biography with tales of torment on the home front, of disgrace and loveless rejection?

He had given an interview to an obscure online arts magazine, *Thought Police*, detailing the trials of his childhood in flights of off-the-cuff fiction:

Thought Police: You've been candid about the ways that your relationship to sexuality has influenced your attitude toward art, and what you have called "a sense of spirituo-sexual revolt" in your paintings.

Christopher Widdicombe: It's a fiction that the trappings of middle- or upper-middle-class life protect gay people from the spiritual cruelties of a society that will, in my view, never truly accept them. When I came out to my mother, who has tons of gay friends—she works with *interiors*, for God's sake—and who had always spoken with compassion and kindness about gay people, she threw a glass of cold milk in my face at the dinner table. She shocked herself, I think— maybe she never imagined herself capable of acting like that. A moment later she began to sob, while I, giddy to see her unmasked in this way, started to laugh uncontrollably. Sometimes before I start a new painting, whatever it is, I like to sit and remember that moment—me laughing like a mad- man, laughing in the face of the narcissistic heteronormative world, my face stained with its hatred—and then bring that spirit to my work.

He figured that by the time any of these fantasias made it back to his parents, he would have set enough of them in motion, and told enough contradicting tales, that the grand joke of it all would become clear. He would have the upper hand. Perhaps he would one day write a book, he thought, of violently clash- ing, incompatible autobiographical sketches. *Confessions*. In the meantime, he still felt compelled to cling to somewhat tradi- tional naturalistic modes of painting. Truth be told, he felt torn: though he hid it as best he could, he felt a sublime connection to history through the great paintings of the European masters and marveled at their obvious technical prowess. Though he worshiped in private, he felt that as an artist he must in public reject to survive.

The water came into view down the hill. Christopher crossed the street at one of the handful of four-way stops in that gingerbread village of a downtown. In the distance the white masts of harbor boats rocked this way and that. He passed the window of a gift shop, where gaudy, bright postcards of a dis- tinctly seaside touristic type assaulted his eyes from behind the glass. As he walked on, however, his grimace gave way to the glow of inspiration. He hastened toward the harbor.

———

Bradford had a bad feeling from the moment he boarded the ferry to Seattle. And though he had a way of feeling doom to be right around the corner more often than not—even on a fine day like that one, pacing the top deck in the sunshine among the commuters, the lawyers, the squealing and romping little kids, the day-trippers, the teenagers, the architects, the mothers, the rest; even in the gentle whip of wind of the Puget Sound that seemed by its nature to forebode successful journeys and breezy adventures; it was what made him so well suited to one day write this script for a horror film—today that soul-sapping interior darkness felt acute. Such hubris, to possess even a shred of happiness; the prospect of a date with Michelle later that evening filled him with enough joy that to be punished by the gods on some other front struck him as only inevitable. How *perfect*, then, to be saddled with what was proving to be an intractable and tortured bout of the hiccups. Just when he needed most to appear to his father responsible, collected, a worthy investment, his body betrayed him, making him squeak and bounce every few moments like a little boy. Surely his father, behind that imposing desk, never got the hiccups; what excuse did *any (hup) grown man* have to go about sounding like a squeeze toy?

He tried to walk it off, he tried to hold his breath for ten, he tried to banish them with ice water, all to no avail. Who was anyone to judge, then, if in his diaphragm-contracting torment he ordered a six-dollar beer from the galley? And then there was that dark little bar he liked so much just down the street from company headquarters; what harm could it do to pop in for one more pint while he waited for his lunch appointment with Daddy, and hope that his hiccups would subside in the meantime?

They did not subside. But alcohol took the edge off, and by the time Bradford took a seat across the desk from his father—who held a finger up as Bradford entered, signaling him to wait as he finished a phone call—he hardly cared that he had the hiccups, and found his father's frowning at him between businessy utterances of "uh-huh" downright amusing.

"Well, excuse you," said his father, a handsome, svelte, white-haired man in maturity. Bradford often looked to him not only with rage or admiration but as a promise that he, too, would age well. "Bless you? Excuse you? I don't know what you're supposed to say to someone who has the hiccups."

"Good afternoon will do," said Bradford.

"Good afternoon to you, then, my son." Because his father had a way of seeming to register the facts around him only after having verbalized them, he then added, with considerably more relish, deploying also a bloodcurdling nickname, "Ah, Biff, my son, my son! Good to see you. I was telling your mother this morning—she was just getting ready for her cruise to Alaska, you know, with that new younger lady-friend of hers, the *folk musician*—that you were dropping by today. How are the Widdicombes?"

"They're (*hup*) fine."

"Nice of them to put you up for a week. Lovely there over on the island. Lovely, lovely, lovely. Getting lots of work done? I remember we used to go to parties there, and we would always be rushing to catch that last ferry back, drunk as skunks. Anyway, I hear the place they have is nice. I'm sure you've been eating well—I know Frank loves to feed his friends more than he loves life itself. Which is saying something. Not the greatest place to launch the job hunt, I don't think, but good to see you among such high achievers. Of course, you know you're always welcome at the condo, once the renovation's over . . . God, whenever *that* will be. The company's had to put me up in a hotel. Which has its advantages, but . . . so, LA didn't work out quite as planned?"

Bradford had been sitting by, hiccupping and listening to the usual parental patter, waiting for this. The fact of the matter was that a little over a year earlier, he had come to his father with a proposition of sorts: after being laid off from his job helping to manage donor accounts at the opera (the arts, they were suffering!), he had caught the show business bug. He felt—he *knew*—he had a screenplay in him (ouch!), and after making a fairly reasonable case for the ways in which residence in Los Angeles could provide him with a creative support network (and a less reasonable but more passionately argued case for having the financial freedom to focus on his new craft alone), persuaded his father to cover expenses for a year while he devoted himself to a suspense-horror script about a bloodthirsty but formless entity that dwelled in the woods of an unnamed town in the Pacific Northwest, seeping into people so that it could control them psychologically. "Just one year, Dad," Bradford had said at the time. "The world needs new monsters."

It was under this campaign slogan that our young man spent one full year drunk and high and occasionally writing in Hollywood, till reason told him it might be best for his health to cut his losses and come crawling back home with half a screenplay and an air of confidence (and an invented agent) that would leave his investor none the wiser. If Bradford had faith in anything, it was in his own incredible talent as a liar, and as someone who could appear to be in total control even as his life was falling to pieces. It was in the spirit of this conviction that he scoffed at his father's suggestion that LA hadn't worked out "quite as planned."

"It was a great success," he said. "The script is close to finished. My agent has the partial now and really (*hup*) loves it. We both agreed that I should come back here for some final research, to give it more authentic regional spirit—just . . . (*hup*) atmosphere, you know. This could really (*hup*) happen—I mean, it's crazy. It really *is* happening."

"You need to do something about those hiccups. So—research? Well, that's great. I'm proud of you. You're closing in. My son, a screenwriter! Have you eaten? We should go somewhere nearby and celebrate. I have a little time for lunch."

While it struck Bradford as potentially strategic to relocate—anything to draw out the occasion, and to put everyone a little more at ease—he sensed from his father's tone that the jig was already up, and that to suggest to him that this period of "research" required a new phase of funding—three or four months at most, a mere season—would prove fruitless. *All Our Fruitless Jigs: A Memoir.* Perhaps it should have been some cause for alarm, or for a good hard look at himself, that the risk nevertheless seemed worth it. His hiccups had vanished by the time they reached the bistro, and, emboldened further by a strong stout with his fish and chips, he asked for the money.

"Huh," said his father after a pause. "Well, it's good to have you back." Bradford then received a gaze of such pained tenderness—a look that burrowed and scrutinized, one that left him fearful that some once-buried aspect of his being was fast becoming apparent to the outside world—that he reached in desperation for his beer. "But to hear you ask me that, well, it makes me feel like I've made a big mistake."

"I've already told you that you haven't," said Bradford, growing offended. "I'm so close. All I need is a little more support, one more push in the eleventh hour."

"Yes, well. As I've already mentioned, I'm very proud of you. I have no doubt you'll finish your movie. To hear you're close, that's thrilling. It really is. But for me to give you more money right now . . ." His father trailed off midsentence, as he sometimes had a habit of doing.

"Would be extremely helpful," offered Bradford.

His father gave him a pleading look. "Well, I don't need to spell it out for you. You're always welcome at the condo."

———

Now that the *boys* were out of her hair (and Carol included her husband in that infantilized platoon; such helpless, fussy *boys*! Even Christopher, for all his lovable, artsy ethereality, succumbed on occasion to the cussed roughness of that clan), Carol could finally seize a precious stretch of afternoon hours to address her most burning desire: the continuing and total redecoration of Willowbrook. Carol took no offense at the Georgian-style home itself, or at the grounds on which it sat. Two acres of woodsy waterside land offered both privacy and the picturesque: from the Ipe-planked deck and backyard lawn, a sparkling whorl of Manzanita Bay; a kayak slicing through the peaceful waters, pushing off from the dock of some other spectacular home; fat greenery striking a jagged skyline, the uneven prototype for some dogged development to come. Carol had urged Christopher to paint this pretty scene for a week before he at last set up his easel on the deck and, hours later, presented her with an impressionistic collection of foul-colored blobs suggesting malignant disease cells seen through a microscope, an interpretation that sometimes brought tears of gratitude to her eyes when she gazed upon it, framed and hanging in the living room. What a talent he was, and her own son!

In any case, while she loved the landscape, the furnishings that cluttered the interior space when she made her first visit still haunted her. The previous owners had marred the spirit of the place with lifeless Americana—quilted pillows with patchwork pinwheels in a patriotic color scheme, a *white* dining room table (it made her think of a cafeteria), bookshelves supporting not only trashy novels aplenty but plastic tubs filled with *Beanie Babies*. Christ! As she had described it with finality to her husband in an argument about the practicalities of a suitable and costly décor overhaul, the hideous scheme that preceded them still cursed the house with an air of "spiritual brittleness"; the ghosts of creaking antique bed frames and star-spangled area rugs demanded that she first burn a bundle of sage and then, rolling up her sleeves, take the steps necessary for a full-fledged decorating exorcism. "We live on a prime piece of property now, Frank," she had said. "It's time to start acting like it."

Acting like it required that she sit on the deck with an iced tea and outbid design-conscious competitors for a shark-toothed bronze mirror frame on eBay. At the insistence of Gracie Sloane, and through the childlike exigencies of that guru's manual for creative manifesting, *The Golden Road*, Carol tacked magazine clippings of jaunty striped rugs, thrilling eighteenth-century paintings of mandrills, and all manner of other interiors inspirations, much of them torn from the pages of *Inside Places*, all of them contributing to her eccentric total vision for Willowbrook. "Source Energy requires imagistic fuel to do the daily work of manifesting," read one passage of *The Golden Road*. "It is to this end that we pin our hopes and dreams to our Vision Boards." The universe, Gracie claimed, would respond in kind. How fortunate, too, that the great, nebulous force in question seemed to reward good taste. Once in its graces, one had only to dream of a shark-toothed bronze mirror frame for it to appear on eBay, a cosmic wink.

Just then, a shape darting across the deck interrupted her online flea marketing. Carol turned her head fast enough to catch the tail end of whatever wild trespasser scampered past her field of vision, through the grass where her quick-to-anger husband had embarrassed her in front of her fellow birders and befriended their new gardener. Narrowing her eyes, she set aside her bids and stepped cautiously onto the lawn. The floppy brim of a straw hat shielded her eyes from the sun's glare; she brought one shading hand to her brow anyway and looked out in the direction of the vanished thing.

The lawn, grown a few inches higher than pleased her, needed cutting. Perhaps she could enlist Marvelous to mow down these mismatched blades of green and stiffened, sun-bleached weed stalks. Then: *Ah!* She spied the culprit of her distraction. Tucked into the too-high grasses, several yards away, a pair of white triangles poked up at attention; beneath them, two glassy yellow eyes returned her gaze.

Carol laughed. "Oh, Carol," she said aloud, wiping her forehead, breathing easier. "Why, it's nothing but a funny little cat." The creature raised its head at the sound of her voice, staring at her still, and Carol returned what she felt to be a smile coming from the stray. Its face, in fact, seemed to convey one of the purest looks of mischief she had ever encountered. There was something to the twitch of its fluffy tail that mocked her, too, as if to say, "Why, is this your yard? Don't mind if I *do* go bounding about in it without a care in the world."

"You're a naughty thing, aren't you?" said Carol. She crouched, went "*tsck-tsck-tsck*," and beckoned it toward her. After a brief assessment of danger, the cat swished through the grass, possessed of what Carol would later describe—when relating the event of this cat's discovery to Gracie, Michelle, and others—as a "positively royal air," approaching her for all the world as if she ought to be honored by its presence. At last it came to her at a speedy trot, slowing as it brushed against her leg with a purr.

"Aren't you a love bug," said Carol, scratching its neck. No collar. "But you *do* look well fed. Do you belong to somebody? Do you? Or are you wild? Are you a wild cat?"

By way of response, the cat rolled over onto its back, baring a magnificent white underbelly, putting its pink-padded paws up in a gesture of rapturous surrender, as if to say, "Why, I belong to *you*, Mrs. Widdicombe!"

Carol broke into a broad smile. This was just the sort of weird and whimsical thing she had envisioned happening at Willowbrook. Pride and triumph swelled her chest; in her hope to make of their new home a summery safe haven for both her family and the arts, had she manifested this sweet varmint's sudden arrival? Yes—the universe meant to surround her with loving creatures large and small, just as she meant to shine the light of her love on the world around her. When she was through with them, the grounds would teem not only with chickens, but with a whole manifested menagerie of kindly country critters. One need never feel alone at Willowbrook.

And to this end, the cat must stay!

The cat augured abundance. Perhaps, too, this would be a step in the right direction vis-à-vis the project of cheering up her husband. She had read somewhere that people with pets tended to live longer, felt less loneliness, and—something about blood pressure. Yes, animals were good for it, that was it. Good for blood pressure. This playful scamp might be just the thing to help Frank *relax*. Frank dandling the fluff-ball on his knee, his old high spirits restored. Frank, his blood pressure settling, his troubled mind calming in time for the Midsummer Feast. So he couldn't go on his precious trip; why dwell on it *sans cesse*? A cat could solve everything.

"I'm going to give you a fun name and some milk," she said, walking back to the house. "Don't go anywhere!"

The cat tilted its head at her with a certain measure of sass, as if to say, "Now, where on God's green earth would I *possibly* go?"

While she spent her journey in and out of the house wondering if cats really did drink saucers of milk—after so many years enjoying the high life in San Francisco, decorating restaurants and the homes of well-to-do family friends (and after compromising with Frank, in the era of Christopher's infancy, vis-à-vis his fear that a cat would climb into their son's crib and suck the breath out of his tiny lungs), she really knew so little about animals—she chalked that voice of doubt up to the wet blanketry of her Inner Critic, a force she aimed to tame with the help of Gracie's book. Her Inner Critic, incidentally, spoke in the same harsh, clipped, doomy tones her mother used to use when young Carol had begged her to adopt a cat: "I will not have a hair-shedding gargoyle in my home, scratching up my antiques and sneaking around every damned corner. Neither will I have a cat." No, they never did get along. Carol forged ahead, returning to her new friend with a blue-and-white china bowl of organic skim milk. (On the chance that it did drink milk, why subject it to an unhealthy diet laden with saturated fats?) The cat grazed Carol's legs with interest as she stepped out to the edge of the deck.

It lapped up the milk.

"Atta girl," said Carol. "You are a girl, aren't you? So pretty. You look like a—" Stroking her new companion's back, she searched her mind for the right name. What to call this mascot of abundance, this harbinger of joy and regulated blood pressure? "Princess Magdalena," she said, her tastes for the exotic and the royal dovetailing in one grand *gavotte* of a word. "You look like a Princess Magdalena."

———

Michelle had opted as usual to ride her bicycle to the movie theater. Riding her bicycle everywhere she could just made sense—unless the errand involved, say, picking up a bunch of chickens from the feed store at Rolling Bay, in which case the task called for a truck. Bicycling fell in line with a more Scandinavian, and thus more natural, more healthful way of life. The bicycle, in fact, was one of the least Scandinavian habits she had made an effort to integrate into "American life," as she called it, after returning from her high school exchange program several years ago. She encouraged a friend on the island to build a sauna that she made use of most every weekend, perspiring as she gasped for breath in the overheated wooden chamber. This ritual she followed with a plunge into the icy waters of the Puget Sound that collared the land. For breakfast she often ate rye bread with cheese or jam, and on some weekends she would bake rundstykker, having discovered that it was fairly easy to whip up a batch of these breakfast buns herself. These indulgences fed her soul, she felt, and helped to ground her in an unpredictable world. In love with this borrowed Scandinavian otherness, Michelle blazed forward in life with the lingering pride of one who, upon their first exposure with a foreign culture, believes they have seen a more brightly shining truth about the world, or have at least discovered a kind of *simpatico* spackling paste with which to fill in the cracks and holes of their own.

Michelle huffed and puffed and pushed her bicycle pedals, climbing the somewhat punishing hill that stood between her and the Lynwood Theatre. To be sure, a touch of nerves made her heart thump a little harder knowing that a night out with Bradford Dearborne, lovable lout, awaited. Since his arrival at Willowbrook her intrigue had grown day by day: who *was* this high-strung son of privilege, this unlikely screenwriter, this peppy, prep-damaged vagabond exuding both spirited curiosity and a ne'er-do-well ineptitude? And how did he manage to look so good whether sporting a few days' worth of golden scruff or shaved to statuesque smoothness? The answer must be, as ever, bone structure. In any case, she forgave his bumbles and his sometimes trancelike awkwardness; he was clearly possessed of a sensitive, creative nature—the kind of innate intelligence that would be given room to breathe and blossom in Scandinavia, but which, surprise, surprise, suffocated in the home of the brave, mercilessly smothered to death under the harsh, relentlessly unartistic pillow of American consumer culture. (A polyester throw pillow from Target, perhaps—one with a gaudy, excessively cheerful pattern.) But never mind that—an adventurous spark such as Bradford's was not something one could just confiscate and throw away at airport security. True mischief makes its home too deep for the pat down of imperial chaperones.

A decline at last made way for coasting, for a deep breath of triumph and the flow of cool air through her hair. Glorious

downhill exhilaration! A twilit tunnel rushed past: large conifers, many houses less resplendent than Willowbrook, wild
lawns bordered by even wilder ravines, a plummeting stream
that led to who knew where, wildlife rustling in the shrubby
pagan interstices. The island hummed with a giddy animism, a
sense of life teeming all around her, of sly gods in the rocks, in
the pinecones, in the woods.

The ground leveled out; Lynwood Center came into view
around a bend in the road. A small, quaint commercial complex modeled, it seemed, after a Bavarian fairy-tale village, its
dark brown roofs angled to steep peaks like a miniature Alpine
mountain range. There sat Bradford on a bench once kelly
green and now charmingly chipped, his legs crossed, his hands
laced in his lap: a sly god in his own right and the picture of
patience. She was surprised he had got there first. But then he
made no movement at her wave hello, and upon closer inspection his head lolled between his chest and shoulder, bobbing up
now as an arrow of panic shot through his sleep. He was either
napping or passed out on the bench, and though she felt this
didn't bode well for the date ahead, it carried somehow an element of flirtation, as though his drowsing was a goofy, amorous
gesture made with courtship in mind.

"Bradford," she said. She shook his shoulder. He blinked a
few times, saw her face hovering in front of his, and grumbled
with satisfaction.

"Just resting," he said. "I had such a long day." He yawned.
"Running around here and there. Michelle, I traveled by land,
sea, and . . . well, not by air. Not really. Not unless you count
being thrown out on your ass by your own father."

"Uh oh," she said. The sweet, spoiled smell of stale beer
greeted her as she sat down beside him. It gave her pause—did

no one around her know when the proper time was for a drink? Then again, there was something real about it, an honesty that flew in the face of the oversanitized self-presentation dominating the culture at large, and it must be noted that, could she have submitted his air to her practical mind for description in that moment, she might have said "there was a whiff of tragedy about him that I found alluring." Bradford, on the other hand, struggled, as he seemed to do more and more lately, to determine what version or amount of truthful explanation his ragged presence required. Should she know, he thought, that after quelling his morning nerves with pills, and then shaking up his quelled stupor with a flight of espresso shots, and then calming his persistent hiccups with a few beers, he had, between the caffeinated adrenal flood, the depressants, and the frustrating encounter with Daddy, settled into a most unmanageable rage? And that this state had called for a couple more beers during the ferry passage back to the island, not to mention a supplementary Valium? (The scripts all came from a trigger-happy psychiatrist who had listened to him speak at length about feeling "simply abysmal—as in dwelling daily within an abyss of some kind.") These shipboard treats had tamed his frustration a bit, and they made driving his Volvo to the theater a careening adventure. Here he had drifted off, taking a ten-minute nap while awaiting his date's arrival. Did she need to know about all that nonsense? No. The hiccupping made for a sufficiently charming and silly anecdote, and he managed to coax a laugh out of her by describing his torment.

"Of course, my hiccups didn't get me any sympathy with my dad," said Bradford. "He has *so much money*. Sure, he helped pay my rent in LA while I was working on my script. But now I'm almost done, and he's going to back out? It's insane. It's rude! And do you know what else? I'm starting to get the idea that he doesn't really believe I can do it. He doesn't think I'll finish—he thinks I'm a fuck-up." Catching the glimmer of pity in her eye, Bradford felt pity, in turn, that she should allow him to draw her into his orbit. Couldn't she see that he *was* a fuck-up, and a fraud? It was his curse to bear that charm came naturally. In spite of any doubts, he made light of his horrid lot, feeling a bit like Rumpelstiltskin: doomed to spin the straw of his misfortune into the gold of first-date enchantment. "Anyway, my family is a bit of a mind-fuck," he said brightly. "I may just have to ship off to one of those dangerous fishing boats up in Alaska for the rest of the summer—chopping fish heads by day, punching up my script by night. I'll probably lose a hand on the job, which is something to consider."

"Do you really think so?" said Michelle, on board with his joking tone. She looked down at his fine, clipped fingernails. "But then how will you play tennis with Frank?"

Bradford put one arm behind his back and leaned forward on the bench. "Well, hopefully it'll be my left hand. Then I can still play, like this." Twisting, he mimed one-armed ground strokes. He stopped, considered, frowned. "Serving may prove difficult."

Michelle neglected to mention other things she imagined may prove difficult with only one hand. "I'm sorry it didn't go well," she said. An urge to defend the whims and neuroses of creative types often clouded her pragmatism; her apology—for the denials of Bradford's father, for the denials of society at large to the creative spirit—rang, she felt, true, and carried with it the sincere desire that anyone with the audacity to "follow their bliss" (it was a sentiment her high school mentor, a statuesque woman and a classics enthusiast, had first expressed to her on the subject of studying abroad in Denmark) ought to be handled with an extra measure of care. While her apology floated in the air, Bradford pulled a small silver flask from the pocket of his shorts and took a nip, then passed it to her. And it was that accommodating aspect just described, along with a romantic sense of wrongdoing, that supported her taking a swig. She then quickly passed the flask to her date, who screwed the cap back on.

"I imagine," he said, "there are ways around the one-hand thing. Ways to live in an almost normal way. There must have been many advancements in medical technology. I could have a hook or a claw, or even an almost lifelike prosthetic hand."

Michelle, her chest warmed and sputtering with whiskey, smiled. She felt a longing to grasp the future prosthetic hand in question and press it to her cheek. Instead, giving her voice the soft, curling lilt of flirtation, she said, "I think I would prefer a hook."

"Yes, well," he said, "that would have a certain piratical appeal." He formed his index finger into a hook and scratched at her shoulder with it as he spoke. "Speaking of the high seas, shall we go see some dolphins get killed and eaten?"

Michelle scoffed at his coarse reduction of the feature awaiting them and slapped away his make-believe hook. "We had better, Captain Dearborne. I want to see the previews. I love previews."

"I always imagined you would."

"And if you're *really* broke . . ."

"Nonsense," he said, waving his hand in a dismissive gesture. "It wouldn't be a date if I didn't buy you a ticket. I like to do things in an old-fashioned way. It's part of my appeal!"

"Which part?"

"It's the hook, of course."

Michelle groaned. Bradford went to the theater window, this little witticism still atingle on his lips. "Two adults for *Porpoises in Peril*, please," he said. Paying brought home what seemed to be the steadily climbing price of everything in the world, and though he was probably a fool to refuse her charity, he steeled himself. Oh yes, he would buy her candy. He would buy her popcorn, too, if that was what she wanted. He would take in this bleeding-heart documentary, this promise of guilt when the lights came up, and, at some point during the parade of on-screen outrages, attempt to slip his arm around her shoulder, which moved ahead of him now as he held open the door for her. He would try, for the next two hours, to forget about his shameful afternoon, and to let the more general injustice of the world pass before him on the screen, on its way to the Academy Awards. There would be time enough to burden his sweetheart with personal monstrosities. His flask was still half full.

———

A Widdicombe loves to disagree. A Widdicombe loves to fight. But when the day winds nearer to its end, when sunset fills the dining room with a rosy glow, a Widdicombe loves most of all to eat. Whether the day has been raucous or humdrum or mild, a Widdicombe at table can set aside competitive sport, unwelcome chickens, self-help, "the community," birding, and all the rest, and can at last break bread in a most convivial fashion with whoever happens to be around. The table served as circle for a sacred rite of forgetting, a warm, miraculous melting away of tensions before a home-cooked meal. Frank loved to cook; so did his wife. Decades ago their relationship had hit its stride in this gluttonous confluence of kitchen enthusiasm. His beef bourguignon, the stuff of legend, had almost on its own lured her from the cold and anemic confines of her parental manse; her passion for fresh, organic produce, while sometimes exhausting to him in its hippy-dippy self-righteousness, still resulted in many a memorable caprese salad and artichoke heart dipped in melted butter. All this, even in its mellowed, so-called midlife form gave the marital bond a sphere in which to flourish more often than not. If Frank felt a kind of confused love-hate at the introduction of a circular green couch with Bundt pan–like central protuberance into the living room (and he did), he also swooned a little when his wife brought home a bag of tender greens from the island farmers market or when she left a brand-new cylinder of unfamiliar sea salt out on the counter—the equivalent of some naughty Victorian flashing her ankle.

Of course, they ate every day, and it wasn't always paradise. In the simmering heat of disagreement even the earthy fragrance of a morel or the shimmer of cellophane around an aged cheese wedge became merely the ingredients in a larger recipe for insult. But today Frank Widdicombe swelled with pride at the sight of his family gathered 'round the table, even if among that nuclear trio trespassed the curly-headed form of one Gracie Sloane.

"On my flight I sat next to a logging baron," said Gracie, speaking in a tone that Frank would come to recognize over the course of that summer: folksy and matter-of-fact, her voice impelled those listening to draw near, to hear some kind of parable, some fabular lesson. "We got to talking, and now *he* had a daughter, name of Annabelle, if I remember correctly—but never mind that. He tells me his little girl's run off with the circus—well, I know it sounds silly, but she took a summer job in concessions when Cirque du Soleil came to town, fell in love with the head of Food and Beverage, and the next thing he knew, *bam*, she's flying after his tushy to Australia. I just pointed my finger at him like so, and I said, hey now, that girl of yours is following her bliss. Don't you dare wet blanket her. Your daughter'll learn more about life with that circus than she ever would at some stuffy four-year school—trust me, *I* went to college, *I* went into the workaday workforce, and where did all that people-pleasing get me?" Carol poured her a glass of pinot grigio; the author of *The Golden Road* gave thanks. "Two divorces, carpal tunnel—unrelated, people! Haw-haw—and a lifetime of inner child abuse that I've been working to undo ever since. I should've joined the circus myself. Well, here's to Annabelle." Gracie raised her glass. Carol, Christopher, and Frank all raised theirs, too. They echoed her: "To Annabelle!"

"I don't know what it is," Gracie continued. "People like to talk to me." Frank served her from a large bowl of paella. He had peeled the shrimp she was about to eat, had crushed the bristly threads of saffron that gave the rice its golden hue. He guessed it might have something to do with her kooky personal style, which all but screamed, "Wretched of the earth, come to me!" Tortoiseshell glasses framed avid green eyes. A cascade of copper curls shot through here and there with white fell to her shoulders. And if her flushed cheeks had a certain brass-tacks set about them, they also broadcast an openness to experience that struck him as both admirable and dangerous. She might jump on the back of a stranger's motorcycle without hesitation—good on her—but might also invite that stranger into their home, taking for granted that anyone who knew her must also possess this zest for the fascinating multitudes. No matter for the moment: a savory waft of garlic and stock reached him, cut and complemented by a sharp undercurrent of lemon juice. Not even Christopher—who, having caught his father's wary appraisal of their distinguished guest, began to fawn over her with the obvious intention of annoying him—could spoil the triumph of this dish.

"Seattle got its start as a logging settlement," said his son, sipping wine—when had his son learned to drink wine with such an air of ease? Europe, it must have been Europe—and leaning toward Gracie. "Of course, after that, it became a hotbed of alcohol, gambling, and prostitution—all lifelong interests of mine . . ."

Now Carol interrupted with a comment about their son's marvelous paintings. The words "inspiringly original subject matter" and "utterly distinct" drifted into his ear, and then Christopher brought a hurried spoonful of paella to his mouth, enduring maternal praise of his watercolor portraits of Polk Street prostitutes. After she had finished, he said, his mouth half full (or was it half empty?), "Oh, did I mention that I went down to the harbor today and did some paintings of the boats?" Carol then waved her hand and added, "You see? We never know what he's going to do!" in a tone near to distress. She took a long drink from her glass.

"I think it's spectacular—this family is so creative," said Gracie. "I can think of no better place to be at this very moment, no better place to hunker down and finish my next book. Meanwhile, Carol turns the house into a gloriously decorated safe-haven for her family and the arts. Meanwhile, Christopher paints his heart out—"

Christopher frowned, looking to his father.

"—and meanwhile, Frank—well, besides this amazing paella—do you have any other projects in the works?"

Many forces came together in an unplanned pause for

effect. The dusky gleam from the dining room windows, the impetuous atmosphere of welcome, the ache of that day's accomplishments. The meal, the wine, the breeze! The strutting Widdicombe pride at having put food on the table; the spectacle of his silly son thinking he could incite disapproval (he and Carol had meant it when, on his coming out, they had both said, almost threateningly, "We love you no matter what"); those two pairs of female eyes coordinated in conspiracy, assessing him for signs of depression, for an answer that eluded disappointing diagnosis; and then—ah!—though France seemed so far away, the encouraging spirit of friendship that had begun to simmer in him, oddly enough, after his encounter with Marvelous Matthews. Giddy with possibility, lost in this rowdy atmosphere of pleasure, Frank heard himself say, speaking as though this riot of elements should be evidence enough of his intentions, "As a matter of fact, I'm writing a sort of philosophical guide to life."

Chatter ceased. His wife and son, so often smug in the assurance that they saw and knew all sides of his character, met this revelation with open looks of incredulity. Ah ha—he had them now! Gracie, peering over her glasses, saw in him a suddenly sympathetic soul. "Is that so?" she said. "Well! You and me've gotta talk."

The game almost ended there, for while the notion had come to him unbidden, it brought with it little in the way of particulars. A guide to life—for whom? True, he had overplayed his flinging in the trash once and for all that copy of *The Golden Road* handed to him by his wife; that offending chapter about the vortex had called out to him from the garbage until, insomniac anyway, he had fished the thing back out and spent what was left of the wee hours poring over its contents. Swinging between rejection and admiration, he had snorted at exercises exhorting the reader to collect scraps of whimsy (fabric, shells, tchotchkes, toys) for a "creativity shrine," but had sat in pensive silence during a chapter on bouncing back from "creativity assassination" that appealed to all his favorite psychological precepts: grit, resilience, stamina, a certain fuck-all flare for going ballistic in the face of resistance. Honest appreciation had soon turned into competitive spirit, and by sunrise, setting aside the book, his thought had been: "Well, for fuck's sake—I could certainly write a book like that. There's nothing to it." He had returned to bed, leaving the idea to ferment. Now, in a moment of repose at the dinner table, it had announced itself, made itself known to all. Perhaps it would be a kind of workbook, he thought. Americans loved to work, especially on themselves.

Fortunately, before further comment on his grand plan became required, attention to new arrivals did: commotion in the foyer, calls of "Hello!" . . . Bradford and Michelle. Looking, he might add, thick as thieves. Well, well—a little youthful romance on the home front? A roosterish if unsteady strut from him, a twinkle in the eye from her? Careful, young lady, he thought.

"People can be so cruel," said Michelle, following Carol's gesture to sit with them at the table. She sighed, shook her head, allowed herself to be served a small helping of paella. "Killing dolphins. *Eating* them. Dolphins, who are so playful and intelligent."

"Let me guess," said Gracie. "You just saw *Porpoises in Peril?*"

"Yes!" said Michelle. "And I am *outraged.*"

"As you should be," said Gracie, nodding sagely. "If you're not outraged, you're not paying attention."

"And if you're not paying attention," Frank said, "you're

going to fail the big test at the end of the semester." He dabbed his mouth with a napkin, and then, as though someone had asked him "What test?" he added: "The outrage test."

"I recently read an Australian study about a wild bottlenose dolphin colony," said Christopher, "which suggested that who a female dolphin associates with determines how successful she will be as a mother. Good mothers tended to spend time with other good mothers. Less successful mothers were less discriminating about their companions."

"I'd rather have interesting companions than be a so-called successful mother," said Carol, laughing and winking at their inscrutable son. Frank topped off both of their glasses with more pinot. He loved it when Christopher got tipsy and tried to work the motherhood angle for disapproval. It never quite worked, owing to Carol's willingness to completely debase the sanctity of motherhood for what she presumed to be her son's amusement. Oh, they were having fun, weren't they? They must have been put on this planet to have as much fun as possible. The two of them could spend entire evenings miscommunicating in this way, dragging motherhood through the mud.

"To interesting companions," said Bradford, raising a glass he had poured himself. A little wine splashed out. Also, if he thought Frank didn't catch the look of flirtatious complicity that passed between the young man and Michelle as he did so, he was sorely mistaken.

It was this look, in fact, that he remembered first when he got out of bed later that night, his sleep again interrupted by the tug of anxiety, his mind cataloguing specimens of fresh memory from earlier in the day. In the bathroom, he pushed at his still mildly irritated nostril, leaning into the mirror with bloodshot eyes (one of them a bit swollen, too, it seemed to him—was he allergic to their new life?).

Why was he awake? Part of a more gnawing concern, no doubt: no matter how much vigorous physical activity he indulged in during the day, no matter how many jobs he did around the house, walks he took around the grounds, meals he cooked, or good times he had at the dinner table, nothing quite seemed to nullify the yawning abyss of inactivity—of insignificance!—spreading from the center of this summer retreat. After a full day like today, his vanity and paranoia should not be tormenting him. He should not have time for midnight terror, should not have time for worries about inflamed nose follicles and the fragility of human life.

In the best of health, he could be a model appearing in a fitness magazine for slightly older men. *Midlife Fitness*, if such a thing existed, although he always shuddered at the word *midlife*, not because it suggested that half one's time was up but because it called to mind that chilling phrase "the middle of nowhere." Here it was, the middle of nowhere, and here *he* was, angling his head to get a better look up his nostril, the unremarkable redness there surely no cause for alarm, but also providing no answers, no road map for the territory in question. Part of the trouble was that out here—out here in the middle of nowhere, with a limited number of ways to tame the hours—he was beginning to fill that void with questions about his longevity. Time to notice things seemed to raise all those little whispers of physical disintegration he usually had such a talent for ignoring to a more yacketing volume: a pop or a crack from one of his kneecaps, a feeling of inflammation where the jaw met the skull that became more pronounced as the day went on, a racing pulse upon waking if he happened to nod off for a nap some afternoon. Unpleasant to think that his body was very gradually breaking down on him. Worse to realize that, under the proper circumstances, he might not have to notice it so often. He thought too about the vastness of the universe, and then felt like a strange and unaccountable animal. What was he doing here, a tiny creature clinging to the skin of the earth? What *was* he? Why was he alive?

He was awake now, anyway—why not check his email? When a lack of purpose gaped, a chasm filling up with physical and spiritual worry, the internet was always close at hand to bridge those shrieking depths.

But even the internet provided little comfort right then. Hunched over the bluish rectangular glow in his office, a search for "nose hair injury" returned only crazy-making articles about abscesses in the nose leading to encephalitis—brain swelling! Just swell. No, that wouldn't do. Two more clicks and a blank word processing file opened. The glaring white stung his eyes; suddenly, he was typing:

The Widdicombe Way—a guide to life.

Who for?
Retired people. People who can't sleep.
People with not enough work to do (body falling apart).
Lessons from sports psychology and hard-won life
    wisdom too.
—Take joy in the little things.

Having made this good start, it seemed only natural to email Channing and let him know how things were going. More clicks, more typing:

Dear Channing,

Well, although it's a shame about France, I'm making the best of the situation. No thanks to your fucking niece! Har-har. Seriously though, I've been wanting to tell you, I started writing a new book. It started as a joke over the dinner table, but now I'm envisioning it as a kind of guide to life—you know, like a workbook, full of activities that help you take joy in the little things. Make the most out of life. Follow your dreams. Keep the fire alive when your friends betray you by letting their country house out to vacuous newlyweds. Worldly wit and whatnot, etc. Healthy, wealthy, and very wise. Early to bed, early to rise. I almost typed "early demise." Fuck. I'm excited about the project and pleased to have all this free time to work on it. It's going very well so far. I can't thank you enough for inspiring me to follow my dreams by not giving me what I wanted.

Yours,
Frank

PS: I might have a new best friend soon. He also happens to be my gardener, which is more than I can say for you.

Finding that this email, like the last one he had composed to Channing, failed to articulate the true depth of his feelings—in fact, it had a surprising air of insecurity; were fears about bodily ruin infecting even the way he composed emails?—he saved it as a draft. Two inadequate messages to his best friend now clogged his Drafts box. Clicking back to the word processing file, he added, beneath the line reading "take joy in the little things," the following:

—sleep on messages composed in high emotion
 (Abraham Lincoln)
—examples from history/presidents/etc.
—don't pull nose hairs (use trimmers) . . . encephalitis

Clicking, typing, clicking, typing: soon our main man Frank Widdicombe had amassed a full three pages of ideas for *The Widdicombe Way*, of which these lines are only representative samples. How freeing that he could include in this guide to life any single subject that crossed his restless mind! There would be no limits, only Frank Widdicombe, *F.W.*, raw and uncensored, come alive on the page, ready with gruff, no-nonsense advice and activities geared toward the mastery of life.

What a clever man he was: within an hour he had rerouted that paranoid mental energy about the inevitable decay of his earthly vessel into an infinitely more productive channel. Lord only knew how many sleeping selves at that very moment were hungry for just the kind of improvement he had to offer.

And speaking of hunger, a fluffy grey creature taken with it jumped just then from some unseen hiding place and up onto the desk. Frank's heart leaped; he startled backward, nearly falling from his chair, and shouted, "Jesus fucking Christ!" Kip the cat, unfazed, began to rub its head against the laptop. (Frank, accepting that Carol would call the cat Princess Magdalena but keen to give it a name of his own, had decided to rechristen it Kip, gender be damned.) It then walked across the keyboard, its paws splaying over the jumbled alphabet with flat clacks, add-

ing to that philosophical masterwork-in-progress these words
of insight:

klpdymwslom'k
'um8u9jgf4r5dtdshyujn

"Well," said Frank, allowing this trespasser purring passage
onto his lap, "I could've told you that."

———

While *The Widdicombe Way* unfurled thus, one sleeping self
in particular stirred at the first sign of sunrise halfway across
the island. No animal companions leaped into bed to warm
themselves by his blanketed bulk; no other soul moved about
the spare studio apartment, grinding coffee beans or coaxing
him from Slumberland with the sizzle of fatback. Marvelous
Matthews lived alone. A band of light fell across his grizzly face,
and there he was: awake. Awake, alone, alone, awake—what
was the difference? His paw searched the nightstand for that
telltale rectangle, that packet half-dressed in plastic, and soon
he lay on his back with the first cigarette of the day fixed between dry lips. The ashtray he rested on the round of his belly.
His thumb flicked the flint wheel on a dollar-fifty lighter.

He had always been an early riser. Two hours remained before one of his clients, a harried Seattle lawyer who lived on the
waterfront and who, after taking Marvelous's number from a
poster on the bulletin board at the Island Gym ("Organic Vegetable Gardening—Landscape Gardening—Community Building"), had called asking if he could "handle a rock garden." "Of
course," Marvelous had said. "I do rock gardens all the time."

He had never done a rock garden. His business, now close to
celebrating its one-year anniversary, was largely improvised—

what began as a therapeutic, Zennish new leaf, a bit of meddling with plant life meant to keep his hands busy and put a little extra dough in his pocket, had fast revealed a natural talent both for gardening and for business. Too humble at this point to call himself an "entrepreneur" (he had done it before and wound up feeling like an ass), he nonetheless took pride when given the opportunity to tell people he ran his own company. A better answer to the terrible question, "So, what do you do?" than wordlessly brandishing a beer can had been.

Before getting dressed, he sat on the edge of his bed, using the nightstand as a makeshift desk on which to do the daily "freewriting" required of him by *The Golden Road*, a sixteen-week program of creative recovery recommended to him by a fellow former drunk. "Today marks the beginning of Week 6," he wrote, "the Week of Growing Awareness. I'm a little tired this morning but am going to spend the day moving rocks . . ." His automatic, uncensored, scrawled reflection tumbled out from there, eventually filling three pages, often returning grouchily to the subject of moving rocks but touching upon other concerns as well: "God, I'm fucking lonely," read one line; "Maybe this weekend I'll see that new thriller about the runaway train, *Hard Luck Express*," read another. Near the end of this exercise, when he realized only one page remained, he felt suddenly panicked that he hadn't yet mentioned his visit to Willowbrook. Scratching at his beard, he wrote that Frank Widdicombe seemed like an interesting guy. The line "Could be there's more than meets the eye there" marked the end of his session, and though he whipped the page over, leaving a blue-lined blank ready for the next day, this idea lingered with him, weaving in and out of his awareness as he showered, dressed, ate a bowl of shredded wheat squares with milk, and climbed into the front seat of his truck, Gretchen. "Come on, Gretch," he said, patting the dash after he had let the engine warm up for a minute. "Let's go haul some rocks."

Already the day promised to punish him with direct sun. Best to start early and quit shortly after lunch, before the heat got unbearable. He was farmer's tanned enough already, and prolonged heat sometimes made leggy bottles of cold pilsner dance in his head, a chorus line of temptation. With the help of a strong local high school boy he sometimes hired, he had laid down a curving, pebbled path, had planted ferns and fir and spruce shrubs along the edge before blanketing it in reddish brown wood chips days prior. All that remained was to put in a series of wood steps along the path, and then—the worst thing—the bigger rocks. They waited for him on a pallet by the driveway. He took his sweet time with the wood steps, walking around them again and again to confirm proper spacing, assessing the feel of the little landscape he was creating until the task could no longer be reasonably postponed.

He and the boy struggled to scoot the first large boulder onto a dolly, sweating as they tipped the burdened thing and rolled it down the drive. At first he felt some humiliation: he huffed and grunted as the two of them ferried stones along the side of this magnificent waterfront home; he entertained some half-baked but basically uncharitable thoughts about the lawyer and his wanton display of wealth. The thrill of his own strength soon won out, though, and for two hours (longer, probably, than *Hard Luck Express*) they moved, dumped, and positioned rocks in the lawyer's imminently complete rock garden, stopping now and then to stand in the shade by his truck and quaff cold water and sodas. He wiped his brow and thought, "As I build this rock garden, I build myself up." He looked over his handiwork. One roundish rock remained, a ridged and grey-white boulder meant to rest upon the slope of the hill. They loaded it onto the dolly.

Perhaps a man who had done a rock garden before would have approached things a little differently. This theoretical man, surely, would have had other professionals on hand, would not have insisted on doing every damn thing either on his own or with the help of one high school wrestler; and then who knew if there wasn't some complex theory unknown to Marvelous underlying the placement of rocks. He probably would not have used a dolly, but a stone-boat of some kind. What did he care? He was a self-made man—evidence of the resilient human spirit—and he did things his own way, learning from his failures as he went. His rock garden looked almost as good as the ones he'd seen in pictures. However, it would have looked even better had he and the kid not, at that moment, on the mildly sloping lawn, somehow lost control of the dolly, battling to right the long cart as that final rock, that cherry on top, rolled just enough to tip the balance of the entire operation, and then, outmatching the duo's considerable combined brawn, slipped from its platform and started rolling down the hill.

Horror gripped Marvelous as the rock tumbled heavily over the trimmed green grass. He ran after it, but what could he do to prevent it from falling over the hill and down onto the steeper waterfront decline? At the edge of the drop he stopped and stared, helpless, as the rock, having gathered speed, launched itself off a short ridge, hurtled through the air, and cannonballed into the water with a loud splash.

His helper turned to him with his jaw hanging open. A storm of swearing followed. Marvelous started to laugh after that, though in a way that he felt probably frightened the boy. "Well," he said, clapping a hand on his helper's shoulder, "nobody saw this but us, and nobody got hurt." In truth, the accident excited him. Now the sun beat down; now the stone was gone; now he stood at the water's edge, one rock short of a rock garden.

————

Heat smothered the island that evening. The sun set behind Mount Rainier, enveloping in a haze of orange and pink that craggy stratovolcano ("One of the world's most dangerous," as Christopher liked to say), but the stars and moon brought scant relief: Frank and Carol both tossed in their sleep, covered by a single and somehow suffocating sheet; Bradford, alone in the guest room, threw aside *his* covering in a nocturnal fit, hugging a spare cushion close to his naked body; Christopher, for his part, woke up periodically to flip the pillows at his disposal, looking in vain for one with a cooler surface.

Elsewhere similar woes were underway. Where no air conditioning had been installed, or where it failed, windows remained wide open, inviting the passage of night air and the ambient sounds of rustling, hushing woodland, the persistent lapping of saltwater at the shore, the long yawn of solitary cars passing by on serpentine roads. Along a stretch of southern coast, a heron, lanky and long-winged, its neck crooked and tucked, sailed past a flock of sleeping gulls, following an inlet to a path of marshland. A river otter, meanwhile, propelled itself underwater, its wet whiskers and gleaming eyes popping above the surface every now and then for air; it passed on its route a large stone new to the watery landscape, coiling past this curiosity en route to land. When the creature found a suitable covered path from the shore, it began to wag its dripping way toward a structure up the hill. (At that moment Marvelous, miles away, started awake at the sound of a raccoon rummaging through the garbage cans in the alley outside his apartment window, but he was too tired from his day hauling stones to get up and look. He fell back asleep.) The river otter had good timing: a full-grown opossum had just passed by the site of interest, having investigated the Widdicombes' yard and found it, perhaps, lacking in the slugs for which that ancient marsupial is said to have a craving. In any case, beneath the deck there was now a vacancy. Had she been possessed of superhuman attention, Gracie Sloane, who sat sleepless at a table on top of that deck, might have sensed a dark shape slinking across the yard and under the Ipe planks. Instead, she turned her gaze from the long reflections of light wiggling over the surface of the bay and looked up at the moon. Then, softly, so as not to wake the Widdicombes—at a polite volume, so that only she could hear—she howled.

PART II

S ome people around here aren't quite as enlightened as others," said Carol. She and Gracie sat sipping cups of smoky Lapsang souchong imported from a Parisian tea merchant. "And by some people I mean Frank."

The two were in the *salon*. (It had been called "the living room" until Carol rechristened and revamped it, creating a charmingly cluttered space for entertaining guests. The television had been banished, much to Frank's displeasure; Carol protested with the point that the two would never agree on what shape the living room should take—how could they, when they could not even agree on a shared definition for the word "living"?) The space now fell more stringently in line with the way Carol imagined her home appearing in some forthcoming issue of *Inside Places*: the controlled chaos of gilded West Coast bohemia shining through quaint, claw-footed French couches with their cushions reupholstered in zebra print, slipper chairs ringed with gypsy fringe, lamps crowned with fluted shades in turquoise and goldenrod. A bold green circular sofa served as centerpiece, its central protuberance now topped with a potted palm. Frank, for his part, found this "protuberating eyesore" not only "fruity" but "out of context." "What context?" "It looks like it belongs in a hotel waiting room—a hotel in Liberace's cerebral cortex!" Carol took this to be an endorsement.

It was just the kind of sofa for people who felt it important to have as much fun as possible. An aggressively irreverent décor nucleus: what more could she ask for? The sofa was a miracle, a piece rescued at the end of the seventies from a demolished luxury hotel and acquired by her longtime decorating adversary Wolfgang Schumacher, who then "gifted" it to her in an ongoing tradition of each presenting the other with treasures that challenged even the most flamboyant aesthetic sensibility. Well, Wolf would eat crow when he showed up to the Midsummer Feast and saw what she'd done with it.

Gracie, dressed in black jeans and a plain white tee—the very picture of chic simplicity, she had lost weight since Carol had last seen her—clutched her china cup with both hands and blew on her tea, troubling the plumes of steam that rose from its surface. "Some people don't respond as gracefully to displacement as you do, honey," she said, speaking in a meaningful, ominous tone, as though beginning one of her case study essays in *The Golden Road*—an all-too-human example of creative potential thwarted by mismanagement. "You may be the *queen* of manifesting—and you are, okay?—but that's because you get the whole abundance thing. You know, it's one of those deceptively simple concepts—but I'll tell you, the moment I stepped foot into this house I was like, '*Whoa*, girlfriend.' You are *getting* it, Carol. You are attracting all that positive energy to you. But it's only natural—and I've found this to be true of men especially—that some people will meet that energy with resistance. No, *natural* is the wrong word."

"*Typical*?" said Carol.

Gracie laughed, leaning over their lacquered tea table in a warm and conspiratorial fashion. As long as Carol had known her—just under six years, since meeting her at that seminar in San Francisco—she had been a woman hyperaware of personal space, and a woman hell-bent on subverting the nervous boundaries of private life with a more intimate, hands-on body language that she felt to be a small antidote—"a tincture of loving grace"—in the face of modern life's rigid, claustrophobic separations. She seemed always to be redrawing boundaries. To this end she reached across the table and laid her hand upon Carol's arm, looking her in the eye. "I mean I feel like I can *breathe* here, you know? What you're doing is really marvelous."

"I just wish he would let himself have a little more fun," said Carol. "I mean, it is *all* about letting, right? He doesn't seem to get that yet. He's still in this space where he thinks he has to go to it, to *grab* life, to *fight* for life. I had a dream last night that we were driving in the country together on this crazily winding road. He was driving us, and there was this terrible storm. I kept yelling at him to put the car in neutral—'Put the car in neutral, Frank!'—and every time I did, he gripped the steering wheel tighter and accelerated into a higher gear. By the end of the dream we couldn't see the road anymore and were driving faster and faster. I was screaming in terror; I woke up screaming. Somehow I knew that if he would just let go, everything would be okay."

"Wow," said Gracie. She moved to refill both of their cups from the high-design Scandinavian teapot—a gift from Michelle—on the table. "This is so relevant to the book I'm working on now, which is all about having fun, regaining a sense of play in our daily lives, and attracting natural abundance. I'm calling it *The Habit of Wildness*. It sounds like our psyches are on the same wavelength right now."

"Completely!" said Carol, throwing her head back in a momentary rapture of feeling understood. "A sense of play—that's exactly what we need around here. And as you can see—" here she gestured around the *salon* proudly "—that's just what I'm going for in my new decorating scheme."

"Honey, it's working."

"And with adopting Princess Magdalena. I mean, we've *worked-worked-worked* so hard, and for so long—isn't it time we relaxed and gave ourselves a little break? Isn't it time we enjoyed ourselves?"

"Amen." Gracie set the teapot down with a definitive *clack*.

"He is so depressed," Carol lamented. "And his workaholism is not helping. Not to mention suffering from what at this point I'm pretty sure is at the very least *moderate* adult ADD. I was looking at symptoms online the other night, Gracie—oh, and it's gotten even worse ever since he started working on that so-called guide to life of his!" Gracie gave her a look of sympathy for all creative endeavor, a look that said, "Hold on now," and Carol, understanding, added, "I mean, I'm glad he's got a project, but I'm a little scared. Where is this coming from? Nowhere—he's acting very unpredictable. Although he does seem to love the cat." In truth, it irked her a little how much he seemed to love the cat. She had hoped the cat would bring them all together; now she had started to feel like he was *commandeering* the cat. The cat, in turn, spent most of its time with Frank. He'd had the nerve to give her a second name.

Gracie nodded sagely, indicating she had seen this many times before. "He needs creative space now more than ever," she said. "We have to trust that Source Energy won't lead him astray. And a little abnormality, that's normal at times like this. He's changing shape. I mean, I get that. I've been there."

"Oh, I know you have," said Carol. "Talk to him, Gracie, please!"

The author of *The Golden Road* had tried to chat with Frank several times since arriving. And while he had responded to small talk with something close to relish—discussion of the weather, of his tennis schedule for the week, or, especially, of what he planned to do with some heirloom tomato or bushel of basil brought home from the market, proved animated—when she tried to coax him into conversation about his new book project, a subject on which she had much to say, he closed off. His face would darken, his jaw set with resistance. "It's nothing," he might say, or, "I'd rather not talk about it right now," adding, once, "Have you ever been to France?" Well, of course she had been to France. What's more, she cherished any opportunity to praise the laid-back sense of leisure time Europe represented to her, shown most gloriously in what she had come to believe was a cultural preference for long, drawn-out baths. In America, one showered, spurred on by the brisk spur of Puritanical shame and efficiency; in Europe, one lingered in the bathtub, returned to the ecstasy of the senses.

She could wax poetic about European bathing habits with the best of them, but that didn't change the fact that Frank's preoccupation with France carried with it an undeniable whiff of deception, and of desperation. Here was a man deeply damaged by decade upon decade of environments hostile to creative play. This France bit, well, it was obviously a cry for help. The man wanted his child-self back; he wanted to be wild again. If only she could convince him that he could trust her! But these things took time, especially when the wound had cut deep. It hurt her, in a way, to see him sneak off to his office for hours at a time after morning tennis, emerging only to fetch a beer late in the day (the stifled creative spirit often reared its head in the form of chemical dependency; frustrated mystics, as Jung said) when the heat began to settle into a languorous evening lull, or to spy him slipping from the house for a lonely, meditative walk. Sometimes, too, banished from the kitchen so that he could chop parsley and scrub grey-shelled clams, all her offers of help refused, a pang of painful empathy would strike her. The stench of minced garlic couldn't hide what she knew was his anguish; she struggled with the urge to throw herself over that boundary of solitude between the man and all those around him, to press that deepening shadow of facial hair—barometer of sorrow!—against her shoulder, let him weep as he surely must desire to do.

All perceived desires to weep aside, life at Willowbrook carried on beyond the sorrowful kitchen and the festooned *salon*. At that very moment, outside, Bradford had pulled one of the deck chairs onto the lawn in order to sit near Marvelous Matthews, who tended to the task of transferring a number of basil starts into the vegetable garden, his suntanned forearms fully sleeved with a thicket of tattoos (roses, skulls, waves, ships). The young man, his long, shaky fingers holding a third cup of French press coffee a few inches from his mouth—coffee *not* of the brand distributed by his penny-pinching father, he would be quick to point out—was in the middle of regaling the gardener with a full report on the intricacies of his romantic life and his finances.

"Scavenger hunts are fun when you're a kid," he said, "but at a certain point, it would be nice to feel like I had *found* something—something more or less permanent. Is it any wonder I spend half the day taking things to break through the haze and face the day, and the other half trying to put myself back into a haze so that I can forget about what I ended up having to face? And that I can barely sleep through the night? I mean, that's when I inevitably get up and write—it's a good time to write about the monster, but is that kind of life compatible with a relationship? Do you know what I mean? On one level I'm like, yes, let's do this, and on another it's like, look, I'm *almost* finished with my script—maybe I just need to focus on that right now."

"Huh," said Marvelous, patting the soil around a basil plant. With a delicate gesture he wiped some dirt from its young leaves. Was all this addled self-revelation and hand waving Bradford's way of asking Marvelous to Twelve Step him? An SOS? A cry for help? He barely knew the guy, but could tell he wanted something, even if he didn't recognize it himself. "What does your gut tell you?"

"Well, I think she's the kind of person who understands that creative people sometimes need to disappear into their . . . creative projects . . ." Bradford recrossed his legs and continued to speak about creativity. Marvelous lit a cigarette, half listening. Did this kid realize he had bigger problems than whether or not he could write the script for a creature feature and woo a young lady at the same time? None of the people who hung around this house, it seemed, had much experience with what he might call "real life." The son painted egregiously tacky watercolors of the harbor, the mother put a crazy couch from some hotel lobby in their living room, Frank had taken to speaking in abstract terms about the symbolic significance of the nose, "what it represented"—

"I'm sorry," said Bradford, "I'm boring you. I'm probably overthinking this."

"Sometimes our brains can be our own worst enemies," said Marvelous. Bradford noted the way in which the gardener's face lit up when, pausing to blow a smoke ring, he looked toward the house as though trying to catch a peek of something through the window. If the gardener thought that just because Bradford had troubles of his own—oh, the sober old regional relic surely wanted to Twelve Step him, draw him into the complex but simple program of recovery from drugs and alcohol. How could he possibly consider making such a major change while on the brink of completing his script? No, it wasn't for him, not now. And if he thought that Bradford hadn't seen the glint in his eye every time Gracie stepped out onto the porch or passed by the French doors, he was sorely mistaken. Marvelous—bending his impressive bulk over a somewhat rusty cylindrical cage, thrusting it around a "grabby" tomato plant, one stray vine from which the green thumb had to pull away from its slow, potentially strangling reach toward a young pepper plant—Marvelous amused him. "What is it's caught your eye over there?" Bradford said. A little thrill of triumph ran up his spine as he turned the tables of scrutiny. "And don't try to say 'nothing,' Marv—I see your eye wandering over to the porch, watching for someone. What gives?"

The gardener frowned and rolled out the burning cherry of his cigarette. He buried the ember under a handful of dirt. "Nah," he said. "It's nothing."

"What did I just say not to say?" said Bradford.

Marvelous rubbed the rough canvas of his gloves. "That woman staying with you all—what's her deal?"

Bradford peered into his cup, as though in the dregs he might divine Gracie's "deal." He swirled them with the express purpose of drawing out the pause. People were such god-awful idiots, manipulatable in the extreme. How satisfying to put this self-righteous, sober oaf in an uncomfortable position. Too many stimulants at breakfast may have left Bradford feeling frisky, mischievous, malicious even. He had caught Marvelous in a moment of lustful yearning. Was there any position more defenseless than desire? Even Buddhists said so; no one had yet proved anything the Buddhists said wrong. How clever they were! He must remember, after this particularly vicious period of his life had passed and he had become a successful screenwriter, to become a Buddhist. "What do you mean, exactly, her deal?"

Marvelous thrust the spear ends of another tomato cage around a flourishing green heirloom start with a grunt. "Come on," he said. "She looks like someone I've seen before."

"Is she *someone?*" Bradford goaded him. "Someone for whom you have eyes? Eh? Someone for whom you have the hots?"

The gardener found this forward tone too all too familiar: Marvelous, with his self-assured bearing, his calm, recovered demeanor (*stay humble, stay humble*) *intimidated* this young man, who he was being overly friendly in an attempt to compensate for his own insecurities. Typical addict behavior (*now, now . . .*). Not one to be pushed around, Marvelous sauntered over to where Bradford sat and took out another cigarette. Aggravation rumbled in his gut. Looming over the young man, Marvelous curled his lips in, a kind of quick self-kiss and a trick that drew attention to the long, diagonal scar connecting his upper lip and cheek. "Is she *someone?*" he repeated steadily, inhaling a waft of smoke. "Is she *well-known?*"

As hoped, Bradford shifted in his seat, jogged his leg. "Well-known? Well, I'm not exactly sure how *widely* known, but, ah, yes, she's written a few books, if that's what you mean. Self-help books. Well-known to a particular set of self-improving people, I guess—women of a certain age, in this most uncertain of ages. She's Gracie Sloane."

Good God! So it was true. Struggling to keep his expression stiff, Marvelous sauntered back over to the garden plot. "I see."

"Do you know her?" said Bradford.

"I thought maybe I had seen her picture in a bookstore," said Marvelous, trying his best to give this explanation an off-handed and conclusive air. "The garden is looking good, don't you think?"

Bradford surveyed the plot, laden now with transplants, his eyes all but glazing over. Better not to continue badgering the poor, ruined man just then, lest he risk a lip-splitting rake blow of his own. "Yes, quite good. The vegetables look lovely. Which reminds me"—he looked at his watch—"I'd better be off. I think I will ask Michelle to come out with me today, after all. Thanks for weighing in."

"When did I weigh in?"

"When did you weigh in!" said Bradford, carrying his chair back to the porch. "Why, when didn't you weigh in?"

Okay then. That second cigarette hadn't been the best thing for Marvelous's nerves, but it had kept his hands distracted from the temptation to smack, strangle, or shake. He buried another extinguished butt deep in the dirt of the garden plot, commencing to pluck out minor weeds and toss them aside, but then—Gracie Sloane! What synchronicity. So synchronicitous, in fact, that his hands began to tremble as he worked. Gracie Sloane, Gracie Sloane . . . never in his wildest dreams had he expected such a thing. He felt a giddy kind of urgency as he dug through the dirt. He should make a note of this later, when he sat down with *The Golden Road* to check his progress during this week—The Week of Synchronicity! This very woman—now a meaningful, cosmic coincidence in the flesh—whose first book, *The Twelve Directions of Positive Thinking*, had kept him busy, kept him company, helped him through a low time in his life. This woman whose written voice he had internalized irreversibly by reading through no fewer than four times her mini-essays like "Reconciling with Your Inner Critic," "Breaking the Art Barrier," and "Listening," and whose activities, from imagining one's ideal day in vivid detail to making a "creativity doll," had salvaged his sense of childlike play. The very woman now sat drinking tea, chatting, gesticulating, separated from him by one mere Willowbrookian wall.

Synchronicity, yes, but then a coincidence like this one was hardly done justice by that dry old multisyllabic mouthful. *God*—it had to be God. Either the hand of God or some other one of God's magnificent body parts that was always doing impressive things the full significance of which eluded Marvelous's comprehension. Yes, this or that mysterious movement of whatever organizing appendage God had free at the moment had undoubtedly brought the two of them together. The blue sky above Marvelous flared, bright and new and strewn with clouds. Making sure nobody could see him, he pointed up at the heavens as he had seen professional basketball players do when they wanted to give proper credit to the man upstairs, and said beneath his breath, "Thank you, Big Guy."

The old Marvelous Matthews might have barged into the *salon* without a second thought, making passionate pleas and all but clubbing the woman and dragging her back to his cave. He might have fallen prey to a heady brew of lust, euphoria, frustration, and lizard-brained impulsiveness. The new Marvelous Matthews, however, had taken steps. And though this revelation gave rise to unusual feelings—feelings that threatened the order he'd worked so hard to erect (Easy Does It, the Middle Way, Buddhism, Tao of Sobriety, One Day at a Time,

Buddhism)—he had a solution; a community; a sponsor. What better time than now to make the call?

———

What good were his paintings anyway? Christopher flopped down on the circular sofa in the *salon*, a summery seersucker suit hanging from his gaunt frame, and, finding no cozy corner in which to curl up with his despair on that cushioned roundabout, slumped. On the wall opposite, on either side of a windowpane lit up with hard light, his mother had displayed a total of eight framed artworks: two photographs by some San Franciscan family friend with a knack for stark, high-contrast urban landscapes; four seventeenth-century botanical illustrations by a German naturalist, stunning in their resplendent precision and vitality; and then, horror of horrors, two new Christopher Widdicombes from a series of watercolors of the harbor. Even against the pale sea green-painted walls, their trim accented in a deeper olive, *Gorgeous Harbor #1* and *Gorgeous Harbor #2* failed to produce the sickeningly strong touristic nausea he had so hoped to achieve. He had tried to suffuse these postcard tableaus—bobbing boats, glittering sea, each friendly seagull a childlike *v*—with a Pollyannaish derangement, a manic, overjoyed idiocy in the face of what was, after all, a downtown dock. Perhaps he had succeeded in this *too* well. The masts of yachts trembled with an irrepressible happiness. The blue patch of Eagle Harbor, which should have been reduced to a watery body of irony, jumped with bizarre life. All of this was meant to strike the note of some bratty child playing an obnoxious game in which they repeated everything their parents said to them, steeping each request or command in jubilant mockery so that the original words returned to them like the cry of a broken ghost. In the end, however, honest-to-goodness watercoloring talent had returned his own pretense at mockery to him with a mockery all its own: the paintings, despite his every effort, throbbed with a pure delight that overpowered any parody or impudence. They were, in a word, lovely. They communicated joy.

Forever suspicious of his own pride, he made himself sick over them. If only he had burned each and every watercolor in the *Gorgeous Harbors of Bainbridge Island* series. He should have known that when island regulars and the occasional tourist had stopped to watch him, had approached him with scrutiny in their eyes only to say things like, "Really great," or, "You've got quite a talent," that the paintings would never unnerve anyone. What more could he have done? He even, after receiving such infuriating praise, took extra pains to imagine the yachts of masts as priapic emblems, to see the water as the very material of smut, the birds as voyeurs at a pornographic peep show of received loveliness. And yet, his prurient eye had only brought out a sense of liveliness, a certain saucy get-up-and-go in the subject at hand. Admit it, he told himself, you've lost your nerve. In the end all you really wanted was to paint something . . . nice. Simple. Sweet. You don't really want to alienate anyone; it's an act. You're an actor. Displaying this series of six at Willowbrook for the benefit of his mother, his father, and Gracie—the latter had insisted they "have fun with it" and throw together a makeshift gallery opening for their own amusement, complete with champagne, and bruschetta prepared by Dad—had proved confusing. His mother, first laying eyes on them, examined them for a surprisingly long time. Her mouth began to tremble, and then she reached for a tissue to dab her eyes. Shaking her head, she said to him, "I was worried when you said you had started painting down by the harbor, but these—*these* are not paintings of seagulls and boats. Oh no. Not at all." What they *were* paintings of, it seemed, went without saying: some hidden giddiness of the human spirit, some core, irrepressible happiness. "Cool stuff, son," his father had said, clapping a hand on his shoulder. "Proud of you." Gracie praised his unfettered creative flow. What could he do but sullenly gift them each a *Gorgeous Harbor* of their own?

If only he could climb aboard one of the boats in these paintings and sail as far from here as possible. Oh, how he had tried to set himself apart. Nude portraits of Polk Street prostitutes, staid realist scenes of Italian streets brimming with garbage, early works concerned solely with the inner workings of milk, ironical treatments of the San Francisco Board of Education—all of it accepted, all of it adored. How tiresome to feel one could do no wrong—that one was, most likely, at bottom too cowardly to do so. Soon enough, in fact, in the days following his show of the *Gorgeous Harbors of Bainbridge Island* series, Christopher flagged. He dragged. The unfettered creative flow so celebrated by Gracie reduced to a trickle.

Finally, it dried up.

While his mother fussed over his father's (so-called) depression, *he* wilted. Did anyone notice that he had not changed out of his seersucker suit since the viewing? Or that he had not drawn or painted anything since, had not engaged in any activity that could be construed as artistic or creative? Typical. Frantic at first, he had looked for inspiration—in a book about reupholstering techniques he found in his mother's room, in a selection of readings on dentistry hauled home from the public library. He had even pored over an LSAT study guide with the thought of working up the nerve to start in on an unlikable series of paintings inspired by standardized law school admissions. But then, his instincts were clearly the wrong place to start.

Tired of himself! Tired!

He banged his head against the pot that held the sofa's crowning palm, then slid even lower to the ground so that his legs splayed out on the floor. Hands over face, he sank deeper, too, into despair. "Cool stuff, son." "What's it like to have such a brilliant son?" Son, *son* . . . The word separated itself from memory like a bird lighting off from a tree branch and flying away into the sky. How funny, all these words for what one person meant to another. *Son*—what did it mean? That he had been an embryo once, had gestated inside the human female that most recently concerned herself with acquiring the very circular sofa on which he now slumped. That he had toddled for some time under the protective influence of this social unit and now cohabitated with them, forever, in a sort of psycho-architectural labyrinth? *Family, son, family, son.* Turning the words this way and that, repeating them, they soon gleamed with mystery, strange artifacts unearthed at an archaeological dig. It was at this moment, holding these newly defamiliar-ized specimens up for inspection in his mind, that his mother walked into the adjoining kitchen.

"Hello, son," she said.

Of course! *Son.* What could be more obvious and yet more unbelievable? That he should exist only in reference to those that created him, those that nurtured him and paid his way to survival—what better starting point for an act of subversive and provoking performance art? He would *hang out* with his parents, throwing himself completely into an exploration of sonhood, son-ness; he would spend the rest of the summer so artificially at ease with his family, so devoted to an exaggerated performance of sonhood that he would eventually surpass the so-called reality of son-ness and enter a realm of tongue-in-cheek filial abstraction, becoming a parody of a son. If nothing less, it would surely annoy his parents. On that he could depend.

"*Mother*," he said, lifting himself from the sofa, staring across the *salon* into the kitchen. Carol stood there, buttering toast. "What are you doing today, Mother?"

She looked up from her toast. Once the words left his mouth, he realized it must have been a very long time since he had made such a workaday utterance in front of her. Accordingly, she scraped her knife for a moment longer than the normal pace of small talk demanded. "Well," she finally said, "I was going to run some errands in town—get some groceries for tonight, pick something up at the post office. Oh, and I have to stop at the bank." She sighed. "Michelle took the day off."

Another long silence passed between them as Christopher ambled across the room, hands in pockets. He stopped on the other side of the counter from his mother. His searching look must have made her uncomfortable, for she soon said, "Want some toast?"

"I'll come with you, Mother," he said. She turned to him with toast in her mouth, crumbs on her lips, surprised.

Son, Part I: Errands with Mother.

———

"The nose on your face is just the tip of the iceberg," Frank said to Kip the cat, tapping the pink protuberance in question. He then briefly touched his own schnoz to hers; the cat scrunched her face in outrage, glaring at him as though she possessed a system of etiquette all her own—one that he could never, coarse thing that he was, possibly understand.

"Do you know what's beneath the tip of the iceberg?" The cat, pleased by Frank's petting, narrowed its eyes into a rapturous squint. Then Frank shouted, "The rest of the fucking iceberg!" The cat jumped from his lap, taking up residence in an antique porter's chair in the corner (yes, Carol's decorating bonanza had spilled over into his office; he had held his ground, insisting that, like that old coot Virginia Woolf, he needed "a room of my goddamn own," but even still, the chair, which she had found in Palm Beach, was what one might call "handsome").

The rest of the fucking iceberg had been concerning him all morning.

Dear Channing Goodman, Nancy-Pants Extraordinaire,

I hope you're well. I've been thinking a lot about noses lately—how the nose on your face is just the tip of the iceberg (yours especially, if I remember correctly . . . although I haven't seen you in over a year, and I'm starting to forget what you look like).

Before you accuse me of impertinence, let me say that my guide to healthy wealthy wisdom, *The Widdicombe Way*, is going quite well indeed. I've completed several chapters, including "On Waking Up Early" (the gist of it is that you should), "On Sleeping on Emails Composed in Extreme Emotion" (as demonstrated by president Abraham Lincoln, who, if recent biographies are any indication, your brainwashing homosexual cabal is trying to claim for its own), "On the Occasional Compromise," which addresses a well-known strategy for marital harmony through the example of a handsome old porter's chair my wonderful wife recently gifted me, and "On the Occasional Surprise Cat," which is all about what, at the moment, may be the most satisfying, low-stress relationship in my life—a cat that wandered in from the cold, so to speak, or was seized and dragged in, but in either case has become a most reliable companion.

How nice to look up from one's philosophical musings from time to time and see a fluffy scoundrel give you a wink from the windowsill where it's sunning.

Yes, I know I've said things before to the tune of never ever wanting a pet (I said the same thing about kids once, you'll recall), but now that this one has sashayed into my life and my office, I find my old presuppositions about my preferences falling away. Suffice it to say, life is full of surprises, as I'm sure you're well aware. Why, just a few months ago I was sure I would be spending part of this summer in France, and then—surprise—life threw me a curveball.

Which brings me back to my original topic, noses. I'm holding mine thoroughly to the grindstone, Channing. I am hard at work on the next chapter of my book, a chapter titled "On the Nose." I must admit it's of a deeper, more abstract nature than my other meditations. At the same time, it is the most concrete. About a week ago, you see, our Michelle (I used the call her our assistant, but I'm not always sure what she does, so now it's "our Michelle") savagely ripped out one of my nose hairs. Since then the tip of my iceberg hasn't been the same. What began as a

little irritation—waking up in the middle of the night with
some intolerable itching and a little redness—has become
a strange affliction indeed. To the naked eye, it would
appear that nothing at all serious is wrong with me (so said
one of the doctors on the island here, who claims I may be
suffering from allergies). But at unpredictable times of day
I now find that my throat flares up. It constricts as though
by some domino-like series of malfunctions prompted
by the extraction of one crucial debris-blocking nostril
hair . . . Hey, that's a good line. I'm using that.

I've never had allergies before, Channing. And suddenly
my throat from time to time feels like it's filled with broken
glass.

One possibility is that I'm allergic to the island, but
another is that the removal of that one particular nose hair
allowed for the passage of some foreign particle into my
nasal cavity, some wastrel rock star of a foreign particle
that is trashing my nose and throat like they were a suite
of luxury hotel rooms. Now, in matters of health, it can
be a very terrible thing when more than one possibility or
explanation exists. Am I just a little sniffly, or am I dying?
This dilemma lies at the center of my meditations on the
nose itself.

In my research so far, I've learned several terrible things.
The nose, as I'm sure you know, is the gateway to the
brain. (That the nose delivers oxygen to the brain,
thus allowing me to think at length about the nose, is
an absurdity not lost on me.) There is a kind of yoga

(naturally) that believes the right nostril is solar or heating in character, and that the left is lunar and cooling. Now, Michelle pulled the hair from my left nostril, which could very well mean, in this context, that I'm now breathing in an excess of lunar energy. But let's set such nonsense aside for a moment, for there are other, worse things to understand about the nose. I have spent perhaps too much time in the last few days reading about Egyptian brain hooks, which those ancient rascals would use to break open the bone that separates the nasal cavity from the brain cavity, then stir up the brain till it was liquefied. They would turn the body over then, so that the brain spilled out the nostrils. As it happens, I've been experiencing persistent drainage from both nostrils, and it's sometimes hard for me not to believe my brain is leaking out of my body.

On the other hand (there are so many hands when considering the nose!), I've read, too, that if it's not just mucus—a runny nose—it could be cerebrospinal fluid draining from the brain into the nose, or CSF rhinorrhea. It's true that this usually is a result of some kind of head injury, but what if the removal of a very important nose hair can have the same traumatic effect on an exquisitely sensitive person as a head injury? The literature on nose hair is scant, so it's hard to say for sure, but anything is possible with the body. In which case an eventual CSF infection like meningitis can't be entirely ruled out.

And then, of course, there is that whole business with people smelling burnt toast before having a stroke.

Well, guess what my wife had for lunch today? Toast.
Who makes toast in the middle of summer? You can
imagine the panic that came over me when, sitting here
at my desk, minding my own business, the smell of toast
suddenly wafted into my office. My friend, for a minute
there I thought it was all over. I turned to the cat and I
said, "So long, pussycat," and then, well, I cried a little.
But some time went by, and, as you can see, I did not have
a stroke after all.

Yours,
Frank

Having also survived the composition of this email without
having a stroke, Frank saved it as a draft. So many drafts lay
in wait; he had not actually sent any of them to Channing. All
the better, for he had yet to achieve that measure of confidence
in *The Widdicombe Way* that would make it possible for him to
speak about it in anything other than cryptic allusions (even
that had gotten him into trouble on the home front; ever since
the spontaneous mention of his project at dinner, both his wife
and Gracie had been eyeing him with curiosity, asking after his
progress in a self-consciously casual way). Nosy—that's what
they were. Quite a nose had that Gracie: the bridge long and
sloping, ending in a beak-like little swoop. And then, to be
certain, he often preferred the innocent button of the cat's nose
to his wife's, which, when he really looked at it, reminded him
all too much of her father's—a snobbish snout that he would
without a doubt never see again. The mouth beneath that pro-
portionate and sensibly pointed patrimonial proboscis once
spoke words to the effect of, "If you marry Frank Widdicombe,

you can kiss your inheritance good-bye." She had done so, turning her back on a California grape fortune to climb in the passenger seat of his VW Bus (different times) and drive as far away from the intolerant Caruthers clan as possible—through Arizona and New Mexico, Texas, Louisiana, down to Miami, where Frank could make good use of his tennis skills for a while. Though they ended up back in California, the damage had been done: Carol no longer spoke to her father, and didn't much like to speak about him, either. She had shut the window, hard, on the past. "I prefer the present and the future. I don't want to become one of those people who sits around remembering better times—life, after all, just keeps getting better the longer it goes on, don't you think? We're getting better and better at life."

After so many years, Dale Caruthers came to mind for Frank only in passing—why *had* he hated the idea of him marrying Carol so much? There were far worse hippies afoot at the time, and far worse vagabonds, not to mention cultists and serial murderers. Not even a degree from Stanford and a crack tennis game could make up for all of the social disintegration represented by his long hair and unkempt beard, it seemed. True, he had been the de facto family tennis pro. But he wasn't a fortune hunter. He hadn't cared about the Caruthers' money. Carol, in fact, had kept the full extent of it from him until long after they'd fallen thoroughly in love. Well, if the man could see him now—a trim, athletic owner of several sweater vests and multiple pairs of loafers (with and without tassels, in black and burgundy), a passable patriarch who, pooling his earnings with those of his industrious wife, had earned enough money and enough good credit to afford multiple homes. Wherever he was, Dale Caruthers could eat crow. And speaking of eating,

Frank had done enough work for one day to warrant an egg sandwich with homemade garlic aioli.

Did a no-good hippie make his own aioli? No, sir. Upstanding and upwardly mobile men of integrity now added garlic to their mayonnaise. The days of the VW Bus had long since passed. And yet, after he had toasted, slathered, and fried in a pan, who should he meet as he wandered out onto the deck with his sandwich but another relic of that era: Gracie Sloane, her nest of curls catching the light; Gracie Sloane, writing in loopy script in the pages of a diary with a floral-patterned cover; Gracie Sloane, turning her head and saying something to him.

"What?" he said.

She shielded her eyes with one hand, peering through what must have been a glare coming from behind him. "Sandwich time?"

"You bet." He declined an offer to sit down at the table with her, preferring to stand at the edge of the deck, to bite into his culinary creation as he surveyed the land. "I've been sitting down for hours," he explained.

"You're telling me," said Gracie, closing the journal in which she had just been taking notes for a chapter called "Making Rules to Break the Rules"—a subject that she hoped to address at length in *The Habit of Wildness*. The notion that one could, and should, take a methodical approach to spontaneity, scheduling regular bouts of "feral romping" and "whimsical savagery," made up the bulk of this section as she envisioned it. This one part would contribute, eventually, to a lush and beasty whole, a guide that promised her legions of readers "a return to nature through creative play, and a return to play through a return to nature." (This last line needed work, involving, as it did, so many returns as to border on the vertiginous. It had come to her in a freewrite, though, and therefore need not be censored. She could work on teasing out a more articulate expression of the idea it contained later.) As such, Frank's bare-footed rejection of table-lunching struck a chord with her, and she opened her notebook once more to jot down a few lines: *Activity – barefoot picnic – table = symptom of civilizing/crippling influence – regular "barbarians' brunch"?* Having scratched behind the ear of the self-help muse with this little stroke of genius, she slipped her sandals from her feet and stretched her toes. "Frank," she said, "What do you think it is that makes going barefoot so gosh-darn delish?"

"Helps the feet to breathe," he said, his mouth half-full. Gracie sighed with pleasure, as though the breathing foot was the most delicious idea of all. And wasn't it, along with all the other delicious ideas about the human body? A delicious miracle, the body. Recalling a friend with a critical streak who hated it when people used the word *delicious* in this way, she redoubled her efforts to apply it to everything around her. The delicious feel of cool grass against her delicious toes (she hopped from the delicious deck now, onto the delicious lawn), the faint, delicious smell of pine needles and saltwater on the breeze, the delicious sun painting her skin with delicious heat: a delicious return to the senses, to the mysterious vibrancy of the big, wild, utterly delicious world. *Ha!* Lunching at a table only deadened the soul— why, why had she lumped down on that chair when she could have been rolling in the grass? Why did she stay at Willowbrook when she could wander the summery globe, sling a knapsack on a stick over her shoulder, sleep beneath the stars? Why write *The Habit of Wildness* when she could just go wild? There it was: the old urge to run, to quit before she'd really started, to keep moving lest some power pin her down and—and what?

"Do you smell something?" said Frank. He stepped onto the lawn himself and sniffed at the air. Like a hunting dog, Frank, his mustache raised to the wind, twitching, turning his head to try and catch some scent. Gracie said, "Could be that I'm wearing amber oil," nonchalant as possible, half hiding any trace of hope or flirtation. Why was it Carol never really gushed about this delicious athlete, his head of cropped salt-and-pepper doing little to disguise the stamp of wildness reformed? "No," he said abstractedly, sniffing around the edge of the deck, "it isn't that. It's like an, ah, animal smell." He peeked underneath, but seeing nothing, he lifted his shoulders. Could be pheromones, but then, she ought not suggest it. What was this impulse in her to draw close to men who had wives, to check and see if the structure had some loose bolt she could shake out? No, Gracie—no, no, no. Feeling a flush of heat in her face, she hurried to the deck, grabbed her sandals, announced she would now take a walk along the path in the woods. "Don't do anything I wouldn't do," said Frank. How silly! That was all she *could* do. Walk away from him, past the curving canes of wild blackberry and onto the path, seek shelter beneath the swaying maple branches and beside the twisted, ruddy madrones, their bark peeling away to expose smooth trunks. Her sandals, worn to shape, slapped her heels as she walked, and soon Nature, as she suspected She would, drew from her a breath of relief. Beyond the occluding trees, slashes of bay called to her, "Take it easy!" Furry rugs of moss, unmoving, said, "What's your hurry?" Odd shapes of light falling over the path declared her walk a holiday. Nature strolls belonged in *The Habit of Wildness*. Perhaps even a Nature Journal to help drained readers reconnect with creation. Why not draw a tree? Describe an anthill? Press leaves between two pages and rub a crayon over the top, revealing their crenulated edges, their thrilling skeletons? In their Nature Journals, readers of *The Habit of Wildness* would freewrite about what it felt like to walk in the woods. Gracie would include a note encouraging them not to overthink their strolls, and not to feel bad or guilty if they couldn't put their fingers on just how it did feel to stroll, but also not to feel bad or guilty if they *did* feel bad or guilty. "Just notice your feelings and sensations, dear reader, whatever they may be. There is no right or wrong way to take a stroll in nature." That was the essence of the thing.

Along a downward slope, a fissure in the path—a tinkling, thin creek ran at the bottom—demanded that she hop across. A fern brushed her calf, casual as an old acquaintance at a party. Across the valley, down and around which the path would soon snake, suggestions of a man-made structure (shingles fuzzed over with green, drooping wood grey with age) teased her eye. Curiosity compelled her, and before long she rounded the bend, the music of the creek fading as she hiked up the other side. A shack—a house—a hut? A shed. A discovery, in any case: stewed-looking planks formed walls at a tilt; wood shingles splintered around a large stone someone had, to all appearances, heaved onto the roof. She paused a couple of yards from a front door that hung by a single rusty hinge. Her pulse quickened. This, however, could only be the enchanted kind of fear so common to serious states of play—dark, spellbound discovery belonged in *The Habit of Wildness*, too. Summoning all the courage that she hoped her readers would, in years to come, call upon if faced with similar circumstances, she plunged forward. She pushed the door, inhaled the still, cool air of the dark interior. For a moment she stood in the middle of that room, waiting with stirred heart for her vision to adjust.

Then, through the tiny window tinted with scum, from the L-shaped crack of the crooked door, light revealed to her four walls in shadow, a dirt-flecked floor, a modestly vaulted ceiling partly broken by the stone. No cobwebs drooping in the corner, no droppings from any wayward raccoons, no cigarette butts or beer bottles abandoned by teenagers. No dead bodies, monsters, skulls, insects, holes, kidnapped children being raised in solitude; no road kill disintegrating in glass jars of acid, no serial killers waiting for a fool to rush in; nothing slime-covered, muddy, damp, writhing, many-legged, legless; no portal to hell; no bottomless pit, no false floor. The muted forest barely reached her in that lonesome, empty cell. What it needed was a woman's touch.

———

What it felt like was breaking free: spirited away by a good-looking, unpredictable young man with a car of his own and sunglasses in which Michelle could see herself, speeding along the twisting waterfront roads on the south end of the island as he, in a happier mood than she had seen him in some time, blasted a sublime and string-heavy film score on the sound system. With all the windows down, the warm air came in sudden, breathtaking gusts. The hum of the station wagon's engine changed as Bradford shifted gears, and in this carefree barreling some heavy, dutiful part of her fell away, as when, coming home after an uncomfortable journey, one crosses the threshold and lets a cumbersome piece of luggage slide off the aching shoulder. A picnic basket sat in the backseat. She could have kissed him then and there for all his recklessness, his generosity. He had been reduced to tearful laughter by her impressions of the Widdicombes—which, she maintained, came from a loving place—as when, just before departing for their joyride, she had started riffing in her best Carol voice, "Bradford, darling, I just want you to have *fun* today—now, where are my sunglasses, would you find them for me, please? I've come to believe we were put on this planet to have as much fun as humanly possible. Shall we have a little spin around the island? Too few people know the value of a spin anymore. We stop spinning at our own peril!" Bradford made her feel not only that her observations were keen, but that her caretaking amounted, in the end, to something meaningful and good.

"Today I'm not going to think about my script at all," said Bradford. "I got up this morning and realized that sometimes you just have to *step away.*" He threw his hands up off the steering wheel—a gesture of letting go that gave her a sharp little moment of distress, seeing as the car was rounding a curve. "When you're working on something like this, sometimes it's work *not* to work on it. Sometimes you just have to step away and take life in—take a drive, have a picnic, listen to some music, jump off the dock. *Relax.* I mean, you have to *live.* We have to live, Michelle." He smacked the steering wheel hard with his palm.

"Exactly," said Michelle. And though she suspected that one lived a little less every time the necessity of doing so made its way into conversation, she felt, on the other hand, that to discuss what it meant to live might in itself constitute part of a full life. What was that famous quotation, about an unexamined life not being worth living? "Although they say an unexamined life is not worth living," she said.

"True."

A swell of strings in the film score reared up, and she had to raise her voice. "I suppose there are many ways to examine life."

"And then an unlived life may not be very well worth examining," yelled Bradford.

"But what if examining is a way of living?" she shouted.

Bradford sighed. "I suppose one can't help but live, in that case."

The two of them certainly couldn't help but live that afternoon, so for the time being they set aside the task of examination in favor of a little fun. After peeling into the dirt parking lot and stripping down to their bathing suits, the two raced down the length of the public dock with all the happy ferocity of children, leaping at last through the air with a scream, plunging into cold water. Tempted as she was to swim right over and grab his waist, or to tease him by the underwater grabbing of an ankle, Michelle enjoyed the sexual tension that continued to build between them. She paddled away from Bradford in an easy backstroke, calling out that it felt so nice to take a plunge. "Just what I fucking needed," he said in return, treading water and doing a passable imitation of Frank.

Once they had hauled themselves up the crooked rungs of the dock ladder and toweled off, the picnic came out: bread and cheese, olives, salami that Bradford sliced with a Swiss Army knife, farm-fresh strawberries bought from one of the roadside stands along the highway, and, unsurprisingly, two bottles of wine. (Michelle, no fool, was coming to see that his nips off the flask were something more than youthful boozy insouciance, and that every meal with Bradford would include a generous helping of alcohol; but oh, the unlived life!) As they lounged and lunched, they spoke about the beauty of the island, which from their vantage point presented itself in a sloping hill lush with green growth and dotted with formidable, architecturally tasteful homes, a curve of dark, conifer-thick land across the water. "It has a certain magic to it," said Bradford, turning his eyes from the landscape to her in such a way as to suggest what else he felt to have a certain magic. "*And* a certain *horror*," he added, "but never mind that." At moments like this her heart would race, and laughter, uncontrolled, would run roughshod over her reason. The surrounding terrain softened her; she wondered how her date could imagine such a setting as home to a mysterious, disembodied, psychologically ravening, forest-dwelling monster. She refrained from asking, for they were not to talk about it that afternoon. She supposed that, at the end of the day, a psychological ravening could take place just about anywhere.

"I want to ask you something," said Bradford.

"Ask away," said Michelle. She had decided there was no real harm in partaking freely of the wine on a day so glorious as this, and had a buzz on.

"I know I said I wasn't going to talk about it—and I'm not talking about it, not *really*—but I want to go away and do some work this weekend. I'm so close, and my friend has a place up on the peninsula that I'll be housesitting."

"Nice," she said.

"It's going to be perfect. I was wondering if you might like to come with me."

In short order, swept up in the reigning atmosphere of surrender, Michelle found that she had half agreed to the weekend getaway. "That sounds so great. Let me figure out if I can." Both were aware of what such figuring out entailed: a step back to assess the depths before diving, instinct meeting hesitation and having a proper tête-à-tête. It freighted the rest of the afternoon with hope and with doubt. Could it be that this added tension hastened them, day-drunk, toward a secluded pull-off on the other end of the island where they could park the car and kiss, at last, in private?

Indeed, the eventual kiss reassured them both, and, if it didn't manage to break the tension between them completely, it cracked it at least. After a bit of this, Michelle pulled away, digging her hands into her hair.

"Oh my God," she said, "I could do this all day, but . . . what are we *doing*? I can't believe this is happening. No, I mean, I want it to . . ." and here she stopped to kiss him again, "and of course I can believe it. I've been wanting to. It's just—oh God, let's go to Pegasus. I need an iced coffee."

Bradford, unable to do anything other than grin since kissing her, started the car again. Apparently, he found no serious threat in her uncertainty, only the upset typical of romance. Irked and enchanted by that dumb grin, Michelle gave his shoulder a solid punch as they drove away. To this he responded with a low hum of pleasure, as though he had just tasted something rich.

———

After Marvelous met up with his sponsor (he also saw Bradford and Michelle, who stopped in at the same shop for iced coffees—both of them seemed a bit drunk and self-conscious to be seen by him in that state), he chose that evening to clean up his apartment. What began as a little nervous tidying soon evolved into an all-consuming summer purge (such was his curse: small things all too often turned, within the space of an hour, into heady exigencies, demanding his total devotion; better that he direct this energy into cleaning than drinking, but still, he couldn't help but notice it): windows thrown open, shirts he never really wore pulled from his closet and thrown into a white garbage bag, old newspapers dropped into a cardboard box for recycling. Wishful thinking, in part: perhaps, as Gracie Sloane had written in *The Golden Road*, if he said "so long" to the dead weight in his life, it would make space for the new. How much old junk did he have to ditch before he had enough room, energetically and cosmically speaking, for Gracie Sloane herself? He pulled stacks of paper—business files, personal mail, and so forth—from drawers and filing cabinets, spreading them out on the floor of his apartment for organizing. A cigarette hung from his lips. He imagined Gracie seated with him at the wobbly folding card table by the window, clutching a mug of cheap coffee and talking to him about the ways of the universe. He imagined waking up beside her in his terrible, un-made bed—note to self/universe: spring for something bigger than a full-size that your feet hang off of—and, comforted by her presence, pulling her into his arms with a satisfied grin as he fell back asleep. So he had not yet spoken to her—so what? Her own books made a case for fate, for hunches, for coincidence as a prayer answered. Surely that meant something.

A satisfying feeling, to have all of your things out of their holding cells and spread out around you, to hum with a sense of putting life to order. With these details in plain view, blockages and accretions stuck out in comic fashion. Did he need to keep these old issues of *Success* magazine? Ridiculous—he doubted any of the individuals profiled in *Success* kept old issues lying around. And would it not serve him better to separate this one file labeled "Important Stuff"—which Stuff included his vehicle registration, his apartment lease, his marigold-colored birth certificate (Swedish Medical Center, Seattle), his passport (would be nice to use that one day), and other miscellaneous papers—into multiple files? Then there was all the detritus from exercises in *The Golden Road*, and *The Twelve Directions of Positive Thinking* before that—reams of freewriting, lists of hopeful manifestations (the words "a stronger sense of self-sufficiency" popped out at him from one of these), broadsheet-sized collages still alive with stock images of satisfaction (a male model—no matter, it was the idea that counted—pretending to take pride in himself as he pushed a wheelbarrow full of dirt), romantic adventure (a leggy, mysterious woman walking down the street of some foreign city, dressed in wildly patterned clothes), and personal growth (flowering branches and vines pasted around a photograph of his own head, as the activity had demanded). These could go in one big manila folder.

One collage, however, gave him pause. For several minutes he sat cross-legged on the floor, smoking, looking at this map of desire. It was all happening, everything he visualized, cut out, and pasted, just like Gracie had said. Like any grown man, part of him doubted always the efficacy of these exercises (though, thanks to AA, faking faith for the desired result was beginning to come easily to him, a new second nature), which yielded its own particular exhilaration. How fun to voluntarily—and with faux enthusiasm—do something your critical mind scoffed at and dismissed, how rewarding to call your own doubts into question by some frivolous sleight of the self-helping hand. Pride tickled him; he folded the collage into quarters, filed it away. Time, he thought, to start another.

He spread that day's newspaper out on the card table and began to flip through those magazines bound for the recycling, ripping out pictures of styled men in sunglasses and suits, women in white bikinis lounging poolside, circles of sun culled from full-page advertisements for booze and profit colleges and trips to Panama, cultivating an atmosphere of heat, skin, torpor. Bodies entwined. Even after all of this, a hole at the center of his new vision beckoned to be filled with—well, he knew what. And though he hesitated, the coaching of those earnest guides to remedial creative gesture soon wrestled his hesitation to the ground. In a happy trance, he grabbed *The Golden Road* and cut the author photo from the back cover. He found a recent snapshot of himself (looking a little jowly, but so what; he rarely photographed well) and pasted her in, a wise, warm head beside his own.

This pretty picture he placed in the center of the collage. It was now, he felt, complete. The two of them looked a bit like the couple from *American Gothic*, except that her stubborn tenacity came across not in frown lines and a hard stare, but in an imploringly frolicsome gaze, a steadfast smile. His own features blazed forth with a dumb, sleepy-eyed half grin, an insult to the drawn resilience of its predecessor. (Rather than guarding a farmhouse, too, the pair stood steady in a maelstrom of coveted objects, a churning sea of luxuries.) Never mind that: he secured the collage to his wall with thumbtacks, pleased and guilty, admiring his handiwork. Of course, she must never see it. Maybe years from now, when they stood together at the altar, he would turn to her and say, "Gracie Sloane, I manifested you." And maybe, too, she would, with tears in her eyes, touch his cheek and say, "Oh, Marvelous—I manifested you, too," and then he would kiss the bride.

God, what was he thinking? He wasn't thinking, not really—and how nice. In the meantime, just to have that collage hanging loose by the window made it a little easier to move on with the task at hand: to "chop wood," to "carry water," to say good-bye to yesterday's garbage and empty out his ashtrays.

———

While Marvelous tended to manifesting his desires and taking out the trash, Carol drew close to completing a full day of errands. All of them, however, had been given a strange, theatrical makeover by her son. At the bank, he had insisted on walking with her to the teller window and, while she deposited a check, engaging the clerk in a long discourse about the bygone days of the pneumatic tubes used to do business from one's car in the bank drive-thru ("When I was a child," he had said, "I used to love those old tubes. Do you remember, Mother? You would take me with you every time you went to the bank because you knew how much I loved watching those cylinders travel through them, between citizen and banker. What ever happened to those old tubes . . . uh, Heather? Oh, I know—computers put an end to all that. Isn't it sad, Mother? Computers . . ."). When they stopped to get coffees to go from Island Coffee, a deranged, overcome look had entered his eyes, so much so that she feared he might start to cry as he looked at her and said, in a trembling voice, "Isn't this nice? Just a mother and son stopping to get coffee together so they can run some more errands!" Then the post office, where he had taken an inordinate interest in the family post office box, pointing at it with excitement and saying, "I need to write down the number of this post office box. I'm going to send you and Dad a special letter from Rhode Island. Yes, that's what I'm going to do. I'm going to sign it, 'Your son, Christopher.' "

It was a treat, of course, to take her only son along on these errands, but on some level his charged, unpredictable behavior frightened her. She admired her son, her brilliant little gay *artiste*. She often wanted to describe things as "fabulous" around him, though she knew he shrank from the word. The more he drew attention to the fact that she remained his mother and not, as she sometimes felt she struggled to be, his friend, the more she felt she had to impress and mollify him, as though he expected her to feel somehow guilty for having given birth to him, as though the filial bond was a kind of outrage, a transgression for which she ought to perform endless penance. Yes, Christopher had an eccentric, artistic nature, but on this occasion his personality struck her as burdened with an additional layer of basic grief, a stratum of pain laid down by life's glaring and essential absurdities. He had come to see the world in a way that hurt him, she felt. A day spent witnessing this anguish disturbed her.

By the time they got to the grocery store, her spirits were dragging along the weight of concern. She saw more, too, than he gave her credit for: did he think, for example, that she couldn't see how terrified he was? Did he think she couldn't sense how he felt about her? That he saw her as part of an all-too human conspiracy to make him suffer? Self-absorbed—but he was at that age. Still, it pained her; it slowed her; the ambient sounds of the market churned around her, thick with sorrow. She had never been called "Mother" so many times in one day.

"Now, what do we need?" said Christopher. "I'll help you shop. Let me see the list. Shrimp, peas, farfalle, parmesan, bell peppers, salad greens, lemon. Oh, I know Dad likes those dark chocolate bars with almonds and sea salt—we should get him one of those. Treats—treats for the whole family! Father, son, and mother."

What exactly *was* going on in Christopher's head? He temporarily extracted himself at that moment, for he had started to feel overwhelmed and needed a moment to think. He left his mother with the cart, swerving away down an aisle stacked high with a rainbow of clear plastic soda pop liters. He needed a breather; his first performance art project, *Son*, was proving fruitful, but it exhausted him. It required that he drag his personal history to the surface—that bit with the pneumatic tubes had been inspired (a real memory, and dear to him), but it knocked something loose. All day since, pleasant memories of boyhood flew to him, lining up like birds on a telephone wire. How weird that the banalities of survival—money, food, driving as a family from place to place, fetching, fetching, fetching—vibrated with so many emotional associations, and that these in turn felt so far removed from their present reality. Perhaps he wanted his mother to delight in his childlike delight at pneumatic banking once more, or to beam when he called her Mother. Long ago, the procurement of a chocolate bar for his father would have been grounds for a day-long adventure of anticipation, culminating in ceremonial presentation and the electric charge of fatherly surprise. Today, he would be lucky to get a "Hey, thanks—nice of you. My favorite."

Not that he imagined the three of them could ever return to that state of delirious play. No: impossible. And therein lay what now clutched at his nicotine-stained, Europhilic heart: he could never again sit on a tall chair as a seven-year-old, making chocolate chip cookies at the counter with his mother and father, could never again feel the somehow illicit elation of finally understanding that his parents, of all people, had names—*Frank* and *Carol*—that they prefer he not use. (For several weeks following, he had by turns amused and unsettled them by playing up this formality, addressing them as equals. "Carol, Frank, can we go to the park? There's a new drinking fountain I want to see.")

He took hold of a bag of shell-on shrimp—grey, frosted, faintly striped. One must go on making new memories. European memories, Rhode Island memories, memories of this island. All new memories, all far from home (home being, it seemed, the past, a shore one perpetually sailed away from, a concept that struck him as more outmoded every day). At that moment, this prospect filled his breast with panic. To step away from the freezer door with this cold, bulging bag of headless shrimp, step into making a brand-new memory, seemed a bravery beyond him. When the idea emerged that he might go ask his mother right now if they could buy the ingredients for chocolate chip cookies, and convince Dad to make them with them, tears almost welled up; he choked on a sound half laugh, half sob. "Christopher, Christopher—you can't cry in the grocery store." He wiped his eyes and sighed. "This isn't like me. What's going on? I move ahead. I leave behind."

Walking down the aisle, the prospect of returning to his mother, her cart filled with items she had picked out herself, set his heart pounding with fear. What if, in the last five minutes, she had changed? He grabbed the chocolate bar for his dad on the way. Yes, most certainly she had, in the last five minutes, changed. It would be invisible—no new line down the center of her forehead, no streak of white in her hair. Time itself would bear the mark, cockled by the memory of each new moment, an orange wrinkling on a windowsill.

His mother stood inspecting cherry tomatoes. She gave him a smile as he approached. The look said, "I know, I know." The voice said, "Thank you, son." He dropped the bag of shrimp in the cart, letting it crunch against metal.

———

Dinner again. Somehow the prospect buoyed Frank's spirits more than it had in recent days. The badgering boobs of Willowbrook had all disappeared down their own rabbit holes—in the case of Gracie with her compulsive walks in the woods, almost literally. Carol, distracted by the concerns of sons and guests and area rugs, turned her spotlight away from him for the time being. Christopher was being Christopher, hanging his head after a day of errands, curling on a sofa in the *salon*, cuddling up with some volume of arcane knowledge. (That boy just couldn't handle day-to-day details, could he?) Bradford and Michelle scampered about somewhere, quite likely with their hands in one another's hair, their eyes full of young, dumb love. And Marvelous—where the hell was Marvelous?

Frank had come to terms with the fact that the gardener wouldn't take a drink with him no matter how much he teased him about his sobriety (all in good fun) or expounded on the virtues of a recently acquired bottle of Montepulciano. He was a good man, Marvelous—could give as well as he took, reminding Frank in this way of old pals like Channing. So, Frank had extended an invitation: "Come for dinner. You can help me in the kitchen. We'll cook up some of those community vegetables you love so much."

The doorbell rang. Frank, already entering "the zone"— that cherished psychological space where slicing onions into half-moons mattered more than the inner workings of the nose or inflamed finger joints, where dragging a lemon zester over a bright yellow rind rivaled the Zen benefits of raking any sand garden (so Buddhists didn't go for onions—did that make him a heretic in enlightenment terms?)—went to the door wiping his hands on a dish towel, and let in the bluff mug of Mr. Matthews with a hearty greeting and an immediate philosophical inquiry. "Marvelous, you know a thing or two about this enlightenment shit. Why do Buddhists hate onions and garlic?"

Marvelous, feeling the free and easy flow of ideas after a full day of cleaning and collage work, offered, "Because they're onion-lightened." Not even the chopping up of the verboten bulb in question could have produced so many tears as the fit into which Frank Widdicombe then fell.

When he had recovered, he wiped his eye and said, "Fucking hell. You're all right. Here, peel these shrimp."

And so began their friendly kitchen adventure. Frank brought Marvelous into the so-called zone with him, acting as though the two had worked in a kitchen together all their lives. He maneuvered around the gardener whose bearish hands he now saw called for extra concentration in the shrimp-shelling department (too bad for him—concentration was the name of the game), sliding a knife from the block. He set up a cutting board alongside him, chopping leaves of basil for the zucchini blossom stuffing. The basil and blossoms both came from the garden, so Frank made a point to praise the former's aroma and to say how thrilled he was to cook with fresh specimens of the latter. Ah, summer! A season with culinary delights all its own, flavors that seemed somehow infused with blue skies and sunlight. As long as he kept on cooking and eating, the terrifying terminal fate of his body kept its distance. Mixing the basil with goat cheese, Frank pondered.

"Have you ever thought about getting a goat?" he asked Marvelous.

"You can't get just one goat," said Marvelous. "It'll make a racket. They don't like being alone."

"Why not?" said Frank, turning to the sink to rinse his hands. "Being alone, that's a wonderful thing."

"You might not think so if you were a goat," said Marvelous. He plopped another unsheathed grey crustacean into a glass bowl.

"Assuming goats can think at all," said Frank. "Maybe if

they could, they wouldn't mind being alone so much." Then, as if to demonstrate the usefulness of thoughtful silence, the two of them carried on for a few minutes without speaking. Marvelous peeled on while Frank halved red and gold cherry tomatoes with a serrated knife. A fruity, tangy smell rose up from the cutting board. You would think this silence had concerned the cat, for it soon came skulking around the corner of the kitchen cabinet and brushed against Marvelous's leg.

"Hello, cat," said Marvelous.

"She likes you," said Frank.

"She likes shrimp."

"Well," said Frank, crouching down to scratch beneath her chin, "you can't fucking have any! You'll get sick."

"Actually, she probably won't."

"What do you know about cats?"

"I know I've fed a raw shrimp to one before."

"Really?"

"Yes, really."

"And it didn't get terribly sick and die?"

Marvelous rolled his eyes. "Come on. Cats have stronger stomachs than we do. They make violin strings out of them."

"I don't think that's true." Frank drew his brows together and frowned. "I think they use sheep."

"Well, then why do they call it catgut?"

"Search me. Maybe once upon a time they used the guts of cats. Not in this day and age."

"Here, watch," said Marvelous. He plucked a pale, raw shrimp from the bowl and dangled it in front of the cat. Front claws and mouth flew to the morsel, dragging it to the floor, devouring it with tiny, wet smacks.

"Well, I'll be a fucking monkey's uncle," said Frank.

"See?" said Marvelous. "Do you really think she'd get so excited about something that could make her sick?"

Frank, turning to wash a pile of lettuce, concluded that this demonstration, while illuminating, probably gave Kip the idea that she could come mincing around the kitchen whenever she desired a taste of the sea. "Then again," he sighed, "why not?" He would certainly be feeding her another fishy treat at some point in the near future, if only to remind her who *really* loved her, who cared for her and fed her and petted her, day after day. As of now, deceived by indulgence, she made a big show of rubbing her flank against Marvelous and purring.

To Frank's surprise, jealousy nipped at him. He plunged his hand into the bag of heart-shaped cat treats they kept on the counter, rustling it to get her attention. The little glutton rushed to him, and he fed her one of the treats from his palm, saying, "You've been so brave, letting Marvelous feed you raw shrimp—here's a reward." From that point forward the cat paced the kitchen, turning her head up first at Marvelous, and then at him. Well, better she be confused than taken in by a charlatan. He kind of hoped she did get sick, just so that he could call up Marvelous the next day and say, "Hey, guess what? There's catgut everywhere."

Frank set his friend to shelling fresh peas for the pasta primavera while he julienned summer squash, and they fell again into silence. Short-lived, thanks to the arrival of one wild woman back from her forest escapades: Gracie stepped in from the porch with the lowering sun ablaze behind her (deep orange, it looked kind of like a wobbling egg yolk), more calm and self-possessed than earlier, when she had fled into the woods. Going through some thing gone through by women of her age, no doubt.

"Evening, gentlemen," she said. She took a seat at the counter. A serene smile lingered on her face, to all appearances left over from some estimable outdoor insight.

"You know Marvelous," said Frank, surprising himself: after several weeks of Marvelous coming and going, he couldn't quite believe that there had been no occasion for the two of them to meet. In fact, as they shook hands, Frank caught the slightest tremble of giddy guilt in the gardener's eyes. Had Marvelous been avoiding her, hiding from her? He *had* started showing up earlier in the morning, making muttered claims to "temporary schedule concerns." Perhaps they had just missed each other.

"Always a fan of men in the kitchen," Gracie said, plucking a plum from the fruit bowl and holding it to her nose. "*Men in the Kitchen, Women in the Woods*—now that's a catchy title."

This comment gave Frank another good laugh, but before he could add any further appreciation, Marvelous chimed in with, "I think it's important to feel at home in the kitchen *and* in the woods. You have to be a well-rounded person."

"I couldn't agree more." Gracie bit into the plum. "I would only add that, for some reason, people are more careful than ever. There are more people stuck indoors than ever, too—men *and* women—in the kitchen, on their laptops, glued to their phones. Screens, screens, screens! Psychological safe zones! That's what they are. Not that people don't need to feel safe from time to time, but really, what ever happened to the spirit of adventure? No one in this country even hitchhikes anymore! They're afraid."

Frank, seeing that Marvelous leaned one elbow on the counter as he continued to shell peas, and that he listened intently as Gracie went on about adventure—she sounded semi-sensible for once, anyway—took the opportunity to slip away for a second. "Come on, little lady," he said, scooping the cat up in his arms, "you can't stay in the kitchen." He did his best not to cast any suggestive glances or wiggled eyebrows over his shoulder, though the temptation was strong. If he had, he might have met Gracie's admiring gaze, which instead followed his back as he slipped around the corner down the hall.

Cats named Kip ought to feel at home in breakfast nooks—all those spacious chairs and couches on which to curl, that bonanza of throw pillows calling out for a fresh coat of hair, armrests waiting to be used as fallen scratching posts. Why, then, did this particular Kip wriggle from his grasp every time he took a seat, and make as if to return to the kitchen? Marvelous and his fucking shrimp. He really did want her out of the kitchen, though. A cat underfoot meant a tail in peril, and Frank's feet weren't known for not stepping on nice things. And so, after several rounds of catch-the-cat-and-drag-it-to-the-sofa-and-hold-it-still-in-your-lap-to-calm-it-down-but-then-it-escapes, he buried La Kip beneath the aforementioned bonanza, where at last, breathing at the bottom of her cushioned pyramid, she seemed to find peace (or, at least, to be stuck). No harm in leaving his little darling there for the time being—she was smart and could break free at her own leisure. She had a growth mind-set.

It was true that cats took care of themselves. How he loved being a cat owner!

Speaking of love and wild beasts, the kitchen all but shook with aftershocks of sexual tension upon his return. Marvelous stood alone, popping the last of the sweet green peas from their pods, a far-off look in his eyes. He looked up at him and then back at his peas, making a big show of business as usual. Oh no, unh unh—that was not how things worked in a Widdicombe household. Frank slapped his shoulder.

"What?"

"*Wild thing, I think I love you*," he sang under his breath, "*But I wanna kno-ow for sure!*"

"Shut up, Frank," said Marvelous. Something had surely passed between the two—some current of electricity beneath the hitchhiking nostalgia and talk of summer peas. Marvelous was *trying* not to click his heels, dance a jig.

Well, he could help with that.

"Here," said Frank, putting a green bell pepper into one of his hands and a yellow one in the other. "Cut these bastards into strips. I'm gonna boil some water . . ."

Lucky for Marvelous, the truly focused final stretch of dinner preparation came just when Frank would have liked to ask him a few questions. Content to let this mystery boil away right along with the pasta water, the man of the house, for the next thirty minutes, launched into a number of delicate operations—shallow-frying the stuffed zucchini flowers in hot oil, sautéing slivers of bell pepper and squash, keeping an eye on the farfalle lest it pass the point of al dente—while Marvelous composed a salad. "Waiting sharpens the appetite." So said the French, and the promise of having to wait, at least for the duration of the family meal, to learn what the hell was running through his new friend's mind added a piquant spice of its own to the dishes Frank brought to the table. The French did not say, "Waiting to see if two people you know are going to get together makes a good meal even better," but they might have thought to do so.

In truth, Frank's own buoyant spirits left him blind to the personal torments that preoccupied his dinner companions that evening. Christopher glugged down a first glass of wine in one pull, settling into a sullen silence for most of the meal. This, at least, could be chalked up to artistic temperament. No clear explanation existed, however, for the fact that when the subject of the Midsummer Feast came up, Carol could only say, her voice flat with doubt, that she hoped everyone would enjoy themselves. And while Frank kept an inconspicuous eye on Marvelous and Gracie, watching for schoolyard signs of attraction, the two kept what looked to him like strict poker faces. He did not notice Marvelous nervously burn through three soft drinks as Gracie ranted and raved about wildness. (This had, in recent days, become her go-to topic at moments, like this one, when she felt cornered; anything to keep her from some stupid slip-up that would shed light on her feelings for Frank . . . and so, just as many friends, finding themselves faced with an evening of potentially revealing talk, resort to comfortable complaints about the shortcomings of mutual acquaintances, she fell back on critiques of American society and its "domesticating agenda.")

Meanwhile, Marvelous felt the opportunity for honest, forthright revelation slipping further from his grasp. For he had failed, when Frank stepped out of the kitchen earlier, to tell Gracie that he loved her work, that he owned all of her books and had done every exercise in *The Twelve Directions of Positive Thinking* and most of those in *The Golden Road*; that he already, in a sense, knew her; that he had put his face next to hers at the center of a collage meant to manifest her presence in his life; that he wanted to jump across the table, crushing the few stuffed zucchini blossoms that remained, and kiss her, as if by such a gesture he could communicate all of this crucial information in one fell and carnal swoop.

Alas! It was not to be. Not that evening, anyway. That evening tumbled away from them, lost to obligatory praise of Frank's prowess in the kitchen, to dissembling declarations of what a marvelous ("Sorry, Marvelous"), beautiful, gorgeous, lovely day it had been, and now this wonderful meal, this great, cool breeze through the window—could anything be better? No, nothing could, not for Frank, who, relaxed at last, flush with ease and pinot gris, growing used to this summer-at-Willowbrook thing, poured himself another glass and raised it in an informal midmeal toast:

"Again—to good food, good company, and good times!"

Glasses clinked. Having satisfied this urge to mark the precious nature of the occasion, Frank sighed contentedly. He looked across the table to his friend. "Hey, Marvelous."

"Huh?"

"Tell me again: why do Buddhists hate onions and garlic?"

An excerpt from *The Golden Road* by Gracie Sloane:

Week 7: The Garden of Unfolding Mysteries

ACCEPTING THE MYSTERY

A friend of mine, a *New York Times* bestselling novelist I'll call Nancy, reports that, at a certain point in her process, her novels inevitably start writing themselves. "I remember the first time it happened to me," says Nancy. "I had written a few drafts of a book. Then I got stuck. It was frustrating. On the one hand, I felt like the book wasn't even close to finished. On the other, every time I sat down to work on it, it seemed to resist being worked on. Finally (or, I guess, *not* finally—what an eternally false adverb!), I put the thing in a drawer and moved on to something else. In time the details of the story slipped from my conscious mind. When I returned to it several months later, I had the distinct sensation of entering a kind of secret garden that had been left to flourish unattended: it was as though everything I had written before had changed shape, shot up, and was now in full fruit and flower, ready to be harvested."

You may be feeling, right about now, like things have started to happen that are beyond your control. And not in the *usual* way that makes us want to bang our heads against our desks, give up on life, dull our senses by turning to our preferred method of muting the troubled cries of the soul. You may find, in fact, that your inner voice is calmer this week, even serene, as though it knows something you don't.

You are a little more than halfway through this journey, believe it or not, and have experienced stretches of powerful

emotion—from anger (Week 3: Wild Thoughts) to exhila-
rating possibility (Week 5: The Joy of Rampage)—as your
creative power becomes unblocked. This week allow the
mysterious process of creation that you have been making
room for to unfold in an unhurried, organic way. Take a
long bath. Go for an aimless walk. Growth is happening all
around you. Strange as it may seem, it needs you to leave it
alone right now for the magic to continue.

It is important to listen closely this week. To listen and to
look. You need not strain your eyes or your ears, only open
them. Over the years, many people have told me that they
begin to see the world in a new light during this week: colors
are brighter, once-familiar scenes more vivid, even strange.
For some, this can be startling. Serene days may turn into
anxious nights as deep and potentially unsettling questions
rise to the surface. *Who am I? What does it mean to be human,
and to die one day? Why are we here? What is the universe? Am
I doing what I'm meant to do with the time I have left?*

Let these questions come. During this week, do not try
to answer: simply notice them. You are now walking in the
mystery. Take a deep breath. Try just to live.

———

A month passed. And in that fine transit through July, Willowbrook saw heartache, anguish, sorrow, redecorating. It all began with that dinner, but as the unrelenting light and heat of the season made one day near-indistinguishable from the next, melting time down to one seemingly interminable stretch of birdsong, iced beverages, and mockingly fair weather, the core grievances of each troubled soul festered, garnished now and then with some supplementary indignity.

Christopher? As if the failure of *Son*, his first foray into performance art (he considered it a failure, anyway, in that it actually made him feel *closer* to his parents), and his touristic watercolor experiment before that, weren't enough to stall the progress of such a raw and tender talent, within the week he received an email from Kreshnik Gropcaj. The Albanian bellhop had met an actor from Madrid who had come to stay at the hotel, and the two had fallen in love, and were going to spend part of the summer in Barcelona and that gay seaside paradise, Sitges. Wasn't it grand? Oh, and, *"Mi manchi, mio uccellino." I miss you, my little bird.* All very well for the party that missed, but the little bird in question had had his wings clipped: why wasn't *he* thumbing his nose at heteronormative life in Sitges, instead of perishing at the parental manse? It interfered with his work; it drained his creative spirit, which, no matter how many block-busting exercises Gracie foisted upon him with the intention of restoring it, inevitably dried up again the moment he took hold of a pencil or brush. Sure, he managed a few sketches—studies of interspecies homoeroticism after Hokusai's *The Dream of the Fisherman's Wife*, diagrammatic calligraphy inspired by the waggle dance of the foraging Western honeybee (title: *Trophallaxis*)—but not even cephalopod head nor the miracle of insect communication could rouse his sleeping artistry. Washed up, marooned upon an island of no interest, he soon developed psychosomatic allergies, as his father had before him, and spent much of the day wasting away yet again on the couch, halfheartedly scratching at a paper pad so that everyone would leave him alone, thinking him occupied in some visionary aesthetic pursuit. Was this ennui? Anomie? As long as he remained here, in this house, one of *them*, every step he took forward was promptly followed by two steps back, back into the nullifying void of family.

Now, evidence of such primitive ancestry might have been enough to cheer up Gracie, were she not burdened that month with two serious tasks: nailing down her speech for Green Dawn next month (she hoped to both inspire the audience and to give them a little taste of the fun to come in *The Habit of Wildness*) and denying herself the animal luxury of acting on her now undeniable attraction to Frank Widdicombe. The repression of instinct represented by the latter ran counter to the carefree spirit she hoped to nurture in the former, and the resulting dissonance threw her into a state appropriately marked by soaring highs and plummetous lows. No sooner would she return from a mandatory nature stroll with the notion of writing a chapter called "Making a Sacred Journey Staff," her head abuzz with activities that would get her readers to decorate and consecrate a walking stick ("Your link to the ancient and sacred spirit energy of trees . . . Why not dress up your Sacred Journey Staff with crystals, feathers, even sequins? This is *your* walking stick. Do with it as you will."), than Frank, his mood jollier than ever, would stick his head out of the sliding doors and ask if she wanted some ice cold basil lemonade—he had just made up a batch with basil from Marvelous's garden! Ice cold basil

lemonade, or cool, peppery gazpacho, a summer dish that just
happened to be one of her favorites. She would sit with Frank
and Carol, spooning down the soup, appalled at its ambrosial
lushness, stewing with unreasonable annoyance when Carol—
her friend!—pushed her half-finished bowl away, complaining
of fullness or the potentially dyspeptic consequences of too
much tomato acid. Did she think she was fooling everybody
with her so-called sensitivity to nightshade vegetables? Such
fits of uncharitable judgment drove Gracie to remorse, and she
soon found herself walking, more often than not, all the way
into town during the day, intent on avoiding the Widdicombes
until she could process her lust and her anger. There, she would
settle in for hours at a time in a corner at Bainbridge Bakers,
nursing a perpetuity of sugar-free iced teas with lemon, freewriting page after page, dredging up free-associative material
such as the following:

> *we all must recognize our wild side, but what if our wild side
> tells us to do something destructive? imagine for example you
> find yourself attracted to someone who you know is bad for you,
> wrong for you—your animal instinct says "that's the one! come
> on! get him!" while your logical mind tells you "wait a second
> i've seen this before this is a pattern of some kind . . ." what
> then? what to do when faced with a wildness both creative and
> destructive, an adventure the pursuit of which could bring pain
> to another?*

Oh, pain! Who knew more about it than that soft-hearted,
gardening fool, Marvelous Matthews? For once Gracie started
making herself even more scarce, spending the day away from
Willowbrook, he began to wonder if he had done something

creepy at that fateful dinner. A relative novice in the ways of manifesting desire, he sometimes still found himself slack-jawed and savage when the universe handed him what he asked for. Had he flirted too artlessly while shelling peas in the kitchen? Offended her with too many covetous glances over the dinner table? Perhaps too she had sensed that he was hiding something and had judged him untrustworthy. If anyone could sniff out his secret, after all, it would be her. A specialist in creativity and human potential could surely spot a lie from a mile away, and if she had spotted it, well, could he blame her for avoiding him? He would probably do the same in her position. How could he even imagine that she would ever come to take an interest in him?

Then again, there had been that exchange between them in the kitchen when Frank, the crafty bastard, had removed himself on some cat-related pretext. Marvelous, usually relatively taciturn, started chatting up a storm.

"I couldn't agree more about screens and the outdoors and everything you were just saying," he said, words tumbling out of him in a rush. "Nature is important to me. That's one of the things I love about living here. You don't find this kind of nature in other places. How long have you lived here?" Remembering it, he cursed himself for this clumsy attempt to appear as though he knew less about her than he did.

"I'm just visiting," said Gracie. Someone as intuitive as she was must be able to pick up on the subtle vibrations produced by clumsy deceptions. And yet, it seemed to him as though her eyes gleamed with the light of fascination. "I split my time between Berkeley and New Mexico, though, so I know *exactly* what you mean. I lived in New York for several years." Her face changed; she looked as though she had just swallowed a spoonful of bitter medicine. "A person can't do anything truly creative there."

"How can they possibly be expected to, when their inner life is under constant siege?" A twist in his gut: was he repeating lines to her from her own work? "How can they discover anything truly . . . *new?*" he added.

"*Exactly,*" said Gracie.

At that point, something mysterious had taken place. After a charged moment of silence, the two of them continued to talk. However, Marvelous began not to understand what either of them were saying. Words poured out of his mouth. Gracie's lips moved, forming, he supposed, sentences. Colors seemed brighter; whatever was passing between them did not depend on language. He likened it to music. He didn't understand what was happening and wondered how he had come to be standing in that kitchen, feeling connected to this woman in a deep and electrifying way. His whole life felt unfamiliar to him.

What further freaked him out was that once they were seated around the dinner table with the Widdicombes, she acted as though nothing strange had happened. He felt sure that she, too, had been electrified—had he misread their entire exchange? In the wake of this, he wondered about himself. Was he crazy? Now a rush of merciless, disparaging self-talk came, alarming him. Once he started beating himself up, asking himself "What's the point?," the threat of relapse reared its ugly rat head, gnawed with its yellowing teeth at the anchor-line of sobriety. No way—not worth it. He went straight away to a meeting, and then to another, and before long found himself back in the rooms on an almost daily basis, as he had been at the dawn of his recovery. He spent more time at the ice cream parlor, talking shop with old drunks, perpetual relapsers, and serene, stable stalwarts. And while he still hung out with Frank from time to time, lumbering over the tennis court for an informal lesson or drinking soda in the *salon*, he avoided dinners and other such festive, Gracie-inclusive occasions, leveling quite clearly with his friend, "I can't be around alcohol right now. Maybe in a while, after I get a few things in order, but right now—no." Frank, bless his normy soul, expressed concern ("Everything all right?") followed, after reassurance, by his usual display of bluff confidence in Marvelous ("Fuck! As long as you're happy, pal!"). Thank God he laid off talking about Gracie, too—aware, after several significant, pleading looks, that discussion of her auburn tresses or expertise in the field of positive thinking did nothing to help.

Meanwhile, he communicated more frequently with Michelle, providing her with the names and numbers of contacts for the Midsummer Feast, offering guidance on the selection of canopied event tents and musical entertainment. Michelle, for her part, resisted the urge to commiserate with the gardener about relationship frustrations, even though she sensed the man had been through more than his fair share of disenchantment on that front. Rather, she surged forward with faultless efficiency, corralling the elements of the big party-to-be: she confirmed RSVPs via email and phone; got specific with sober jazz quintet the Steady Five about how much equipment they needed to set up; bartered with competing customer service representatives over the cost to rent an event tent, striking a two-for-one bargain; and even persuaded Frank, in the course of several days, that the Midsummer Feast would be a splendid opportunity for him to show off his cooking skills by personally catering the shindig.

Now, if she could accomplish all of that and more in a mat-

ter of weeks, why was it that Bradford—who she was beginning
to think was an even more extraordinarily sensitive talent than
she had at first imagined (the way in which he spoke about his
screenplay showed such intensity of feeling, such incandescent
vision that the "nameless, numinous entity of horror" at its
center came mysteriously alive for her when he described it,
formless though it might be)—why was it he couldn't finish
his script? In fact, he could barely write a word. During that
weekend the two spent housesitting for his friend on the peninsula, he showed himself to be so tormented that her pained
tenderness for him only grew. Yes, perhaps it had been fringed
on occasion with annoyance—anxiety, even; had she given
up *too* much control?—but then he would come sulking over
to her when he felt "blocked," and it seemed a true relief in
those moments to make love. She did find that sex with him
satisfied not just a sensual longing, but a more abstract desire
she couldn't quite put her finger on (only once so far had his
drinking or his having taken some odd cocktail of prescription
downers spoiled the event). If by taking her own pleasure she
could somehow bring him closer to artistic success, all the
better. Michelle considered herself, as it stood, a kind of good
influence on her fussy beau bound for greatness. Over that
weekend filled with lovemaking, too, he had taken to drinking
a little bit less, medicating himself with what might even be
called moderation.

In spite of this, she wondered: was it good for her? So she
mused over video chat with her dear friend Jens, with whom
she used to hop from one Copenhagen bar to the next, falling
into drunken conversation with smart Danes, practical Danes,
working Danes with purpose and pride. And their mysterious
air of self-control and acceptance! "Everyone in America is so

fucking stressed out. It kills me to see him beat himself up, but then sometimes I just want to slap him and say, 'Will you shut up already and get to work?'" Jens listened, though provided little in the way of insight; he told her to be sure and consider now and then whether she was being treated fairly.

"*Fairly?*" she said. She burst into laughter. She pulled back for him then, painting a bigger picture of her time with the Widdicombes & Co. up to that point, drawing a connection between the topsy-turvy atmosphere of her job and the romantic straits in which she suddenly found herself. "I'm not sure I know what fairness means anymore. Was Alice treated fairly in Wonderland?"

At the end of their conversation he added that he would be flying out to New York for work at the end of August. Wouldn't it be nice if they could see each other? He had the time and the money to pop over to Seattle for a week. He had family there he wanted to visit anyway. "Yes," she said, "and I want you to meet Christopher—I think you'd like him."

Bradford's anxieties bore a notable resemblance to the chilling entity that, in the so-called script for his still untitled horror film, plagued the residents of a made-up island in the Pacific Northwest: "represented by a thin fog, the entity seeps into their pores, into their noses and mouths and ears, into their *minds*, and from there induces them to carry out its twisted bidding, driving them to act out their most psychotic, depraved, and self-destructive impulses." Though he had not yet expressed his fears to Michelle (for whom, incidentally, he had started to feel a needy, all-consuming attachment), he at last had to admit to himself that his day-to-day existence stank of a chaos he had once considered part and parcel of the creative process and now found increasingly cumbersome. People were such idiots, and it was unfortunate that he must include himself in that judgment. For it was not only fears that remained unexpressed: Bradford, having completed his proposed residence at Willowbrook, had told Michelle that he would be staying with different friends in Seattle, on the island, and up the peninsula. In fact, he had been sleeping in his car, showering at the gym.

What's more, the very thought of his screenplay sickened him. In what he took to be the warm, illuminating light of his obsession with Michelle, the undertaking struck him as childish, lost (never mind that he had, to boot, hardly tended to it for some time now). He despaired of completing anything more than the addled draft he'd brought back from LA, and his stomach knotted when he thought that he only kept the thing alive with lies to please Michelle and others. (It was as though he had to *feed* it lies, as one might feed defrosted mice to a pet snake.) What, after all, would remain of him were he to release the ghost of his now-dead dream? A house free of hauntings, and all the more empty for it. He supposed that things might end up fine—he would get a job again and give up on all that. At other times, surges of resentment left him sure he could finish the thing if only he had never *met* Michelle or if he could just get *away* from her. Yes, it was people like Michelle, people who allowed him to inflict his byzantine neuroses and his rotten character on them, who continually distracted him from his true aims.

One can imagine the toll such a terrible inner fugue took on the young man all that month. By the end of it, he had opted, in a kind of fit, for a weekend of solitude and of separation, informing the object of his affection that he was driving down to Portland for a couple of days to "see friends, and just . . . clear my head a little."

Other fugues occupied the mind of that woman whose most burning desire was to see her home appear in the pages of *Inside Places*. Thank goodness, since the prospect of any internal work to be done weighed heavily on Carol; she preferred, for the moment, to direct her energy toward a full realization of her aesthetic vision for Willowbrook's interior. Even still, no matter how many hours she spent rearranging the furniture—did her collection of Frederick Kunsthoff ceramic vessels look better on the mantel, or on the hall table? Did the master bedroom, aside from the obvious rogue element (Frank), scream "bohemian Paris meets California cool meets Pacific Northwest casual" at the appropriate volume?—none of it relieved the sinking sensation, most unbearable at night, that her husband and son had become more like strangers to her than ever before. The moment Frank's insomnia disappeared—the damn fool all of a sudden sleeping through the night like a baby, even smiling and making self-satisfied humming sounds like some dog swept up in a happy dream—her own rushed in to take its place. One evening she shot awake a mere hour after nodding off, stricken with the disoriented feeling that she had never seen their bedroom in her life. With her bedside light on, the sight of her undisturbed, dozing husband affronted her sense of justice. *Why*, when just over a month ago he had twitched and grunted with signs of adult ADD and depression, did he seem so pleased with himself all of a sudden? She fought the urge to shake him awake but fumed all the same. Did he not care that a terrible, yawning gulf prevented any of them from truly knowing and understanding one another? Their son may have been a great talent—whatever that was; sometimes she wondered if she had spoiled him—but his whole fragile little mortal coil shuddered with pain, horror, and loneliness. She felt it every time he passed through the room. Had RISD done this to him? Had she and Frank? Had they coddled him too much? All things considered, they had done well—accepted, respected, even celebrated his decisions at every turn. Who expected a mother, though, to accept or celebrate her son's sadness?

The unpacking of antique treasures struck her as somehow widening the rift. How could she be expected to entertain a legion of friends, acquaintances, and strangers when the very thought of the two people supposedly closest to her threw her into paroxysms of doubt? Old memories counted for so little, and imagining the Midsummer Feast, with its whirlpool of social activity, its chatter, canapés, and sober jazz, its parade of essentially unknowable individual souls, exhausted her. Nobody needed her help now, it seemed, after all. Not even Princess Magdalena.

Frank, meanwhile—well. The thought of the party floated his boat, especially once he came around to Michelle's suggestion about his whipping up edibles for the event. (Not *that* kind of edible!) After that dinner he'd cooked with Marvelous—a success—he felt capable of anything. His mood leveled off at a properly epicurean plateau. The morning after, deciding to skip tennis, he composed the following email:

Dear Channing Goodman, Faerie Queen,

Well, things around here are getting better every day. Too bad about France—all in all, though, I think it's for the best. A little extra time with the fam has been good for me (I'd say it's been good for them too, but modesty prevents me), and I've made a few new friends around here. (One of them is a cat. Again, more than I can say for you.)

I thought I would mention that we're throwing a little
shindig here—or hosting a shindig, as the case may be.
A shindig will be had. A "Midsummer Feast." Anyway, if
you and Ray wanted to come crash the party, you'd be
more than welcome. I can't remember where you are next
month (party's on August 8). Don't say Auvergne or I'll kill
you, you lying bastard. But the Widdicombes would love
to have you if you're in our neck of the woods.

Hope all's well.

Yours,
Frank W.

PS: I'm sending along a barrage of other emails I drafted
over the last few months and never sent you. In them
you'll see that I've started writing a book called *The
Widdicombe Way*. I'd like to show you a few chapters, if
that'd be copacetic.

He sent this email, along with all the others. Later that day,
much to his delight, a reply came:

Dear Frank Widdicombe, Closet Case,

Great to hear from you. Glad everything is working out for
the best out there on Berrybush Island or wherever the hell.

As it happens, Ray and I will be in LA around that time.
Maybe could pop up your way for the party. Let's see how
it works out.

Attached you will find a picture of my niece and her
husband on their honeymoon.

Your Obscure Object of Desire,
Channing

PS: Happy to read any of your illiterate scribblings.

Though the attached photograph showed, in truth, a
close-up of Channing's middle finger, the email cheered Mr.
Widdicombe considerably. He carried the joyous anticipation
of seeing his old pal as he went about his affairs that month.
Spurred on by Channing's willingness to read bits of *The Widdicombe Way*, he also started writing more. A chapter titled
"The Widdicombe Table" sang the praises of that spirited togetherness fostered by a good family meal, "whether family to
you means parents and their kids, a few of your closest friends,
or a heap of freaks brought together in some kind of twisted
fucking social experiment." His enthusiasm for just such spirited togetherness over the month, along with a decline in his
fitness regimen brought about by a relaxing acquiescence to
the flow of things, eventually led not only to almost complete
abandonment and amnesia in the fear-of-bodily-decay-and-
death department, but to the writing of a chapter titled "On
Putting on a Few Pounds." These he sent off to Channing with
the hope that their lively wit and philosophical savvy might win
him over to the idea of coming for a visit, along with a somewhat lengthy chapter on animal companionship titled "The
Company of Cats."

The moniker-rich cat that had inspired this meditation
(Christopher had gotten in on the act, too, privately christen-

ing her "Tlön, Uqbar, Orbis Tertius" after the story by Borges, abbreviating the name to TUOT and pronouncing that some- where between "Too-Ought" and "Twat"), well, she eventually emerged from beneath her pyramid of cushions in the break- fast nook. And yet even she fell into a more listless state that month—a sorrow that could only issue from a creature fed one single delectable raw shrimp and then left to dream of the day when her good luck would return.

———

The hour before any party typically limps along; so it did for Carol. Frank, Marvelous, and Bradford—that prodigal rogue—all worked in the kitchen (*Men in the Kitchen, Women in the Woods*). Christopher showered for what must have been the first time in many days. Gracie, taken with a sudden fit of inspiration, ran off for a last-minute walk through the woods, saying, "I'll be right back—I've just had a thought about tree communication that can't be ignored!" Michelle changed, declaring that it would be unsuitable to put anything but her best foot forward after spending so much time coordinating the event. (There was more to this story: she could not believe she had to see Bradford there after he had admitted to hooking up with someone in Portland. BRADFORD: "I thought we were on a break." MICHELLE: "We are now!") Carol's young assistant had thrown herself into the task with such zeal, in fact, that it left Carol little to do with the day now arrived. The urgent need to straighten rows of tchotchkes and to smooth out buckles in the Persian rugs no longer possessed her, and with her home's interior ready for its close-up, a malaise settled in. What was her life that she had come to this point of sitting in her *salon* and waiting for her guests to arrive? Had she no cute little rope bridge of a purpose over which she could teeter, could cross this deadly hour? Then she might not have to deal with such morbid thoughts, might not feel so weak and frayed.

She turned to her phone for solace, holding the thing in her lap. The sun coming through the window behind her revealed streaked fingerprints on the screen, and in those, aggravating dust motes, like flies trapped in honey. At once these flecks went from aggravating to depressing: no amount of industry, all-purpose cleaner, or rubbing of plastic displays against blouse sleeves could free her or anybody else from the ubiquity of motes, dander, debris. (The fabric technique often only pushed the offending particles into that fine, dark fissure around the screen that set it into the body of the phone, that feature being like a crack in the earth that led to hell.) Disquieted further by the impossibility of a mote-free existence, she stared at the device for all the world as though it might provide a way to move through time without this ache of despair. Instead, as she idly (but importantly) pressed down on the directional nub that guided her through her address book, highlighted names jumped out at her without meaning, appearing first at the bottom of the screen and then floating up into oblivion as others arrived to replace it, a silent waterfall of acquaintance rushing in reverse:

Abbey Jenson
Adam Park
Alexander Wu
Anne Keeling
Anthony (Salon)
Ava Liebowitz
. . .
Hal Caruthers

Hanna Sacco
Harry Worrell
Helen Down
Hiro Kawasaki

As the names moved past, she played a macabre game with herself: who could she call if she was thinking about jumping off a bridge? Who occupied that space between the too-overwhelming intimacy of family (at certain times, the sound of Frank's voice might make her even more likely to jump) and the alienation of the half known? Gracie, maybe, although as of late her friend exerted a remarkable amount of energy avoiding her company, disappearing into town to work on her book, slipping away as though she found Carol difficult to be around.

Fine: she would call no one in her final moments on the bridge. A regretful shudder ran through her, as though this last thought was no different from the fatal leap it suggested. She battled darkness so seldom—why had it come to her now, a hunched, uninvited guest loping into the house like a professional mourner hired to fill the space with wails of grief? As far as she knew, the occasion called for no mourning. Unless, by some terrible fluke of daily circumstances, she had died without knowing, and her ghost had wound up here in this purgatorial parallel universe, the Midsummer Feast a cover-up for her own cosmic funeral. Though she rarely told anyone, she often wondered if she might already be dead.

Such sepulchral speculation served as her rope bridge in the end, and the hour extinguished itself. People, as they so often do, showed up. First the Steady Five, who set up their instruments (cymbals and snare with brush-ended drumsticks, upright bass, a saxophone on a tripod-like stand, a trumpet

reserving a cushioned stool, a clarinet) on the makeshift bandstand out on the lawn; they fished cans of soda from a cooler
full of ice. Then a trickle of eager early arrivals invited by
Marvelous and Michelle; Carol shook their hands, smiled at
them, and offered them drinks or snacks if Michelle hadn't, in
her efficient way, already swooped in and asked, "What's your
poison?" In time this unswinging liminal atmosphere gave
way to a span of perpetual influx, the atmosphere picking up
a rhythm as each new guest appeared. At this juncture—half
swing—the Steady Five started up a conscientious rendition of
"Summertime," and Frank, along with his team of man-cooks,
set the tables beneath the peaked white event tent with those
delights that had required longer preparation. A fleet of folded
placards identified each dish:

Chevre, Figs, and Sautéed Onions on Toast Bites

Heirloom Tomato Gazpacho

Pesto Pasta Salad with Sun-Dried Tomato and Pine Nuts

Grilled Shrimp Skewers

Melon Squares with Salted Cheese

Mediterranean Spinach Salad

Homemade Pickle Slices

German Potato Salad

Baked Miso-Glazed Tofu

Cold Shredded Carrot Salad with Orange Juice

In addition to ample quantities of all this, the men had set
up a large, boxy grill on which lamb burgers, various vegetables,

and salmon sizzled to instrumentalized lyrics (*Your daddy's rich, your mamma's good-looking*, etc.). Carol found herself drifting first to this corner of the party then that, making noncommittal small talk with families from the neighborhood, young college students home for the summer, recovered alcoholics, other homeowners served by Marvelous Matthews's Community Gardens, decorating colleagues (these she gave tours of the house, pointing out a pair of glamorously grotesque and menacing dolls she had picked up in Bali, Christopher's paintings of the harbor boats, and the incredible vintage sofa), all the while keeping an eye out for Leanne, the editor of *Inside Places*. During one of these flits from group to group, she ran into Christopher on the stairs. He had emerged from his bedroom at last, washed, shaved, wearing respectable khaki pants and a white linen shirt.

"You look nice, honey," she said, smiling as she passed.

"Thanks," said Christopher. He brushed his fingers over his sleeve and greeted the cluster of guests his mother had with her, weaving past them so they could continue up to the second floor. "All of you look nice, too!" he added, a cheery parting shot, and wandered through the *salon*, through the door and outside, onto the deck.

The evening air patted his cheeks. He had scraped them free of stubble with one of those disposable razors, wondering all the while if some untapped artistic energy didn't wait concealed in the ribbed, gendered blue handle, the grinning double-stripe of blade. Like the rest of his most recent ideas, this one landed (perhaps prematurely) in the trash. Now he walked out onto the lawn, wonderfully camouflaged in chinos, desert boots crushing the grass, and watched the jazz band start into a new tune, playing, playing—the beat came in; he knew; he would have known it anywhere! "Aquarela do Brasil," "Watercolor of Brazil." Known more often simply as "Brazil," maybe because that was the only word in the song understood by the English-speaking world. This merry musical watercolor danced around him. Not yet keen to make conversation, he stood there in the shade of easy listening, observing the scene: over there, Dad looked jolly and was grilling with Marvelous, joined by a miscellaneous flock of men and women praising meat. (Nearby, Bradford held a beer—surely, judging from a slight sway, not his first of the evening.) Unknowns milled under the tent, over the lawn, in the colorful frames of *salon* he could see through the windows, their edges warmed by buttery light. (Had his mother, in private, stood out here and taken into account the way her *salon* looked from the yard? Probably. Though it made him smile, he doubted this little twinge of joy would last him through the evening.) The party was really picking up—fifty people, maybe more. Times like this he wished that there were a switch at the back of his neck (a therapist told him to imagine this once, as a mechanism for "switching the brain off" when he felt overstimulated), and that he could by flipping it kill the light that illuminated social ritual in all of its spine-tingling absurdity. As it was, the best he could do was attempt by a willful overload of perception, an edging toward the impossible comprehension of everything happening around him, to short-circuit his senses. Maybe then he could eat a hamburger without feeling inexplicable.

To this end he wandered from the bandstand to the well-positioned middle of the deck. He held his phone to his ear in order to strike the appearance of making a call, and from this privileged perch of masquerading normalcy he expanded his circle of awareness, trying, at first, to hear every conversation within earshot at once. The scrambled result somewhat resembled a radio submitted to an endless turn of the tuning wheel:

"Okay, who wants a—"

"—spent two weeks in Beirut—"

"She seems a little depressed, doesn't she?"

"—seven years next month—"

"—it's sort of a memoir about growing up with two child psychologists for parents—"

"The house is amazing."

"—I'm like, Jesus, does he cook like this all the time?"

"—out on the water today—"

"—any mustard?"

"—you're kidding!"

"Now, now, you know I don't have a soul anymore . . ."

This Brazil, beautiful and swarthy / Is my Brazilian Brazil

"Christopher!"

This last outburst came courtesy of his father, who waved a metal spatula over by the grill. Doubtless he wanted him to eat something. What had gotten into *him*, anyway, looking so happy, his mustache curled into a mischievous smile?

"Want me to grill you up a burger?" his father said. And though Christopher could, at that moment, just as soon imagine cutting his own tongue out, or pressing his own face down on the burning hot slats of the grill, the pleased, proud look in his father's eye—he would really rather be doing nothing else than standing here flipping burgers for fifty; lucky man!—shook his insolent resolve, and he said, defeated "Would you, please?"

"Gladly," said his father, slapping Marvelous on the back as he moved past the gardener to slide another raw, pink patty onto his spatula. Marvelous fanned himself with his cap, looking sweaty (a few locks of hair matted along his forehead, dark with perspiration), and shifty-eyed, as though at any moment the police might burst onto the lawn and arrest him.

"I'm gonna go grab something to drink," Marvelous said, flapping the hat back onto his head. He left the Widdicombe men to bond over fire and made for the tent, where cold and sugary refreshment in a can awaited. How good to take a cool swig of soda after working all day alongside Frank, chopping, mixing, arranging, plating. Quite a hot day, too. He looked to the Steady Five, but Mike, Morgan, Sean, Rory, and Joe each kept close to his chosen instrument, absorbed in the single-minded conjuring of some dizzy, Gershwinian spell the name of which escaped him. Fascinating music, whatever it was. (Oh, it was "Fascinating Rhythm." Duh.) Finally, soda in hand, he levered the tab, heard a satisfying *snap* and the hiss of carbonation, pressed the iced, wet aluminum briefly to his forehead, took a sip.

In *The Golden Road*, it was the Week of Strength, and while he felt stronger than ever on the sobriety count—a month of meetings and more time spent in the company of recovering drunks had bolstered him somewhat—one thing still chewed at him: Gracie. Conspicuously absent from the festivities thus far, which saddened him. "We must reclaim the strength of character to declare our creative intentions out loud, and to stand by them," read one mini-essay in that week's chapter. He had stared at the words that morning, fixing to think of them when, in conversation with Gracie, the moment came to tell her at last that he knew her work, her vision, her own struggles with the creative life.

Frank said that Carol had said that Gracie had gone off walking in the woods before the party. A woman like that, Frank said, was "subject to whims." Ah, to be one of her whims! He did want a cigarette; a stroll down the path into the quasi-wild beckoned both him and the pack in his pocket. Before that could happen, though, here came Ingrid, the young woman from LA who he knew from AA, flipping her shiny brown hair and walking with purpose.

"Hey, M," she said, "I'm taking off."

"Cool. Everything okay?"

She looked behind her. "Yeah," she said, "some booze bag tried to hit on me a minute ago. I'm just tired, though, and I have to work early."

Before she slipped away, she pointed out the culprit: across the lawn, Bradford sat on the arm of a deck chair, drinking a beer and, to all appearances, hitting on someone else.

"What did he say?" said Marvelous.

"Some line about nameless horror, and a screenplay he was writing," said Ingrid, wrinkling her nose. "Typical drunk nonsense. Anyway—take care."

"Yep, bye. Call if you need anything."

The Steady Five started in on "Mack the Knife," and Marvelous finished his soda, fanning himself again with his hat, the inner front band of which was buckled from a whole season of sweat absorption. Poor Ingrid. Maybe today, during this Week of Strength, he should go ahead and do what he had started to suspect he might be called upon to do: take Bradford aside, man to man, and tell him if he ever wanted to talk to anyone about his drinking, Marvelous was there. The very thought reassured him: he was there, he was strong, he was a rock, he was dependable. Who would have ever imagined? Yes, he'd just go over to the deck and say hello, get a read on the young man, investigate, flaunt his dependable presence a little.

Now McHeath spends like a sailor / Did our boy do something rash?

The sun by this time had dipped behind the Olympics, leaving as it vanished a diffuse, wavering band of orange on the horizon. Twilight agreed with Bradford, for it meant that soon nightfall would shroud his manifest drunkenness in hours better suited to it, justify his passage into oblivion. One-way ticket to oblivion, please—and yes, just one passenger, for Michelle Briggs would most definitely *not* be coming with him. Wherever she was—oh, he didn't care! His sordid sojourn in Portland had decided it for him: he didn't *need* her. In fact, what he needed was to set fire to the flimsy structure of their relationship if he was ever going to recover his creative potency. He needed her to see just what kind of man he was. No one owned him. Other women waited on deck chairs, in the kitchen, on the sofa, smoking by the rhododendron bushes (although he had clearly better avoid the sober ones at this point). And if Marvelous thought he was going to corner him and rip up his ticket, he had another thing coming. The moment he perceived that lout lumbering over the lawn, he pretended not to notice him and disappeared into the house. See, even after a half-dozen beers, Bradford Dearborne kept his wits about him.

Still, what the hell song was that floating through the doors and windows, assailing Willowbrook from all sides as he mounted the stairs? *That sly come-hither stare / That strips my conscience bare . . .* No escape from the plodding, relentlessly light jazz of that teetotaling quintet. That he remembered the lyrics at all astounded him—in what dusty archive had he filed away the words to such a sappy, stupid ditty? People were such idiots. And that penultimate line, could it possibly be right? To strip the conscience bare struck him as such blunt psychological violence for an old standard. He supposed they called them standards for a good reason.

A lie-down in one of the second-floor guest rooms suggested itself to him, insinuated itself as the most natural, obvious idea, the action most appropriate in every way to his circumstances, and he staggered down the hall. What better way to help along oblivion, after all, than closing one's eyes? Provided he had eaten enough to keep the spins at bay . . . oops—there went that old naturalist's painting of a mandrill, knocked from the wall by his shoulder. He propped it up and went on his way. Surely the editor of *Inside Places* or whoever it was Carol kept talking about would understand that interiors sometimes suffered surface damage during successful parties. Finally, a door handle!

What appeared to him next, in the dim guest bedroom, took a startled moment to piece together: two people, standing, man's arms around woman's waist, woman's hands clasped behind man's neck, fish-faces mushed together, but one of them, fuck, one of them Michelle's. The other some scruffy young thing's: a stranger, a stranger! He shot back, shut the door, said, "God damn it," and lurched down the hall, heart beating, hoping she'd failed to identify him, paused by the painting of the mandrill—but no, they would come out soon, and he'd be a damned mandrill himself to lurk there. He hurried down the stairs, eager to elude discussion, escape even a word with anyone.

Out the front door, as though fleeing a monster in some childish nightmare, straight to his car, into the driver's seat, slamming the door shut. No sober jazz reached him here, at least. How could she! But then, why did he feel this way—outraged, as though her making out with some fish-faced punk violated their marriage vows? "No such vows!" He slapped the steering wheel, achieving mild relief by shouting. But mild relief never saved a soul from plunging ahead in torment, especially when the torment concerned the violation of a *cosmic* marriage. God, what was he talking about? He had been the one who wanted out. He had been the one to throw the first wrench. He started the car. He needed to be away from other people—who were, as had been well established, idiots.

Down came the automatic windows, automatic for idiots, in came the cooling flutter of air as he cruised carefully past clusters of parked cars, each of them owned and parked by a different idiot. He would just drive around on back roads built by idiots, safe from idiot cops, head to the beach, something, somewhere. *That sly come-hither stare / That strips my conscience bare* . . . idiots!

Back at the house, Michelle returned to the party, sending Peter to get her a drink outside while she took a breather in the *salon*. Apparently during her make-out break (she had been working for a long time to make this party a success, and had spent all day guiding, finessing, coordinating, confirming, double-checking; she would be damned if she would let the night pass without indulging in a little devil-may-care celebratory behavior herself, especially after Bradford had betrayed her in such a cavalier manner) the party had tipped over into full swing. Strings of tiny paper lights outside glowed in the dusk. Bradford's dumb stunt had not escaped her notice. Had he followed them, swung the door open to catch them in the act? Also: so what? She felt a bit bad for him—who wouldn't?—but she wasn't sorry. Oh, how she had wanted for all these weeks to take care of him, how she had felt in some way part of the creative process by being there for him. And then for him to simply throw that under the bus! Well, if he thought that just because she liked to take care of him that she had no interest in taking care of herself, he had another thing coming. *She* worked hard; she deserved everything she earned and the little extra that she seized when the spirit took her. And what the hell was the band playing now—"Tea for Two"? How fucking appropriate.

Carol entered the *salon* alone, her forehead curiously un-lined. On Carol, the occasional blank mask could mean frus-tration, resignation, plain and simple unhappiness. Michelle touched her shoulder.

"Need anything?"

"Oh no, I'm fine," Carol said, her eyes betraying a lost look. She took a seat on the circular sofa, brushed one of the palm fronds with her fingers. "She's not coming."

"Who?"

"Leanne," she said. "From *Inside Places*. She emailed her regrets."

Michelle croaked with disappointment. "Well, shows how much an RSVP means to her," she said. Noticing Carol's weak smile, she added, "I'm sorry. I know it meant a lot to you. But we can still get her over here, right? Another time, I mean . . . just because she's not here tonight doesn't mean you can't get Willowbrook into *Inside Places*. It deserves to be, after all you've done."

"No, you're right," said Carol. She rubbed the bright green fabric of the sofa, finding it somehow gaudier now that no mag-azine editors would be seeing it that evening, as though Leanne had condemned it, specifically, by her absence. "We'll get her in here soon enough. We'll just have to have another party!"

Her assistant laughed, set free at last by this effortful out-burst of good humor, and a few minutes later drifted out to the deck. Carol watched her join the others outside. It was a fine, clear evening. Their party shined, a jewel in the crown of high summer. Willowbrook, doing what she had meant it to; Willowbrook, filled with the murmur of happy people exchanging pleasantries, jokes, ideas, and flirtations as they listened to "Corcovado." Only she took this moment alone, shipwrecked on an overgrown tuffet salvaged from an old hotel. *Little Miss Muffet / Sat on her tuffet / Eating her curds and whey.* The shape of the sofa offered no protection, no crannies or borders of any kind. It displayed her, it revealed her, it crucified her! Her own wrists, though maddeningly creased from years of bending, flopping, and flicking, remained pale at their tender undersides— no nail-holes, no red rivulets zigzagging from the punctures of martyrdom. Oh, to be punctured: sometimes her skin felt stretched so tight over her, like a balloon inflated to its maximum capacity, capable of rupturing at the slightest pinprick. Low laughter shook her as she imagined her body popping with one loud *pah!*, one bitter, fed-up declaration of a burst, leaving behind only a ruined rag of skin, everything else gone—where? Where did the spirit, the soul, the blasted-out mouth bones go when a person exploded? Disintegrated, reduced to dust motes, maybe all of it survived as dust motes sticking to the human oil streaked across the screens of our cell phones, swept eventually into those thin, purgatorial fissures that surrounded them.

Disturbed by this psychotic turn of her imagination, she rose from the sofa. Though plenty of party time remained, she made for the stairs. Tired, aching as a balloon must when it has remained inflated and taut for weeks, she floated to her bedroom. It screamed "bohemian Paris meets California cool meets Pacific Northwest casual," all right. A huge, hairy palm dominated the corner by the window. Playful Cocteau line drawings were there on the wall above the dresser; the dresser itself radiated strength, built from warm, heavy wood. A rug decorated with thick blue and white stripes tied the room together, gave it a lively air. The nightstand on Frank's side bore a large volume of Montaigne, and slim ones of La Rochefoucauld and Gracián—predecessors to what he hoped, she knew, would be his big, manly triumph of personal philosophy. She had to admit it: he seemed to be getting more out of Willowbrook than she was. He was outside, positively *soaked* in fellow feeling. Later the cat would probably leap up onto his lap as he took a breather in the breakfast nook. It simply wasn't fair.

She locked the door to their room and then fell back on the clean, made bed. She told herself that she would face the world again in ten minutes. In ten minutes she would cheer up, would come back out full of good humor, a smile on her face. Until then, eyes closed in the darkness, haunted by an instrumental version of "What a Little Moonlight Can Do," Carol Widdicombe hated her house.

Frank, meanwhile, gave his old buddy Channing a bear hug. "You dumb motherfucking son of a bitch—come here! I love this guy!"

"Ah, good to see you too, y'old freak," said Channing.

"I knew you couldn't last a whole year before you saw me again," said Frank. "Look at you—you haven't changed a bit. You're still a short, fat, bald old queer." This hit the mark pretty accurately: Channing, as ever, wore his hair in a trim white half laurel that gave his pate no covering. His bullish bulb of a nose turned up slightly—a feature Frank might have called a "boxer's nose" if his friend had ever been of the roughhousing persuasion. Bushy brows, collared shirt bulging out a bit at the belly, jeans cuffed by a tailor to account for the shortness of his legs—yep, Channing through and through.

"Food looks good, Frank. You can guess the kind of trash I've been eating." Frank took his friend through the gustatory gauntlet under the tent, filling a plate for him as they talked, for he knew the man had little interest in what might be called "good food" and preferred to eat chips and cheap sandwiches unless his poor boyfriend urged some more healthful helping upon him. As such, he always praised Frank's cooking to high heaven, baffled that he knew someone with not just culinary competence, but flair.

"This is incredible," he said, munching a toast bite. "These might be the best thing I've ever eaten. What's this? Shrimp? Don't mind if I do. Mm! Really good, Frank. So good."

Frank hesitated to bombard his friend with questions, or to scrutinize the delight he felt at their reunion. As ever, the two fell into easy banter, exchanging few words about anything that might have passed in their individual lives since last seeing one another. They sat on the edge of the deck, side by side, eating, drinking, shooting the shit while the Steady Five, returning from their break, launched into an anodyne rendition of "Anything Goes."

"Look at this!" said Channing, waving his hand and fork over the grounds and the gemmed, moonlit bay. "You've got water."

"Yup," said Frank. "It's all around us, Channing."

"No kidding. Nice house," said Channing. He looked up and over his shoulder at Willowbrook, as though he had just noticed the structure but wasn't quite sure what it was.

"It's not bad," said Frank. "It's grown on me."

"It's a fucking paradise. Where's Carol? And your kid's here, isn't he?"

"Off someplace. You'll see 'em. Hey, where's Marvelous? I want you to meet a friend of mine."

"His name's Marvelous?" said Channing. He wrinkled his nose. "Isn't that kind of . . . I don't know . . ."

"Marvelous?" said Frank.

Channing bobbed his head from side to side. "Well, yeah, so to speak."

Good authors too who once knew better words / Now only use four-letter words

"Fucking hell," said Channing. "Hey, did I mention? I loved that stuff you sent me."

"What stuff?"

"Your stuff. Your *Widdicombe Way*."

"Oh, right. Thanks."

"It's so—*you*. It's like hanging out with you, only better for your health. Less likely to result in broken bones or sheer aggravation."

They both laughed.

"Yeah," Channing continued, "I want a whole book of them! So, I hope you don't mind, but I sent it along to a friend of mine in publishing."

Frank choked on his beer. "What?"

"I sent it along to an editor friend."

In the kitchen, Christopher stood at the sink, washing a dish. This one dish had been "his"—he had, earlier, dipped into the stock of proper plates (part of a set of blue-and-white china that had occupied the family pantry since as long as he could remember), shunning those paper monstrosities (with their weird-feeling, rough undersides) as inadequate to the task of holding the ceremonial burger his father had fixed for him.

Incidentally, the burger had been good: rare, succulent with bloody juices, stacked with pickles, lettuce, and tomato, slathered with homemade aioli. Soul-satisfying, that burger, even if a cow's death prefigured it. In fact, shortly after devouring it, fine, basic feelings of contentedness and appreciation returned to Christopher. Perhaps he had just been hungry all along—how ridiculous! (Not that this possibility brought so much relief; a dread of the body and its power lurked just beyond the protective ramparts of satisfaction.) In any case, he had set the plate on the counter, thinking he would leave it for whatever platoon of altruists came to clean up the whole collected mess of the party. He had then returned to his experiment of trying to understand and perceive discrete facets of the party-going experience in a kind of rapturous simultaneity, and had, after an evening spent listening, seeing, smelling, and synthesizing, encountered inspiration: tomorrow he would paint this party, capture its essence in livid gouache. (It might not end up looking like the party looked—a bunch of bipeds standing around, pounding drums, babbling, playing with fire—but would reflect its spirit.) Pleased, restored, he had walked back into the house with the intention of absconding to his bedroom. The plate, however, conspicuous where he had abandoned it, grabbed his attention. He ought to clean up after himself, take full responsibility for his mess!

Now, in the middle of tending to that virtuous act of follow-through, something happened so fast, and so unexpectedly, that he would later spend a not-insignificant amount of time trying to re-create the event by the millisecond, imagining the sudden collection of microscopic fractures inside the blue-and-white china, a light-speed sequence of structural failures that knocked one another like dominos until the plate cracked in half. He dropped it immediately, swearing, grabbing his right wrist with his left hand. There, in the canyon between thumb and forefinger, blood welled up like crude from an oil field; air stung the exposed laceration where, he would later learn, he had severed a tendon (this he would revisit in great detail as well, imagining the snap of those white, fibrous cords that united muscle and bone). In great pain, and never one for the sight of blood, he screamed over the insouciant, bopping rhythm of "Anything Goes." Then he fainted. When he came to, Michelle was pulling him up from the kitchen floor.

His father and Channing stood by, the former already calling an ambulance.

While Christopher waited for professional medical attention, Marvelous walked deeper into the woods, his way lit by moonlight and the orange ember of his cigarette. Sometimes strength requires you walk alone. Sometimes the Week of Strength leads you into the woods, away from a big, jubilant feast, draws you down the dipping path toward the water. He needed space to reflect, a moment away from playing the hero. Bradford, wherever he snuck off to, would no doubt still be in need of an older, wiser hand tomorrow. Gracie clearly wanted nothing to do with him today, tomorrow, or any day after that. A self-sufficient woman, Gracie Sloane—what could she possibly see in a ruined man like him? Easy now—he rounded a bend in the path, began a hike uphill—no need for miserly self-talk during this, the Week of Strength. But God, how pathetic, these desperate collages, this milquetoast course in remedial humanity. Self-help! God give him the strength during this Week of Strength to suffer the slings and arrows of self-help. The Buddhists, in addition to shunning onions and garlic, said that life was suffering. That's right, big sigh—Buddhists said that, and they said in meditation not to resist the passing-through of negative, cranky, hateful thoughts, just to acknowledge them with an arch old nod from the inner something: "I see you, hopelessness. I acknowledge that you want me to think I won't amount to nothing, that I am a fool, doomed, that everything I do is wrong, wrong, wrong." Easy now. "Led down the garden path"—wasn't that a saying?

A small shack loomed ahead, a flicker of light teasing out from the openings, the cracks in its walls. He stopped—had he wandered, lost in ungenerous thought, onto somebody else's property? Turning back suggested itself for a moment only, dismissed forthwith by the miserably impetuous spirit of Gracie Sloane as communicated through the Week of Strength: "Say *yes* to risk, *yes* to creative danger," read the chapter. "Your reward will be adventure." Steeling himself, he crept closer; a woman's voice from inside the shack reached his ear, absorbed in soft, unintelligible song. It coaxed him nearer to the door, if only to try and parse the words, which undulated with alien fluency. He recognized the voice then. He stopped in his tracks.

"Gracie?" he called.

A pause in the song. "Who's there?"

"It's Marvelous."

Another pause, as though behind the wall she struggled to remember who he was. "Oh! Marvelous," she cried out at last. "Well, *you* can come in."

Seized with the sense that he stood on the brink of an ordeal that might outstrip his precious, hard-earned strength, he hesitated. But then, what could he do? He had already announced himself, already walked all the way out here more or less by mistake. Social logic—alive and well even out in the woods—dictated that he go ahead and open the door.

Gracie stood naked. Well, sort of. Though no clothing covered her willowy figure (her breasts, with their steep downward slope, their surprise terminal perk, drew his eye immediately), orange, white, and black paint on her face made the striped and whiskered mask of a tiger. He hung back, slack-jawed at the threshold of the room, and said, "Oh."

"I'm having a summer transformation ceremony," she said, the clip in her voice communicating that she was too deep into the throes of said ceremony to provide further explanation. "You can come in, but you have to take your clothes off."

Social logic once again coaxed him along. When invited to a party-in-progress on the host's very doorstep, and with no convenient excuse at arm's length—at arm's length, only dark, rustling forest—what could a self-respecting, self-loathing gentleman do? He disrobed, praying that he might survive this little ritual without getting turned on. The night air did feel thrilling against his naked flesh. He stepped into the shack, which was ill-lit enough to provide him some relief in the exposure department. He laughed a little.

Door closed, Gracie began to beat around his shoulders and head with a large white feather. "It's okay to laugh. I'm just going to clean your aura a little," she said. "Close your eyes, and while I do this I want you to imagine yourself as an animal. Take your time, and when you're ready, I want you to say what animal you see yourself as tonight."

More laughter threatened to shake free as he stood staring into his own darkness, the feather tickling his ears and shoulders. The palpable gravity with which Gracie performed this task got the better of him; he gave in to the power of suggestion and witness, and from the churning depths of his mind's eye, a creature took shape, swaggering out of the darkness. Black and white, it had a haughty self-possession. Its appearance gave him pause.

"I can tell you're seeing something," said Gracie. "Speak it."

"Skunk," said Marvelous, opening his eyes. As the word escaped his lips, some measure of his embarrassment left along with it.

"Excellent," said Gracie. "Skunk." She moved to grab a long plastic palette of finger paints, and only then did he really notice the extent to which she had decorated the interior of the shack. A table in the corner held brushes, a stack of paper, a collection of rocks, a jar of feathers, and a small black boom box. Candles burned on a shelf around the edges. Drying fern fronds formed a kind of molding where the walls met the floor.

As she dabbed his face with paint-smeared fingers, presumably anointing him with the long white nose-stripe of the skunk, he wrestled with the desire to grab her, then occupied himself with shooing away the thought, fearful that his dick might spring to attention and interrupt his totemic animal transformation. She sang a nonsensical song, and he joined in to distract himself, letting sounds come out that, while certainly not in English, struck him as somehow appropriate to the moment. Comprehensible in context. The harebrained harmony they created together brought on an irrepressible smile, and once she had finished with his new face, she said, "Okay, now we've sung a skunk song—it's time for a skunk dance."

She pressed a button on the boom box, and a tape of drumming started to play. Primeval, unadorned. Once again some critical part of Marvelous reeled with resistance, appalled by the invitation to act a fool, and once again he surged ahead, intent on following this wild, bewitching woman deeper into the realm of madness (where, it must be said, he assumed there would be grappling, groping, tasting, caressing). Every time he did surge ahead, in fact, it became easier—easier to dance around instead of turn and run, easier to hoot and howl instead of say to her, politely, "Well, it's been fun, but I'd better get back." Get back to what? The party? *Pah!* He danced, becoming a skunk of a man (his sweat contributed to this somewhat), flaunting what he pictured must be his furry, feathery tail, circling the naked tigress as she strutted and growled, the two of them agitating the candle flames with their untamed motions. The drumming mounted in urgency, carried them into a dance more frantic and uninhibited still, and at some point during this spellbound strutting, Gracie grabbed a glass bottle from the table and took a violent swig. Marvelous, enraptured, abandoned, totally gone, stole the bottle from her hand, taking a pull from the glass mouth that had touched hers; he tasted the warm, spicy ferment of whiskey; he swallowed it down. Caution flew out the shack window then: he threw his head back, dancing, glugged down some more, wiped his mouth and let loose a satisfied "*Ahhh!*"

To Gracie he gave what he could only hope was a smoldering, hungry look. When her eyes mirrored back his own roiling greed, he tossed the bottle aside and showed his woman wildness.

PART III

The middle of August meant more heat, and when the air conditioning at Willowbrook suddenly stopped working, the scene there became one of fussy, snappish sloth. This technical catastrophe only gave more life to the melancholy that was consuming Carol, as though the latter were a bacterial menace built to thrive in just such swamp-like conditions. It weighed upon her as she wandered from room to room, trying to remember where she had left her copy of *Wonderlust: How One Woman Turned Her Back on Everything to See the World*.

The title in question provided her a shred of hope, and a little bit more than a soupçon of escapism. For in the weeks since the Midsummer Feast she had felt restless and somehow wronged: the house no longer needed her, so what use did she have for the house? Every detail tended to, and still no spread in *Inside Places*. She felt "as a ghost," see-through with confusion, doomed to haunt her own island home. A home, a home, and full of her *things*—the stale, precious detritus of domestication (how Gracie put ideas into her head!) taunting her from every corner as she went on the hunt for *Wonderlust*. Perhaps it was she, and not Frank, who suffered from ADD; that might explain why she found it so hard to focus lately. Had she left it on the foyer table? No: there, a family of pegs held all of their key rings, rings of keys that let them in and out of their jail of a house ("All literature is prison literature, Mother," Christopher had said once), started the cars that carried them from the house to the store and back again. A bench made a roof over a pile of shoes: small tennis shoes belonging to Frank; a new fleet of slip-on affairs that made it easier for Christopher, with his temporary use of only one hand (poor thing—although, she had *tried* to be helpful to him in the wake of his injury, and had met with adolescent rebuffs; she guessed it wasn't *her* tendon that had been severed—only her tether); Gracie's sensible shoes, well suited to nature walks; and her own comfortable gardening clogs, the ones she stuffed her feet into when the house compelled her to wander the grounds, abstractedly plucking weeds or, in thrall to some still-intractable, cyclical beautifying compulsion, clipping flowers.

A long, rectangular runner led her past the breakfast nook, where there was also no sign of the book. Only a claw-footed couch reupholstered in an electric plaid of pink, yellow, green, and blue (the discovery and application of that fabric had, not so long ago, provoked a twinge of pride, but even the most shocking design features lost their vital spark with time), a contrasting suite of seats in comparatively tame olive, a slipper chair, a boisterous, tasseled ottoman on which Frank often stubbed his toe, and a long vintage trunk serving as a coffee table, stacked with issues of, yes, *Inside Places*, and empty inside.

A shame, for she had just finished the chapter about Henrietta "Henny" Gibbs traveling to Brazil to experience Carnival after a messy divorce, and the next chapter promised a trip to Lapland, a stay in an ice hotel. Why couldn't she stay in an ice hotel? The closest thing she had was the eye-level chamber of the freezer, which she opened on the off-chance that, overheated and confused, she had placed the book in it while fetching an all-natural all-fruit popsicle. No cranny of the kitchen offered up her book—not the corner of the marble counter, not any of the drawers filled with Frank's odd culinary gewgaws (did he really need *multiple* lemon zesters? He loved lemon, it sometimes seemed, more than life itself: "Lemon *is* life, Carol"). Nor did the adjoining dining room, with its tall, rustic, mint-colored china cabinet, its sturdy table at which Frank now insisted they eat together every evening, if they weren't eating outside. His dogged, quintessentially male insistence on rules of his own creation reminded her, the more she read *Wonderlust*, of Henrietta Gibbs's ex-husband, a man of business who stifled her need for adventure with merciless time management mandates, even on vacation. Frank wasn't as bad as all that, but ever since he had gotten it into his head to write a book of his own, and to do it methodically, here, at Willowbrook, she had felt sort of at a loss. If he could do it, and Henrietta Gibbs could do it, why couldn't she?

In the *salon*, she circled the circular green sofa, noting that the palm on top needed water. Then again, why not let it wilt, brown, die? It would make a nice wick from which to begin the total immolation of Willowbrook—just a match to one frond and the fire would soon spread from the sofa to the pale, fibrous rugs, then collapse the hand-carved and cane chairs, scorch the mirror on the mantel, lick up the walls, and melt the frames that held her favorite art (photography, naturalistic drawings, enviable watercolors painted by her son's once-good hand). She followed her flaming fantasies upstairs and searched the master bedroom.

The book itself must have developed a desire to roam, inspired by its own contents to wander far from prying eyes. Unless of course some guest or another had snatched it up and sat in the punishing sun, poring over what she felt to be her own private discovery—a book that spoke to her own immediate need, her longing for an elsewhere, an otherwise. If she could meet Henrietta Gibbs, she knew she would want to tell her, "Your book changed my life," which meant she wanted it to change her life, which meant she must find it and read the rest of it in order for her life to change. She drew a line at searching people's rooms. Why compound the psychic strain of sharing space by breathing life into such paranoia? She could, however, ask around.

"Frank?" she said, rapping at his office door.

"Come in," he called, "but don't let Kip out."

She pushed the door open just enough to slip in, and held it closed behind her. Frank had all of the lights off. He sat by the window in his porter's chair, reading by the diffuse natural glow. A rotating fan in the corner cooled the room, and *Princess Magdalena*, curled on a fainting couch, perked up at her entrance.

"Why don't you want to let her out?" she said. "Wow, it's surprisingly cool in here."

"I like having her around while I work," said Frank. "She helps me think."

Carol sat by Princess Magdalena, petting her. "Have you seen my copy of *Wonderlust*?" she asked.

"No," said Frank. "How is that, anyway? Did you look out on the deck?"

"I looked everywhere," Carol said, gazing through the rectangle of ghostly light on the wall. The fan, torqueing its head, blew cool air on her neck. "All over the house. I was just getting into it, too."

"Is it good?"

"It's fabulous." She looked at the cat as though it had been the one to ask her. "It's giving me the travel bug, though."

"Oh yeah?" said Frank. He rested the back of his head against the chair, angling his chin at her. "Where do you want to go?"

"That's just it—I'm not entirely sure." With the cat so close, her voice shaded a little into the babyish twang she used to talk to pets. "I only know I want to go somewhere. Do you know what I mean?"

"Of course, my love." Frank went to the desk to check his email. "Why don't we go to Mexico?" he said, staring at his laptop screen. "You've always wanted to go there. You could bring back some trinkets. Learn Spanish."

"Trinkets," Carol said. The thought of a donkey figurine dressed in colorful papier-mâché, or a skeletal Day of the Dead tableau, offered up little excitement. Then again, who knew what other unexpected delights awaited her in Guanajuato, in Oaxaca? She heard it was artsy there. She must remain open to the outcome.

"When's the air-conditioning guy coming?"

"Whenever he wants to. You know how they are," said Carol. The cat stood and stretched out, arching its back, then hopped from the fainting couch and padded over to Frank's feet. "Why does La Principessa love you so much?"

"I don't know. Why do you love me so much, Kip?"

For a moment, only the whir of the fan filled the room.

Carol sighed. "How's your book going? Hit upon any valuable lessons today?"

"You kid," said Frank.

"I wonder if self-help is popular in Mexico."

"Self-help is popular everywhere. Everywhere there are selves."

"Where aren't there selves?"

"I wonder."

"Maybe that's where I should go." Carol stood. Frank looked at her, and his eyes seemed to say something along the lines of, "Yes, maybe you should go where there are no selves, my darling, if that will make you happy." Her heart soared for a moment, pounding with both exhilaration and a kind of competitive envy. Frank thought he was so clever, so special! Typing away, speaking his mind, being creative. Well, she could do that, too; writing a book was as easy as having an idea and a laptop. And what made her so different from Henrietta Gibbs? Plenty of people had been to Brazil before her, and yet she went anyway, charting no territory other than her own so-called bliss, her self-discovery. Yes, it was her own bliss needed exploring, the map of her own experience that required filling in. She walked from the room, saying as she went, "Well, I'll see if Christopher's seen it. Don't work too hard."

"Love you," said Frank, glancing up to make sure she closed the door. Don't work too hard? What a thing for her to say, when she knew very well that *The Widdicombe Way* occupied almost all his waking moments since the party—those moments, anyway, that were not occupied by gorging himself on spinach salads, grilled shrimp, or honeydew melon balls wrapped in prosciutto. What was too hard, anyway? He looked back over the email he had been typing:

Dear Twinkletoes,

It may interest you to know that ever since your ill-fated visit to my country estate, work on The Widdicombe Way has become more difficult than ever. What began as a practical joke, a little bit of trickery, is now a millstone round my neck. That is the right saying, isn't it? That's the thing they hang around your neck?

I blame myself for sending you excerpts that clearly were not ready for public consumption. But I also blame you for sending them to your friend in publishing. I blame your friend in publishing for existing. I blame everyone, Channing! The shelves of my local bookstore are filled with trash. Living Right at Every Age. Count Your Blessings: A Quantitative Approach to Happiness. Yes You Khan: What a Mongol Emperor Can Teach Us About Fulfilling Our True Potential. Okay, I made that last one up, but it may as well exist. Do you think your friend in publishing would be interested in that?

Did Montaigne, in his day, have to reckon with the moronic forces of the marketplace? Maybe. I don't know. But then what I don't know could fill a book, and I intend it to do so. What I don't know about cats, what I don't know about solitude, what I don't know about tennis, noses, pleasure, and the comforts of a convivial meal. About friendship with traitorous gays. About sons and wives and alcoholic pals.

Well, I'm working on a new chapter now, Herr Goodman. It's called "Keep Your Ideas to Yourself," and though I write it with a righteous and important impulse toward discouraging foolishness, I do so too with little joy. It's hard to take joy in the little things, you know—which is a topic I return to again and again in this little thing—

with a phantom looking over your shoulder. Even if it's a
phantom looking over your shoulder and saying, "Take joy
in the little things already, you miserable fuck! Why aren't
you having any fun? Ready . . . set . . . relax!"

Look, old buddy, this thing started out as a lark. And
I intend fully—you mark my words!—I intend fully to
preserve its essential lark-ness, by hook or by crook. So
you can send your minions, your dumb flying monkeys,
till the cows come home. Meanwhile, I will go on fighting
with every fiber of my being to prevent this thing from
becoming a serious endeavor.

Yours,
Frank

He sent the email, too swept up in the fighting spirit to
save it as a draft. Did Genghis Khan draft his declarations of
destruction before galloping in? *Hell, no*, thought Frank. He
just galloped in and started lopping heads. How to keep the
essential lark-ness of the thing intact remained an open question, but Frank was sure that solutions would soon rush in to
support him, sure as the fearsome Mongol cavalry stampeded
forward when their emperor rode into battle.

The other problem of the moment, however, was that he
had started feeling a little funny that morning—loopy, spaced
out, disturbed by a tickle in his throat—and feared that he
might be getting a cold. A fucking cold! Widdicombes so rarely
came down with colds, or flus, or anything of the sort. Symptoms felt like insults. His own body was insulting him. In this
early stage it was more like a whisper campaign, an insidious

take-down of personal character like those perpetuated at the old French court. Well now, he had gone from Mongolia to France in the space of a minute (*quelle grande vitesse!*), but never mind that. The point was, he must crush his adversaries, and quash any rebellions beginning to stir in his body, which was a goddamn temple after all, a temple of pleasure and fun and strength—no place for a rebellion.

Kip the cat jumped onto his lap just then, stepping unfeelingly over his groin in search of a comfortable seat. "What do you think, Kippo?" Frank said. "Do we fight, or do we give in?" The cat stared up at him with glassy, merciless marbles for eyes. He liked to think that if she could speak, she might say, composed as a warrior queen, "Gather the horses, my liege, and summon the men. For tonight we offer them no quarter. Tonight the village streets shall run with the blood of our enemies."

He stroked her back. "You can be so cruel, my queen—but so be it."

Down the hall and descending the stairs, through this home that he had come to love so much. The shape of it, and the attention to detail for which he had his wife to thank, all seemed custom-made to fit him, to reflect back the joy, the splendor filling out that summer. At least, it *had*, before thoughts of phantom eyes prying into *The Widdicombe Way* had threatened to plunge him right back into the bad mood that had marked the start of the season. Fie on phantoms! He rattled a handful of chewable orange vitamin C tablets into his hand. Then, owing to some deep-seated part of him that longed always to have his gestures of resistance witnessed, he wandered out onto the deck to see if anyone was around.

There, at the far end of the lawn, Gracie's thicket of curls caught his eye.

Approaching her unnerved him less now that she and Marvelous had struck up an affair. (The fact that Gracie meant to depart from the region in a matter of weeks concerned him for Marvelous's sake, but then the man was grown and could make his own decisions. Annoying, however, that the old garden gnome refused to provide any juicy details, or even air any concerns of his own. Such reticence would never fly among the men of psychology, gathered in Auvergne.) Even still, he cleared his throat loudly as he walked over the shushing green grass, for her posture—bent over a sage bush, muttering as though rapt in conversation with it—struck him as arcane, absorbed in a secret intimacy that he must now interrupt.

"Afternoon to you, wild child," he called. Their banter had taken on a casual liveliness since the party. He assumed that romantic attention had put her at greater ease, and that unspoken honesty, apparent in manner alone, in turn cast her in a more sympathetic light, a human glare to which he could relate. They were all fighting for their lives!

Turning, she shielded her eyes and smiled. "Hello, you," she said. "I was just talking to this sage."

"I see," said Frank.

"Oh, I know it sounds funny. It's just an experiment. One must try things out and see what sticks. I'm good on the Nature Walks, good on the Wildness Dates. Now I'm trying to figure out a chapter about something I'm calling Spirit Gardens, which will involve cultivating a little plot of plant-companions."

He nodded slowly, as though listening to an unhinged individual and concerned the wrong response might send them flying off the handle. "For your book, then."

"Yes and no," said Gracie. She looked up at the sky, thinking. "For my book, but really, for my soul."

"For your bliss."

"Yes," she said, her voice firm. "And for my beautiful readers. What about you? Taking a break from the old self-help grind?"

"Yup," said Frank. He felt the lure of mischief making a surprise return, and added, "I had an extraordinary breakthrough today, a real revelation about why I've been put here and why I've been called to devote myself to *The Widdicombe Way*."

Gracie's eyes, as he had imagined they would, lit up with hunger. "That's fantastic, Frank. How exciting for you, to start to see a guiding sense of purpose. Care to share in greater detail?"

"Thanks," said Frank, "but I'm still processing."

Snapping a sprig of sage from the plant with which she had just been speaking, Gracie brought it to her nose. Her patient nodding seemed designed to express tolerance for aggravating people like him. "Well," she said, "there is something to be said for that, for waiting until it can be most powerfully articulated. Patience is key. Oh, but breakthroughs—I do love breakthroughs of all kinds."

"They're truly of the essence," said Frank, at a loss for anything else to say.

"When I had my breakdown several years back, after finishing *The Seven Directions*, it took me some time to move from thinking of the whole episode as a 'nervous breakdown' to thinking of it as a 'nervous break*through*.' Often what looks like total collapse is just a new, more suitably aligned life purpose that can no longer be ignored, coming in to clear away the brush. And sometimes we—or what we call 'we'—are part of the brush." She chuckled at this last insight, as if to demonstrate that she had mastered and moved past whatever trauma it was she had experienced around the nervous breakthrough, and now found her own former self laughably unenlightened.

"I'm not sure what brush I'm a part of," said Frank, "but I do know that I woke up feeling a little under the weather today." He stuffed the handful of chewable vitamins into his mouth at last. "The breakthrough didn't really seem to help that any."

"What are you taking? Vitamins?" Gracie wrinkled her nose.

"Vitamins," he said. He then added, in what he thought of as a British pronunciation, "Vit-a-mins."

"What you really need is astragalus. Trust me—this stuff will kick the ass of whatever it is. I take some any time I start to feel a cold coming on. It's all-natural and it's all-powerful. I take it as a tea—I have it in the cupboard in the kitchen, by the sink. Help yourself to some."

"Very well, then," said Frank. An exhausted and vaguely sore feeling had started to creep up on him, and now, besieged by the threat this represented, vocal protest against astragalus struck him as a misappropriation of his precious resources. He resolved to reject astragalus, to curse the very name of astragalus, and then added, "I'll give it a whirl."

"Do!" Gracie watched him retreat to the house. The absence of any desire on her part reassured her. Since finding companionship with Marvelous, her attraction to Frank had slipped away, revealed itself as a momentary desperation at a weak point in her life. Thank God that was over. He had put on weight since her arrival, and even since the party—though that hardly mattered, since she liked men with some meat on their bones. She shook her head, proud that she had weathered that storm and found a more appropriate outlet for her primal energies.

Not that Marvelous served outlet duties alone. Willful and wild in his own bearish (or was it skunkish?) right, he doted on her with all the fervent affections of fresh love, inviting her for walks along the pier or through Bloedel Reserve (the grand forest garden in which his favorite poet, Theodore Roethke, had died at fifty-five—much too young), asking about her work over steamed mussels at one of the harbor restaurants. And she could not discount stupendous lovemaking as one of the highlights of their affair; they both knew she would leave before long (though here doubts began to tease at her, and temptation told her to snatch him up, drag him back to Berkeley or halfway 'round the world on a Far Eastern journey), and this inevitability gave their bedroom antics a kind of urgency, an effervescence. In the sack they earned their stripes as both tigress and skunk— two totem animals well matched in strong, earthy sensuality. They called one another by these pet names—"Tigress, tigress, burning bright," "My big, strong skunk"—in silly postcoital raptures that now and then unmasked themselves as pre-, too. The time they spent tangled in the small bed at his apartment, or in her walled-off wilderness shrine, however, soon showed in her tendency toward dreamy distraction: her speech for Green Dawn needed writing still, and as yet she had only hit upon an illustrative subtopic for her exploration of wildness: "Secrets."

Well, what about them? Walking down the forest path, her thoughts emerged in half-formed, drowsy imagery: her under a sunlit sheet, turning her head to Marvelous and telling him, bashful but thrilled, that she had once entertained a troubling lust for Frank Widdicombe; her reading to him from tender, rambling new meditations written in a transport for *The Habit of Wildness*; her sitting up in bed, grave, blurting out that some domesticated part of her wished she didn't have to leave, wished that she could stay with Marvelous, even become *Mrs.* Marvelous. When to tell our secrets—drag them from hiding, present them like coached youngsters at a pageant—and when, why, how to keep things to ourselves, to carve out hidden nooks and fissures? Hidden places like those the woods around her had—patches tucked away from light, tunneled into the dirt of minor and miniature cliffsides, shaded over by untamed canopies, the light at this time of day, the way it fell upon the path in jagged jewel shapes shaken by the wind—all of that buoyed her, chimed in her a note of elation and of rightness. What purpose, however, served the untouched, the unseen?

Of course, sometimes one must walk simply to proliferate such questions, to coax them into the atmosphere and let them hang unanswered. Like seeding a cloud, one waited, knowing that, having put a little pressure on Nature, she would sooner or later oblige with rain. And so she walked, letting her thoughts fly by like creatures of Queen Nature themselves, alighting on the branches of her mind for a moment only, as though stopping for a rest before flitting back to the unknowable, concerted undertaking in which they all colluded. To extend her walk, she followed a fork in the path that led away from her shack and down toward the water. On this stretch, however, the benign creatures of mental process cleared off, and the notions passing through her field of awareness became things with fangs, hunched backs, and glowing eyes, things that darted between deeper shadows.

How she dreaded returning to Berkeley! The work she had done here hummed with a refreshed vitality, cleansed of the self-conscious spiritual striving she sometimes felt in the Bay. In ten years, too, she had failed to find love there, or had failed to let it find her—must she remain a stop on the way to something else for any potential suitor? She had overheard somebody months ago say in New York that thirty was the new seventy (the person, of course, looked about twenty). And though she put little stock in such idiocies, and hardly feared for her liveli-

ness, her automatic writings, inner voices, and flourishes of synchronicity as of late goaded her more and more in the direction
of traveling more, of leaving behind her comfortable hilltop
nest for—for what? Here guidance ended. The vast uncertainty
of the territory frightened her, and so she had been committing
what she felt to be a capital crime in her own written system
of cosmic law: she was ignoring the urge of intuition, setting it
aside as an inconvenience to return to later when she had more
answers. The universe was asking her to jump into the void; a
test. Now more than ever the prospect troubled her. She liked
her home. She liked her routines.

A drop of water dashed against her arm. Rain? Rain!
Through the sheltering vault of foliage blue-and-white sky still
peeked, but then a staccato patter against the leaves sounded
out across the wood, the sense of a new world opening up
inside the old, a pleasant overture before the drenching down-
pour. No proper shelter presented itself, and she had come this
far anyway—the lip of the beach hovered at a stone's throw—so
what could she do? Out of the forest and onto the accumulated
crunch of rocky shore, where the rain, lit up by the sun, came
at her from all sides. What at first tickled her arms and neck,
cool and wet, soon became a dull barrage. She stood at the edge
of the bay while the water, bright, crackled with falling drops.
The desire to live life suddenly beat in her like a drum—her, a
soaked woman, a sodden wanderer! Shirt darkened and heavy,
clinging to her skin like a peel. But what a boon, too, to be
sopping wet, when knowledge could be a kind of dry death.

———

Christopher made a half fist with his right hand, closing the left
over it for a little assistance. This sorry excuse for a grip he held
for ten seconds then released. The cast at least had come off,

though he had enjoyed drawing all over it in a sloppy, second-ary hand for a couple of weeks. On it, in colored pen, he had executed a crude version of the party scene he had imagined painting just before the accident. And though his nondominant hand had imbued the abstract, multihued scribblings with a naïve agitation (the finished result looked like nothing so much as the energetic and violent scratches of a child given art sup-plies), it stood as a testament to his perseverance. Nevertheless, when it came time for the doctor to break out his medical saw and free the hand that had once painted the *Gorgeous Harbors of Bainbridge Island* series, he said good-bye to the cast without regret, and hello to that pale, atrophied length of him that had spent so many days in mummification. One went on making new memories after all.

Being limited to his left hand not only made it that much more difficult to appreciate Thomas Eakins (not, it seemed, an acceptable course of physical therapy), it also called his artistic future into question: he feared throwing himself too gung ho into bending and straightening, into the squeezing of a stress ball, and courting irreparable damage. Even if he proceeded with caution, his next supposed semester at RISD started in early September, and he would not yet be able to draw or paint. Not as he used to, anyway; nothing like the realist watercolors of the Naples garbage crisis now, he was recently informed, being taken down from the walls of the gallery back east. Some comfort returned when he threw out the idea of an artistic future in favor of an artistic present, but even that called for an almost heroic denial of dread. His sketched portraits of mother, father, Michelle, and Gracie came out looking like a psychotic rogues' gallery. An ambitious series of left-handed watercolors about the fading memory of Kreshnik looked muddy and amateurish; his brush zigged when he meant it to zag. His fingers trembled, cramped, and spasmed, unaccustomed to the motions of art making.

All of this wreaked havoc on his self-confidence, and the suspect promise of Michelle's (that a friend of hers, some Dane, was coming to visit, and that the two were destined to meet), while meant to cheer or distract him, only made him feel more like some freak in a Coney Island sideshow. "Step right up, step right up! Come see the painting prodigy laid low by a fluke dishwashing accident—he's only got one hand to work with, folks, and he's doing the best he can!" What if some cultural or language barrier led the Dane to seize his hand in greeting, crushing his right-handed art career forever? What if they hit it off, and he ruined his future during an episode of vigorous intercultural lovemaking? On second thought, the latter possibility held significant appeal, for what better damage to overcome in pursuit of art than the crippling wages of love? Better, at least, than the crippling wages of housework.

He sat on the deck, allowing his weak hand and forearm—pale as drawing paper next to his sepia-toned left—to receive a little sun. Whatever happened as his lame limb warmed, its cells probably as giddy as far-north Alaska dwellers after a two-month vigil of winter darkness, it must have been healing. How else to explain the thrill of sunlight, except to fall back upon a worshipful prejudice for its life-giving qualities? Dipping a medium-sized brush into thinned yellow the color, almost, of the Scotch broom flowers he saw all around the island, he painted another imperfect circle on the paper before him, continuing a series of solar still lifes. Apparently, he had read online, the sun could always explode. And if it did, it would take something like seven minutes for it to become visible to human eyes, all of which would be incinerated by then anyway. The yellow glob throbbing in his still life reminded him of the crayon suns he used to draw over house and family as a wee lad, long before solar storms and flares had become part of his mental landscape.

He toyed with the idea of leaving school altogether. True, he had already threatened to do so twice, calling home in drug-induced stupors to discourse dryly on the lack of excitement at art school. Each time, however, his mother or father—supportive to the end, to a fault!—wound up agreeing with him, encouraging his half-baked plans to drop out in order to embark upon a "time-bending, multiyear artistic walking tour of the entire contiguous forty-eight states, ending at Plymouth Rock." "A brilliant idea. Follow your bliss." Try as he might, he could never quite work up the nerve to pursue any truly radical course of action. If only he could sell his watercolors to buy crystal meth, disappear, and never call them again. Alas, they had instilled in him an instinct for self-preservation that dovetailed with their own apparently nurturing ideals, and so, at this point, he despaired of ever persuading his family to disown him; anything he could do to court their disapproval would offend his own sensibilities, and it was this unfortunate truth that led him to believe that there was something to the idea of success as a family curse. As this thought barreled toward him, terrible as a heavyweight boxer, his left hand faltered. His brush slipped from his hand, clacking once against the side of the table before falling to the deck and rolling into one of the gaps between planks.

He pushed his chair, leaving behind the ruined blob-sun he had been working on, careful not to do anything stupid with his right hand in the heat of frustration. His last hope was that Michelle's friend Jens would inspire repulsion in his parents while making himself irresistible to Christopher. In this case Christopher might salvage some shred of essential difference between the Widdicombes *pére* and *mére* and their progeny, and in doing so find assurance that his life remained his own.

In his room, sunk in heat—when *was* the air-conditioning guy coming?—a nap beckoned. Fifteen or twenty minutes of shut-eye, whether he drifted off or not, usually did the trick in terms of restoring his faith in the day and its capacity to yield meaning or pleasure. The useless patchwork quilt covering his bed (it served no purpose in the heat of summer; he kept it around for aesthetic reasons) felt rough against the back of his arms and legs. His pillow, sinking under the pressure of his skull, gathered heat and gave it back. The bed's being a single, though of little concern up to now, alarmed him, as though it were a tomb designed to his precise bodily measurements, threatening to engulf him for eternity. Confusion and panic over filial annihilation, plus dread and anticipation of Jens' imminent arrival, plus a passing train of thought about TUOT the cat, suddenly took form in his mind's eye as a six-foot-tall dapper feline sitting cross-legged in a chair across the room, dressed in a clean linen suit.

"Christopher Widdicombe," said the giant cat, drawling the "ist," the "er," the "id," and the "ombe." "Young man, young man—" It dropped its chin, shook its head. "You're as lonely as they come." The creature had a bright, insinuating voice.

"So what?" mumbled Christopher. His own voice reached him from far away, weak and stripped to the vowels.

"Single men have a twenty-five percent higher mortality rate than married ones." The cat's whiskers twitched. It tilted its head.

"So what?"

"Married people also make more money. You say you don't mind being alone, but I know you have your doubts. Who will nag you to monitor your cholesterol levels? Did you know that married adults are three times more likely than single people to survive heart surgery?"

"Go 'way."

"I'm trying," said the cat, casually inspecting the claws on one of its front paws, "to explain to you the link between gay marriage and well-being."

"Shut up!" shouted Christopher, and in doing so, startled himself from half sleep. The broadcasted syllables hung on his lips. Soon, a knock came at the door.

"Christopher?" His dad's voice. "Everything all right?"

"Yeah," said Christopher. "Come in."

His father stepped into the room, scratching at his mustache. "I heard you screaming 'Shut up!'"

"A giant cat spirit visited me," said Christopher, rolling his head over on the pillow. "It told me single men are more likely to die."

"Hmmm. I see. Well, everyone is likely to die, son," said his father, who took a chair, picking up a pile of sketches from the ground. He did not seem perturbed in any way by the idea of a giant cat paying Christopher a spiritual visitation. "These are nice. Is this the garbage disposal?"

"I meant die earlier. Oh, Dad, we're all so fundamentally alone."

"I wish I could tell you that feeling went away. But then Marvelous tells me, when he's feeling very parroty about his AA slogans, that it's important to remember that feelings aren't facts. In any case, I'm sure once you're back in school you won't feel alone anymore. You might even start wishing you did."

"Neither being alone nor its opposite seem very satisfactory, do they?"

"It certainly feels that way sometimes," said his father. After contemplating in silence for a moment, he added, "That's why it's so important to keep moving. Do you need anything? How's the hand?"

"I need to know if it will always be so painful to feel so fundamentally alone," said Christopher. Watching his father consider this, he added, "God, I hate feelings! They're utterly humiliating, each and every one of them."

"I recommend deciding which answer you want and then settling on it until you change your mind," said his father. Christopher couldn't help but laugh. He felt his father's hand clap his shoulder. "All this just means you're a Widdicombe, son. We're a sociable clan, like it or not. As you've pointed out before, it's a matter of survival. A survival instinct."

"If this is survival, give me extinction!" Christopher cried, regaining dramatic flair in the wake of his nap. Seeing his father shake his head, perplexed and potentially disapproving, refreshed him a little. He watched him go, and as he did so, wondered what it would be like if they didn't see or speak to one another for the next ten years. What if he just walked into the wilderness, went off the grid?

"I'll bring you some iced tea."

———

When Frank came into the kitchen to pour a tall glass of iced tea, Michelle, seated at the dining room table with her laptop, kept her eyes fixed to the screen. They had already said their hellos that day; no need to speak every time he came in and out of the room, which, owing to the man's constant puttering around, was often enough. She carried on working.

Charged with tending to the details of her final task for the summer, their upcoming "family outing" to the Green Dawn Expo in Seattle—tickets must be procured, restaurant reservations made, ferry schedules figured out (not a big or taxing job, to be sure; aside from handling the Midsummer Feast, Carol's never were)—the absence of one in their party haunted her. How long had it been now since the Feast? And still she hadn't seen Bradford. Oh, she had heard from him: drunk-dialing episodes (drunk, or worse—high, low, truly wretched) in which admissions of undying love and unmoored apologies factored highly. She could hardly squeeze in a demand to know where he was without him protesting, "No, no . . . I'm taking care of something now, honest I am . . . No, I can't see you till I clean up my act . . . I have to do this, Michelle—will you wait for me?" He sounded worse than ever, more like a man speaking into the howling winds of his own self-destruction. She feared for him. She longed for him, too. It felt kind of gross.

Four tickets for an inspirational speech given by Gracie Sloane, author of *The Twelve Directions of Positive Thinking*, *The Golden Road*, and, coming soon, *The Habit of Wildness*. Behind Michelle a fly buzzed, caught between a raised pane of window glass and the screen meant to keep insects *out*— buzzed a one-second complaint, quieted, buzzed a longer, more aggravated cry of struggle. Perhaps it was wrong to love an imploding man, a man who chose—chose!—to thrash in the water when a hundred lifelines floated around him, waiting for him to simply reach out, seize something, and be carried to safety. Danger hummed with more magnetism than safety ever could, though, and this composed part of Bradford's charm. Yes, he was gorgeous, and well dressed, and had been given the gift of star quality, of charisma. That he carried this gift into chaotic circumstances, a glass vase in the middle of a bloody barroom brawl, baffled even as it seduced—who couldn't feel compelled by instinct to jump up, reach out, and pull the priceless specimen out of harm's way? But then the vase brimmed with a toxic sludge; to pull it close so suddenly meant to risk upsetting its foul contents. Did the Widdicombes need tickets to a panel called Help Yourself: Writing Self-Improvement for a New Epoch?

Why yes, they certainly did.

Thinking about Bradford all day achieved nothing; this much Jens had assured her during their most recent video chat. "It's not your responsibility," he had said. His lilting accent made even banal statements sound taut with certitude, almost offended. "If he wants to be with you, he has to learn to take care of himself." The on-screen image stalled every so often, reducing her friend to pixelated blocks; between these glitches he swiveled in a chair in his studio in Copenhagen, wheat-colored hair swept up in a choppy pompadour, blue eyes deadly earnest, reddish-blond scruff along his jaw catching light from the kitchen window. How many times she had sat at that kitchen table, smoking cigarettes with him and sipping caraway-laced akvavit! God, she missed the simplicity of that time, so in contrast with the present emotional climate, more than ever. The limp hang of his tee-shirt collar exposed a patch of chest hair, and Michelle stirred with anticipation.

"I just can't wait for you to meet Christopher," she said.

"I know you can't," said Jens. "You have mentioned it about five times. Well, I'll be there next week. I leave for New York tomorrow."

In New York, Jens would enjoy a week of vacation from his work at the firm where he specialized in maritime law, resolving squabbles over shipping commerce. Then he would fly out to Seattle to see her (and, she hoped, fall in love with Christopher; she had a strong feeling that the two would either adore each other or fall into instant, bitter enmity). Though she couldn't quite admit it to herself, she hoped that this visit might help her snap out of the spell she felt she'd fallen under. The idea of leaving the island, of starting a new chapter of some kind, had started suggesting itself to her, advocating for itself in a small, insistent voice at the back of her mind. Ever since things had soured between her and Bradford, she had started to see her job with the Widdicombes in a different, almost paranoid light. It wasn't like her to court that kind of drama; had she, swept up in that weird clan's affairs, lost sight of herself? Had they *hoped* for that? It made her tense and jumpy to think that her job description might have changed without her noticing, and that Michelle Briggs, Widdicombe Watcher, might have become a source of entertainment herself. Carol, for one, liked to ask Michelle lots of questions about her newly tumultuous love life, to make a show of mothering her in this department, to test out psychological theories about Bradford that always, in the end, referred back to herself. "Do you think he might be an actual sociopathic narcissist?" she had whispered at one point, and then, not waiting for an answer, shuddered. "I used to be drawn to that type when I was younger. It took me years of therapy to deprogram myself. There were a lot of intense people around back then. The Coed Killer. People in cults. Poets."

And speaking of Carol, how about a panel on Decorating for Enlightenment?

Mrs. Widdicombe had indicated a clear "yes" for herself and a "maybe" for the others—she would have to ask.

"No, I don't want to hear about decorating for enlighten-ment," said Frank, sitting in the breakfast nook and fanning himself with a copy of *Tennis* magazine. "Is there a support panel for the friends and family of enlightened people? Like an Al-Anon sort of thing?"

Christopher, who had come downstairs to perish in the *salon*, slumped on the circular green sofa, said, "No, I don't think so. Will there be any faith healers there?"

Michelle, pacing, paused to look at Christopher's lovely, joyful paintings of the harbor. She then walked over to the window. "What kind of guys do you like, Christopher?"

"Case-by-case," he said, "though I have a soft spot for any-one that I'm not supposed to have one for."

She snickered. Then she thought, Why do gay men always have to turn everything serious into a joke? "So you don't have a type?"

"I like the atypical type," he said. "Why, what's yours?"

This last question taunted her, and she responded to it with an impatient look. "Let's not. I want you to meet my friend Jens."

"I know you do," said Christopher. "You talk about it enough."

"That just shows you how sincerely I want it to happen."

"What a lot of pressure to put on a first meeting. But then, a first meeting without any pressure would be unnatural. Or rather, natural, which is worse."

"Now I think *you're* overthinking this."

"I hope he likes cripples."

"Oh, you're hardly a cripple."

Frank wandered into the room looking aimless, lost in thought.

"Frank," said Michelle, "would you call Christopher a cripple?"

"Christopher, you're a cripple," said Frank.

"Thanks, Dad."

"No," said Michelle, "I mean, would you describe him to someone else as a cripple?"

"It depends on the circumstances," said Frank.

"Wait, what?" said Christopher. "Michelle, what's Jens like?"

"I would only call someone I knew really well a cripple," said Frank, "and only if they said I should. People should get to choose what you call them. And then there are certain things that certain people can only call themselves, like—"

"He's a maritime lawyer," said Michelle.

"Very intriguing," said Christopher.

"Who's Jens?" said Frank.

"Do you think he and my dad will get along?" said Christopher.

"Do you like lawyers, Frank?" said Michelle.

"It depends on the circumstances," said Frank.

"Michelle wants to set me up with a Danish maritime lawyer," said Christopher.

"Well, that sounds very intriguing," said Frank.

"I don't know." Christopher sighed. "Suddenly I feel markedly less intrigued."

"He's nice," said Michelle.

"Nice is nice," said Frank.

"Nice for who?" said Christopher.

"For all concerned," said Frank. "You ought to branch out, son. Have you ever dated a Danish person?"

"They're *called* Danes," said Christopher.

"I always get that mixed up with the Dutch," said Frank.

"Well, don't do that to Jens," said Michelle. "It makes him furious."

"And what do I care if I make some Dutchman furious?" said Frank.

"A furious Dane? Well, now I'm intrigued again," said Christopher. "But what if we do fall in love? He lives across the ocean."

"I'm sure you'd figure something out," said Michelle.

"People always figure something out if it's important to them," said Frank. "If it's really important, the ocean doesn't make the slightest difference."

"I wonder if he'll want to talk about Somalian piracy," said Christopher. "Because I have a lot to say on the subject."

"Was Somalia ever owned by the Dutch?" said Frank.

"Dad, this has nothing to do with Holland," said Christopher.

"Who said anything about Holland?" said Frank.

"Dutch things come from Holland," said Michelle. "The Netherlands."

"Well, which one is it?" said Frank.

"Both," said Christopher. "But Jens is from Denmark. He's Danish. And I love him!"

————

"Want coffee?"

Bradford, bundled in a blanket on the couch and feeling quite dry in the mouth, stirred from whatever kind of nap he had been taking. He was not even sure that the variety of unconsciousness he now slipped into on occasion qualified as sleep, or that it could be exalted by that innocent old word *nap*. It felt much more like some disciplinary punishment his body resorted to in order to restore some semblance of control. The world outside his cocoon of blankets threatened, at present, to burn through everything, to skewer his eyes with light if he emerged. He tried to ignore the siren song of his father's voice offering him coffee, to feign further sleep. But then, his mouth felt very dry, and the word *coffee* carried with it such an irresistible promise of good feelings. He peeled back the cocoon and slowly sat up, half swaddled in its broken remnants.

"Yes, please," he said, his voice low and ragged. "Want coffee."

"Some people say coffee isn't good for you when you're sick," said his father, who was moving around the nearby kitchen (walls had been knocked down in the remodel, so that the kitchen, the living room, and the dining room all flowed into one another, part of an open plan). He was in a blur of business attire, making horrendous sounds with various implements. "But my feeling is, why *compound* illness by giving yourself withdrawal syndromes. Sometimes the best way to take care of our bodies is to keep giving them what they've grown used to being given. No need to incite a mutiny in the middle of a siege, so to speak."

"I'm with you," said Bradford. His eyes, unable, it seemed, to open fully, ached from the view offered by the wide picture window. Beyond buildings bright with glare there was the sparkling Puget Sound. The familiar aroma of coffee—coffee harvested, roasted, and distributed at his father's command—gradually drew him from what he had started to fear might be a state of permanent flatness. "What time is it?"

"Five forty-five," his father said. "PM. Did you get up at all today?"

"I did for a while," he lied, exaggerating the weakness in his voice. "I watched a movie." Why he felt it necessary to embellish his initial lie with this detail he would never know, but once he started in on needless decoration, it was hard for him to stop. "A movie called—what was it called? *Say Something Lovely*, I think. A nauseating romantic comedy about a—voice-over actress, who falls in love with a man she thinks she hates who's working on the same cartoon she is, one of those educational cartoons." Ridiculous this sounded, it seemed to pass muster.

His father brought him a small ceramic cup of coffee. "Huh," he said, "never heard of it." Of course, you haven't, thought Bradford. When will you learn? "So you're watching rom-coms now? What happened to horror?"

"What happened to horror," repeated Bradford, not sure immediately how to answer such a large and open-ended question. "I feel it's good to watch all kinds of movies, to get a sense of how they're put together," he said at last. "And anyway, I'm thinking about writing a romantic comedy after I finish this horror script. You've gotta *keep 'em guessing*, as they say."

"Well, I'm glad to hear you're thinking about the future," said his father, who was already carrying his own cup out of the room. "I'm going to take a shower. Then let's order some food. We'll get you some soup."

Bradford agreed to this thrilling evening plan. He let himself collapse a bit further on the couch, sliding into a posture so uncomfortable as to be almost enjoyable, and closed his eyes again. An exhausting performance, the last five minutes. No one could say he wasn't well rested, anyway; he supposed he had slept for about fifteen hours. It was helpful that he at least appeared and sounded as though he had something like the flu. Too much ecstasy, crystal meth, and "artisanal crack cocaine" would do that to you. It had been a fun lost weekend in Portland, but now it was supposed to be over, and he still felt to a certain extent that he would like to die. The ecstasy had been sheer ecstasy, live music and live sex with a live young woman named Marjorie. In the crack- and crystal-happy days that followed, however, he had talked so much and inhaled so many cigarettes that it seemed his soul had poured out of his body a little more with each meaningless word, replaced by plumes of carcinogenic tobacco smoke and worse. What fun he had had spending three days indoors, in his friend Kyle's windowless apartment.

When his coffee cup ran dry, he got up from the couch to refill it. Not even this fairly traded pleasure could he resist transforming into the most desperate of compulsions. Over the next twenty-five minutes, he would exhaust the entire contents of the rather large French press, thinking all the while that maybe it hadn't been fun after all, this last weekend in Portland—or that it had, but that it had also been all too much like his year in LA, though with considerably more drugs this time. He felt oddly inspired by these binges—ready to get back to the old untitled horror grind—just as much as he felt regret and rage begin to coat him all over with their scummy plaque. He had missed or ignored many texts and calls from Michelle while he was stuffing steel wool into a glass pipe and talking about how his agent was in Hollywood right now, whipping up a bidding war between studios who were all losing their minds over his completed script. "Fucking amazing," that guy whose name he couldn't remember had said.

He was avoiding Michelle, anyway, as it had become all too clear that he would never finish his project with her around. This was not the time for a complicated and long-term entanglement—his *screenplay* was that, after all, and so to become emotionally involved with anyone or anything else meant infidelity. His screenplay, with its evil psychological mist, understood if he strayed for a dalliance here and there, knowing full well that he'd come crawling back eventually and every time. After bigger lapses such as this last one, however, the relationship felt as though it might be suffering just a little from his various indiscretions; what the two of them needed, and soon, was to get away from it all for a while, to take a trip someplace where they could relax, cuddle up together, and return to the original task of completing each other.

All of that would have to wait a short while, he thought, running his fingers through his hair and finding it to be rather longer and greasier than expected. For he was now not only a screenwriter but a dishwasher as well. A screenwriter first, to be sure, but a dishwasher nonetheless. What was more, a dishwasher who must show up for work in two days' time, free from too *very* many visible signs of degeneration and decay.

———

During this long week in question, the apartment building where Marvelous lived rang out often with the sounds of uninhibited lovemaking. While as sweltering there as it was at Willowbrook (Marvelous had no air conditioning, only a trio of cheap fans strategically placed), their discomfort only drove the new lovers to more ardent and frequent exertions in search of relief. Between these slick, heat-mad entanglements, Marvelous and Gracie would roll apart, returned to the inconvenience of being two separate people, both eager to escape the other's thermal flesh. This rupture could only last so long, however, before a joint trip to the shower led to kisses, caresses, and at last a reinvigorated groping that erupted once again, a lustful cycle in full, unwavering revolution.

Tons of sex, in other words. The two might find themselves

pressed together against the shower wall, or on the tile of the bathroom floor, or, as they did just then, throwing towels aside to fall back in bed together.

Rug burns, calf cramps, aching necks and backs: all that disappeared for Marvelous when he knelt over her, kneecaps depressing the mattress, making a beast with two backs or whatever other zoological metamorphosis might suggest itself. Sweat oozed along his hairline, ran down his flanks, dropped from his body onto hers, lubricated their thighs. The space around them thickened with life, that redolent musk drawing even time into their slow and sensual rapture—a welcome third presence in the bedroom, and a master of the art. In their steady outbursts, too—grunting, sighing, goading, yelping, barking, humming, whimpering agreement—the recent past evaporated, which suited Marvelous just fine. They said yes to the moment until it burst with happiness, no longer a moment at all.

"You," said Gracie. Curled on one side of the bed, she reached and scratched behind his ear. "You, you, *you.*"

His chest rising and falling, Marvelous took a cigarette from the pack on the nightstand. Disturbed by this bright spotlight of a pronoun, he turned to her and countered with, "No, Gracie—*you.*"

Thus, put in their places, they stared at the ceiling. Marvelous smoked and let the airy drone of the fan in the window lull him while Gracie Sloane—of all people!—stirred as though grappling with a series of important thoughts, each one complicated by its successor. What brilliant idea could she be gestating? Whatever it was, it might distract him from the violent one now jigging around his own head: that he had really slipped in his sobriety (again), and under the usual circumstances (lust). This had been the third time. Words came to mind about that:

punch line, pattern, running gag. Maybe, though, this time was also a charm—maybe, having made the mistake enough times for it to seem like something other than an accident, he could finally fucking learn something. Like the other two times, he had called his sponsor not long after, verbally flagellating himself, in response to which Mitch had—and this had startled him—laughed, then said, "Looking for an audience? Don't beat yourself up for my sake." He went to a meeting that very evening. Gracie, for her part, had listened to him struggle to explain, watched with moving patience as he bent himself out of shape trying to put words to it. She thanked him for his honesty. Later, after taking some time alone to think, she met up with him again. "Life is slippery," she said. "Even the most graceful dancers fall from time to time." She added that, while flaws made life more interesting, she could not become seriously involved with someone committed to self-destruction. To this end, she trusted that he would take a good look at what their nascent connection meant to him and make a decision for himself. A slip was a slip, but *she* would not be cast in a fixed and limiting role by him. She wanted to see how things would unfold between them, she said, but was not afraid to walk away if she felt herself beginning to abide by or enable his ruin. Marvelous's respect for her had deepened at this.

He turned to her now, stroked her shoulder. "What are you thinking about?"

"My speech, of course," said Gracie, her hand flying to his. "It's stressing me out a little. Though this is helping." She drew his hand to her lips and kissed it, keeping it there.

"Well, we could always just run away." Though he said it as a joke, it was the kind meant to unfold into full-blown fantasy, advertising its riches as an open flower attracts a honeybee. "We could get in my truck and drive down the coast to California, then on down the Baja Peninsula. We could spend September in a little fishing village—eating seafood, going to the beach, making love, lying in hammocks."

"Mmm," said Gracie. He could see she was weighing whether or not to say something about pulling a geographic. She was, of course, fully conversant in the language of recovery and relapse. "Then when we got tired of that, we could carry on to Machu Picchu, then Brazil, then Argentina. We could settle down in Buenos Aires for a while. I've always wanted to go to Buenos Aires. The architecture, the food."

"*Buenos Aires*," said Marvelous, giving his pronunciation proper inflection. Happiness seized him at the thought, as though the two of them had in fact just reviewed actual vacation plans. "*Buenos Aires!* We could learn to tango."

Gracie laughed. The sound of it both pleased and disquieted him. It saddened him in part to provoke joy in someone from whom he was keeping so many secrets. It confused him, too, for how much disclosure did a good life together require? Possibly very little, but then disclosure served an important purpose—a kind of insurance against future damages, around-the-corner revelations that might barrel unforeseen into them with all the blunt force of a car wreck. They were not big, dramatic secrets, but the banal, embarrassing kind that make up a life. He was simply suffering from that gnawing need that came over him in times of crisis: the need to be known. This, of course, accompanied always by the suspicion that one could never feel known in a satisfactory way.

"What are *you* thinking about," Gracie teased. A serious, weighted look must have come into his eyes. Ridiculous that what had begun as a joke, a flight of fancy down through Mexico to Buenos Aires, had him thinking about the future. That particular realm of thought never had been his strong point, and now more than ever was the present so full of rapture as to make any straying from it seem like an insult, corruption. The circumstances demanded intimacy, however, and an intimacy in which past, present, and future all came together to complete one another. To this end, he blurted, without so much as a plan for what came after the blurting, those six time-honored words, "I have to tell you something."

"Okay," said Gracie, wriggling up against the pillows. She propped herself against the wall, folded her arms across her chest, and then promptly unfolded them. She looked unsure whether to defend herself from or embrace what came next.

Marvelous propped his naked self up, too. Would now be a good time for another cigarette? Yes, though in procuring one he delayed continuation of their chat in such a way as to give the moment more suspense.

"Another?" said Gracie. "Whatever you're going to say, for the record, you smoke too much."

"I know, I know. So—" Marvelous took a deep breath. "I don't know why I've been keeping this from you, but . . . I knew who you were before I met you." No sooner had the words left his mouth than relief welled up in him. Why had he kept this a secret so long, when saying it was as easy as stringing together words? He wanted to laugh! Gracie, however, did not laugh. Her eyebrows lifted, and she folded her arms over her chest again.

A secret is more than its size, she would later write. *What may feel to one person like a massive, tortured revelation can, to the person who receives it, seem like a mere molehill made mountain. One woman's offhand confession is another woman's knife to the heart. Yes, timing comes into it, and mood, and history, and the general State of the Union between intimates. More than that, though, secrets speak the drama of the self. They show us how we imagine our bodies, our lives, our worth. The curtain opens on an inner stage. In some cases, the substance of the secret itself may end up meaning less than the fact of its concealment.*

"I'm not sure how I feel about that," she said. "Say more."

Relief came up against a wave of shame and panic. This should not be a disaster. Was it a disaster? "Well, you see, I found *The Seven Directions* during a hard time in my life. This was several years ago. It helped me a lot. It changed the way I think. So, later, when you put out *The Golden Road*, I read that one, too. I did all the exercises." He stopped for a moment, frightened by the words coming out of his mouth. They struck him as vulnerable and weak. Desperate, even. Yes, she would probably hate him for his enthusiasm. "Anyway, when you showed up at Willowbrook—"

"You pretended none of that had ever happened," Gracie interrupted. She kept her gaze on him; Marvelous plainly perceived the unhappiness there, though its nuances eluded him.

"I don't know why," he said. His own voice sounded defeated to him.

Gracie had gotten out of the bed. "That's what I'd like to know, too," she said. She went to fill a glass with water and ice, then came back, sipping from it. "Of course, I'm flattered, in a way. I'm glad my work was helpful to you. But I can't help but feel there's something else going on here. And I'm not sure I like it."

"I can understand that," said Marvelous. "I'm sorry. I kept the truth from you. That was wrong."

Gracie looked thoughtful. Her eyes no longer bore into

him. This left him even less certain about what would happen next, though being left alone (again) came to mind. "I don't know. Maybe it's easier for you to say you were wrong. More convenient."

Marvelous kept his mouth shut. Something in Gracie had softened, but not in a way that he felt translated to his being forgiven or embraced. He had a sudden, violent desire to start yelling, to argue with her, to take control somehow. He wished he had never said anything. He noticed himself starting to sulk, to fume. He took a deep breath.

"I can see you're getting angry," said Gracie. Mostly dressed now, she picked up a chair and carried it to the corner of the room opposite him. It surprised Marvelous, her still being in the room, her not having stormed out. "I don't think that's really about me. Do you?"

Ah ha, thought Marvelous: a test. He considered how to proceed. On the one hand, a window had opened through which he could, if he chose, start to shout. "Of course it is," he could say. "You think you're better than me." On the other, he could keep the spotlight on himself here, and start to grovel, to lash himself, to beg forgiveness. Though seething now, he was grateful in that moment to recall a useful truth: he need not trust himself. He brought the palms of his hands down on his naked thighs. "I think I need to take a walk," he said, "before I try and answer that question."

Gracie stuck out her lip and started to nod. She looked impressed, though her face betrayed some guru-ish condescension as well. "I love that idea," she said. "In fact, I think I'll take one, too. Shall we meet back here in an hour or so?"

Marvelous pulled on his boxer briefs. He needed new boxer briefs. "That should do," he said.

"Great. Then we can both try and tell each other what we're going through."

Though he wanted nothing more than to flee *that instant*, Marvelous stood and waited for her to gather her things. He stared out the window. They would walk out that door together, damn it.

Then she was standing next to him, smiling. "The work starts now," she said.

Marvelous answered with a low, loud grunt. He walked ahead and held the door open for her.

———

The day that some of them had been waiting for, and that others had been dreading, came. A bright day on the sharp edge of August, as only seemed appropriate given the promise of spiritual illumination organized, concentrated, and delivered. Gracie had gone ahead on her own, expressing a need to "husband as much focus and intensity as humanly possible," a task that manifestly required several hours of solitude. Who could husband intensity in the company of others? Carol, Christopher, and Michelle sat together, then, in the so-called galley of the good ship *Kitsap*.

"Why they call it a galley I'll never know," said Carol. She leered around her at the other passengers, many of whom were crossing the sound with children in tow and felt the need to snack. "It's more or less a snack-ateria. Though I guess that lacks a certain maritime ring."

"As do I," said Christopher, extending his hand toward Michelle. He waggled his ring finger. "Do you think a certain someone might be able to remedy that?"

"A full cure in your case might be asking a lot," said Michelle. "But if anything can help you at this point, it's the law."

"I just adore the law," said Christopher. "*Law-law-law-law-law*—it's one of those words, where if you say it too many times in a row, it starts to sound utterly meaningless. Like music."

Carol excused herself, for she felt compelled to take the stairs to the deck, and there to stroll a lap or two in the sun, and to take in the sea air. This passage between island and city never ceased to amaze her. Leaning on the green rail at the end of the boat, watching the low mass of the island curve out of view as they sliced through glittering water, she mused that daily commuters must eventually take even a marvelous scene such as this one for granted.

Of course, this put her back in mind of travel. She had found her copy of *Wonderlust*, and finished it, and now felt in a way both vague and furious that to take the world for granted was a grave mistake, and to see it—to touch it, to taste it, to smell it—an almost spiritual imperative. It had been too long since she had laid eyes on a foreign land, and that had been just another pedestrian visit to Europe. Could she summon the courage to go to Bucharest, to Guadalajara? Moved to act, she had taken Gracie's advice and written out a statement of her intentions and a request for divine guidance. Even though she didn't quite believe in God, she did believe in answers. Divine ones, preferably. Better still than answers were signs—gentle suggestions that one adjust their rudder this way or that. Accidents that weren't. And so she waited for one of these, sure that if one was ever to come it would be on a day like today.

Below deck, Michelle had temporarily ensconced herself in a bathroom stall in the ladies' room, and there sat staring at the screen of her phone. As a general rule, she avoided pulling the thing out at the table, which was rude, but took what opportunities she could to steal away from time to time and give it some attention.

She had not heard from Bradford for a week. Whatever he was going through might very well be necessary for his growth and for his recovery, but did that really require him to cut off all contact with his loved ones? Must recovery always call for this cultlike whisking away from the people who bore witness to one's folly? Her knee knocked against the cream-colored wall of the stall as the boat gave a slight tip. Oh, shame was at the heart of it. Men and women hid themselves away, licking their wounds and polishing their armor, hoping to return to the battles they were fighting with a renewed sense of holy mission. Why was he so afraid of looking ridiculous? Her thumbs swept the keypad.

> Hey B, haven't heard from you in a while—everything OK? Know you're going through some stuff but just know I miss you and, if it's possible, I want to see you. Also, I'm on the ferry with the you-know-whodicombes headed for New Age expo. Thinking of you. If you need any magic crystals let me know. xoxo M

This message seemed to strike a tone of sincere good humor without revealing any of the anxiety or rage she felt about his unexplained absence, and so she sent it. " . . . the you-know-whodicombes" was a nice touch—a light, amusing united front, a shared worldview when it came to that delightful and disorienting bunch. Then again, this turn of events had left her wondering if maybe his feeling toward them had been more bitter than she'd perceived; though fairly confused at present, she knew her frustration with them—and her impressions, her spontaneous parodies—still sprang from a place of love. Perhaps when he was good and well, she would give him a piece of her mind about all that. For now, her mind was in too many pieces, period, and she was doing what she could to reserve the largest one for Jens.

> Will meet you at Artists and Lawyers: The Homosexual
> Future panel. Can't believe we are going to this thing but
> whatever. Long live America. Hope you look pretty today.

Considerably cheered, she got up and left the bathroom just in time to pass a stall inhabited by what sounded to be a young woman making herself vomit. Seasickness might serve as a solid excuse in such circumstances; in spite of herself, she thought of that day at the beginning of the summer when she held back Bradford's tie as he, too, retched, though certainly for different reasons. Just then her phone chimed: a message from Jens, who was always prompt in these matters.

> Pretty pretty pretty pretty pretty pretty pretty pretty

Jet lag, she supposed.

———

As the heat of the day mounted, Frank began to regret not giving the astragalus a whirl. Gracie Sloane might be a fool, but she probably knew a thing or two about medicinal roots and berries—more than he could admit to knowing. Perhaps if he had swallowed his pride that day and brewed a tincture of the gnarled-, wizened-sounding thing, he could have saved himself from this ignominious defeat. Now he sat on the circular green sofa in the *salon*, staring into space as he first wrapped himself in and then cast aside, according to fluctuations in his unruly temperature, a brown blanket from Peru that his wife had picked up in a shop. He had come downstairs for a reason, but between illness and what must surely be the initial *and* final descent into dementia suggested by the misfiring motor of his brain, he would be damned if he could remember what it was. Soon the problem of memory would become moot, he thought, for death's scimitar was already in him, and would sink deeper in with each fleeting year, drawing him closer to annihilation.

I should have some more of the orange stuff, he thought. The orange stuff is amazing.

He rose from the vortex-sofa with the blanket around his shoulders like a cape, not sure whether chills or malarial fever ruled the moment, and shuffled toward the kitchen. It seemed such a forbidding, far journey, to shuffle the several yards to the counter upon which the sexy bottle of generic cold-and-cough syrup, day-glow orange, stood. And it *was* sexy—its upper half sloped at an attractive angle, like the most severe of nude shoulders. There was such sexiness in severity. "Severity is sexy," he muttered, trying to make a mental note to address this subject in another chapter of *The Widdicombe Way* when he got better. "Sexerity . . . sevexity . . ." He coughed a hacking, swampy cough. By the time he had made it to the counter and managed to outsmart the childproof cap on the good and sexy orange stuff, the shelves and see-through cupboards in the kitchen, filled as they were with bottles, drinking glasses, and other shining shapes, had united in a campaign of devastating beauty meant to coax him further toward madness. Champagne flutes caught the light, which in turn effervesced as surely as if it had been the very celebratory liquid with which the vessels were meant to be filled. Countless gleams issued from any and every reflective surface—water glasses, sink necks and basins, stainless steel refrigerator panels, shiny bowls, some sublime shapes that surpassed identification due to this very special effect. It seemed reasonable to think of light as a living creature, a slow-moving and pretty thing that had started to slither into the house, and whose predatory habits were disconcertingly unknown to Frank.

The orange syrup tasted bad. Truffle oil it was not. Then again, astragalus probably tasted twice as bad without being half as much fun. He had come to believe that people had been put on this planet to have twice as much fun as possible. He washed down the bitter, clinging taste with water, then wandered out onto the deck, where he settled into a long chair.

Even as his mind lurched and reeled, poisoned by illness, the secrecy and solitude of the already-ruined day before him brought a smile to his face. Alone at last! Alone with the variegated girdle of greenery separating their land from the sea; alone with the organic vegetable garden, its formidable tomato vines weighed down still with ripening red globes—there had been nothing but dirt there before! It was, in a word, marvelous. *Marvelous!* He chuckled to himself. The whole panorama at hand, from the grass to the gull-crossed water, writhed for his amusement. In his chair he felt as though he had stumbled into the first and only showing of a film, one that only he had had the foresight to attend, and that he would never be able—never *have* to—describe. Could you have seen it, he thought, closing his eyes. Ah, but then: you didn't.

Frank dozed for an indeterminate amount of time (minutes, at that point, capable of expanding to an almost gleefully dangerous degree, like puddles over which a person could step growing into lakes—lakes in which they could swim, or even drown). The medicine, laced as it was with whatever speedy ingredient made it possible for sick people to continue working, prevented him from actually falling asleep but kept him in a state both restful and delirious. In this blessedly defeated, lucid condition—for he had decided that defeat of this kind was not so bad after all; even if he did feel glazed with warm, damp disease, duck à l'orange, sore all over as though he had been tenderized with a mallet, there was a kind of luxury to it; plus, he got to have the orange stuff—he slowly became aware of peculiar sounds beneath him: scratching, shuffling. By the time he managed to care enough to open his eyes, it was because the source of this disturbance had shifted, swishing away from him and into the grass.

"A magic moment exists," he would later write, drafting a chapter in *The Widdicombe Way* titled "Here's Truth in Your Eyes," "when the mind, for whatever dumb reason minds have, falls behind the eye, and for one brief, terrifying, thrilling moment, you gaze upon whatever surprising thing it is you happen to be gazing upon right then with sheer, unchaperoned sight. You have no fucking idea what you're looking at. You stand there staring at it like a child who, blind to danger, sees in the horse galloping straight for it not the threat of a fatal kick to the skull, but a magnificent mystery. The mind, suddenly panic-stricken, sweeps in then, yanks the child from the path of disaster, lifts it into the arms of safety, which are also the arms of terror. In that cut-short moment, magic, and the death of magic."

The germ for that gem, so to speak, began when Frank opened his eyes. Looking out on the lawn, he saw five grey-brown shapes, three of them much smaller than the other two, all of them covered in bristled fur, crawling over the grass and away from the deck. He started up in his chair. The creatures must have sensed this disturbance, for they quickened their pace, and one turned its head in the slightest of backward glances, revealing long whiskers and the black bead of an eye.

Otters: they were otters! Just as Frank's mind burst through the door, frantic as the condemned men in films who tear apart their apartments looking for some important, exonerating, maliciously purloined document ("Where is it? What have you done with it? I know you have it!"), they slipped into the brush and out of sight, presumably toward the Puget Sound.

The thought crossed his mind that he might be hallucinating. He had exceeded the recommended dose of orange stuff, as the nausea brought about by standing up made all too clear. He was going to have to force himself to eat something; where all summer long he had devoured various culinary delights without a thought for the miracle of appetite, now that miracle had gone missing in action. It had disappeared at the first sign of whatever bug was wreaking havoc on his system. For a couple of minutes Frank just stood there staring across the lawn in the direction of the vanished otters. Would they come back to their nest beneath the deck? Or had it been nothing more than a summer home to them? The rascals!

Inside, who knows how many minutes later (Twenty? Two hundred thousand?), Frank sat at the dining room table with a bowl of reheated Vietnamese pho that his son, of all people, had picked up for him yesterday. He had heard about a Vietnamese restaurant on the island and had wondered if it would be any good. The broth, though, soothed him, warm and rich, spiked with a hot chili pepper and garlic sauce that may or may not have been advisable in his current state—who cared? Succulent hunks of chicken proved more challenging, if only because with this particular illness his taste buds seemed not to recognize chicken as a scrumptious foodstuff and responded to his eating of it with curious indifference. When he ate the chicken, it was as though nothing happened at all—an effortful but flavorless extravagance, an action devoid of meaning or purpose.

In the middle of all this hallucinatory soup eating, the phone rang. They all had cell phones, but they had a landline, too, and they used it plenty—Frank especially, who found the prospect of getting a brain tumor from cell phone radiation horrifying. After three rings (he had no intention of answering; if it was Carol he might grab the phone once she started to leave a message, but why waste the energy now?), the answering machine picked up:

"Hi," said Carol's voice, far-off and canned, "you've reached the Widdicombes at Willowbrook—" she never could resist alliteration, and he thought, again, that they should change their outgoing greeting to something less *whimsical*; it was not the place for whimsy—"please leave a message and we'll get back to you as soon as we can. Thanks!"

Beeeeeeeeeeeeeeeeep.

"Oh, hello," said a man's voice, a voice Frank would later describe as "fancy-sounding, but annoying—someone used to getting what they want, when they want it," "I'm calling for Frank Widdicombe. This is Nick Jacobs at Jacobs and Holstein Literary. Channing said I should call rather than email. Anyway, you may know he sent me some of *The Widdicombe Way*. I read it with great pleasure. Would love to speak with you about it. If you'd call me back, my number is two-one-two . . ."

Frank let the rest of the numbers melt together. He lifted his bowl of soup with both hands and brought it to his lips, slurping the broth with such gusto that he could barely hear Nick Jacobs say, "Thanks, and I hope to hear from you soon," over his own noisy delight. The answering machine clicked off with another beep.

———

It may comfort some of you to hear that just as old Frank Widdicombe was tripping on generic cold medicine, Bradford, mere miles away on Capitol Hill, was walking out of a matinee. He was, on the other hand, not walking out at the end of the movie, but the middle.

What would do him the most good at that moment, he felt, was movement. A long walk in the summer air might quell that restless anger and disbelief he had found flaring up in him as he sat in the back row of the dark theater. The sun stung his eyes when he stormed out onto the street. If nothing else, he might exhaust himself. Exhaustion would have been preferable to the riot of feelings he was going through right then—rage, primarily, but rage climbing over the squirming, shouting body of self-loathing, rage being elbowed aside by the not inconsiderable presence of injustice, *all* of whom stepped aside from time to time to make way for the foreboding, silent, authoritative arrival of doom. Yes, the sensation of physical doom had overcome him; he had felt himself growing larger and larger, as though the room would not be able to hold him much longer, as though the sheer vital energy of revolt coursing through his veins would mix with stillness and the struggle for self-control in some chemically reckless way and cause an explosion. All this in the middle of *Green Vapor*, a horror film, set in a small, rural town in the Pacific Northwest, about a nebulous mist of sorts, a malign spirit that haunted the pines and Douglas firs, emerging as a result of excessive logging and then briskly getting down to the business of possessing one resident's psyche after another. The mist seeped into them, it took control of their minds, it drove them to commit acts of unspeakable depravity and violence. Or perhaps, he thought, *speakable* depravity. The shamelessly moral environmentalist twist had insulted him. The resemblance to his own work-in-progress in all other ways went beyond insult.

Walking helped, as far as anything could. Hands shaking, he lit a cigarette. On the path through Volunteer Park he passed a couple of lesbians playing in the grass with a brown baby that he assumed they had adopted. Though keeping a respectful distance so as to spare the child his second-hand smoke, he could still catch a whiff of parental smugness from the women. Infuriating. In truth, he was in such a bleak state of mind that the thought of any combination of people choosing to have children repulsed him. He would have liked to walk up to those lesbians and say, "You know, I hate to tell you this, but someone had this idea before you did. In fact, I just met another lesbian couple that look just like you, with a child just like your own. And theirs could already speak in complete sentences."

Idiots. Neither he nor his sister intended to reproduce, although he had to admit that his sister could turn on him in this respect at any time, and he took some morbid comfort, mixed with a sense of doom, in the consideration that together they represented the extermination of their genetic line. It was as though his parents had, drunk on good intentions, lit a tall, proud candle of hope by bringing him into the world, and that he had then come along with his jauntiest step, licked his thumb and forefinger, and snuffed out the flame. The thought of this gave him a wonderful feeling of control. He may have been doomed, as they all were—as he *especially* was, given that his pet project was now *destroyed*—but if that were the case then he would play out his doom on his own terms.

"Play out his doom." The words made him laugh. When had everything become so fucking serious? A sense of play was just what he needed, har-har, even if play meant hopscotch in the shadow of a beast about to devour him. He shook out his hands, troubled by a familiar tingling feeling in his extremities. Panic was upon him at last; after having stalked him for the whole of the day, it pounced, unable to resist the suddenly overpowering scent of failure. Bradford rushed in the direction of a tree in the middle of the park, secure at least that there he might fall to pieces without eliciting the sympathy of any passersby. And, having reached it, he did just that: he curled up on the ground and he wept, shielding his face from the world as panic broke like a fever, allowing unbearable horror to stay true to its name by flooding painfully out of him.

Nobody *owned* horror, he thought. Somebody had just gotten to it before he did.

After a few moments, the worst of this particular fit had passed. He knew that reinforcements would be called in soon. He rested the back of his head against the tree, sweating from both the adrenaline and the warming day. "Very soon the planet will become so warm that all of us will die," he thought, but the weight of this possibility could not reach him in his exhaustion. "I'm just going to have to let this go," he thought then, and wiped his leaking nose on the back of his hand. "There are more ideas where that came from. There are always more ideas. God, I can't fucking believe this. I have nothing left. No. Count your blessings: I've got a job, I've got a place to stay, a car." Never mind that the place to stay was in his father's guest bedroom. Never mind, too, that these blessings

easily turned from comfort to aggravating interdependence as
he imagined the authorities that brokered them: father, boss,
traffic cop. He had given himself so many people to answer to;
as life carried on, one only went on meeting more people to answer to. And then there was Michelle—God, he should return
her text message, let her know he was alive at least, if that's what
he was. In a fit of doing-it-now, he pulled his phone from his
pocket and thumbed the keypad, looking for her name, finding
it, writing her:

I'm OK. I'm sorry. I'll call you after work.

That would intrigue her, at least. Work! Work! Work! Call
you after work. Very impressive. Except not, and except he
probably wouldn't. He already felt the germ of some heartless
rebellion working its way into him, slipping all too easily past
his panic-bombed ramparts. He felt such contempt for Michelle for wanting him, such loathing for himself for wanting
to turn to her now, in his hour of offended pride. What low
standards they all had! Understanding, infatuation, support—
all of these made him feel ashamed. They were nothing more
than sophisticated forms of procrastination. Other people, with
their wretched intimacy, stood in the way of his getting back
on track. He could have finished *his* script long ago were it not
for other people. Furthermore, where once he had thought it
essential to return "home" to get inspired, it occurred to him
now that maybe what he really needed was to be as far from
that vampiric abstraction as possible. The impish notion came
to him, as it often had before, that nothing could be easier, once
it had been done, than simply turning one's back on everything
and walking away.

This imp stuck by him through the entire work day that followed, leaping from his shoulder onto the bowed swan's neck of the faucet as he loaded sauce-smeared plates into the dishwasher, dropping down into the pocket of his stained apron when he wiped the filth from his hands on the stiff white fabric. It even accompanied him into the alley outside when, toward the end of his shift, he had to drag out the heavy, web-like red mats that he stood on all day and hose them down. Mischievous companion to the fast-growing threat of his rage, the imp prodded him now and then with its little pitchfork of encouragement, putting on an especially impressive show when the café manager, a goateed Australian who just last week had told him in an aside that he must travel to Sydney one day to experience Mardi Gras, said that there would be a surprise birthday celebration after the restaurant closed that day. Could he stay for an extra twenty minutes or so after his shift? One of those questions that did a shitty job of hiding its own preferred answer. Yes, he could stay, and so could his imp. Together they would draw strength from this mysterious twenty minutes, seep into it like a mist, control it psychologically, and drive it to commit acts of unspeakable depravity.

Bradford, the three waitresses, the busboy, and the two chefs gathered in the front of the restaurant. Bradford was still in a muddle about their names, though the hottest of the waitresses, the brunette who seemed to have a desperate and suggestive desire for escape in her eyes—another one who longed guiltily for a liberator, a destroyer—her name was Cassie. It was her birthday.

"How's it going?" Cassie said to him, turning from her chatter with one of the other waitresses. "This must be what, week three? You're practically official now."

"Totally," he said. He was about to flourish some other pleasantry for her benefit, in the manner of an amateur magician producing plastic flowers out of thin air, when all heads turned to a flickering light that floated into view across the room. A cake, lit up with several tall, skinny candles, carried by the Australian manager who felt it imperative that Bradford visit Sydney for Mardi Gras one day. This man's goatee was now contorting itself into various effortful shapes as he sang the first lines of "Happy Birthday."

The staff joined in, smiling as though at last relieved of a terrible secret. He contributed his own voice to the celebratory droning. Cassie was saying, "Oh my God, you guys!" She was covering her mouth with her hands, emphasizing her surprise. It was oddly thrilling, Bradford felt, to sing her name out, like casting a spell.

"Happy birthday, dear Cassie . . . Happy birthday to you."

She blew out the candles; thin trails of black smoke snaked up from the wicks as her successful effort met with applause. Bradford was growing giddy. Somehow it felt like a relief to have everyone's attention on Cassie, who was thanking everybody and telling them how embarrassed she was. He watched her with a grin.

"We got you pretty good," said the Australian to Cassie, clapping her on the back. "Bet you thought nobody knew it was your birthday."

"I hate my birthday," she said, bursting into a mix of laughter and tears. The others jumped in with compensatory merriment; Cassie seemed to recover herself, and added, smiling bravely, "But this is so wonderful. You're amazing."

Bradford found this display of instability more alluring than he felt he should. An *invitation*: that was the word that described what he read in her bearing. Part of him wanted to stop this, to remove himself from the situation before he did something regrettable, but the temptation teased at him, and his spirits continued to rise. Just as wisps of ragged cloud burn off before the intensifying glare of the sun, leaving clear skies, his depression soon retreated before the full force of his charm coming out.

"Have some cake," said the Australian, handing him a plate.

"Don't mind if I do," said Bradford, and from that point forward a feeling of mounting control took over. Though he had sulked through his shift, silently fantasizing about the deaths of his colleagues, about scoring some OxyContin and maybe pawning one of the Lichtenstein paintings that sat bubble wrapped in his father's condo so that he could annihilate the memory of *Green Vapor*, he now moved from one coworker to the next with chatty finesse. How were the tips today? Where did you learn to cook? What *is* Sydney like during Mardi Gras? Happy Birthday—any special plans? He felt like an unstoppable cat. Had there been a baby sleeping in the other room, he could have easily slipped in, jumped into the crib, and sucked the living breath right out of its mouth, as cats are said to do. Instead, his *coup de grâce* in this impetuous embrace of misplaced festivity was to corner Cassie with every intent of conquest.

"Ugh," he said, rubbing his stomach and making a pained face, "that cake made me feel *so* fat."

"Stop it," Cassie said playfully. "I'll bet you've never put a pound on in your life."

Bradford winked. "Born this way, baby." That felt a bit too far on the mania scale, and so he attempted a quick recovery, covering his face with his hands. "God," he said, "I can be so cheesy sometimes. I'm the worst. *The worst!*"

"Stop it," said Cassie. "You're not the worst. I'm the worst. I just cry-laughed at my own surprise work birthday."

"Actually, I was very impressed by that."

"Oh, shut up," said Cassie. She wrinkled her nose in a way that he felt obscurely promised success. It took an eye as sharp as his, and a mind as intricate, to see such things. He felt himself making dozens, perhaps *hundreds* of wordless microdecisions and calculations even as he gestured and spoke. Instinct could be a fine thing. He did see with some clarity that a little fear had entered the mix between them; that could prove useful.

"No, I really was, Cassie," he said. "You see, I hate my birthday, too. There's too much pressure to celebrate and be happy. It's a wicked trap. Like when it's a beautiful day out but all you want to do is stay inside and binge watch crime shows. May I ask you what bothers you about yours?"

Cassie tucked a strand of brown hair behind her ear. She laughed again, as though it had all been a big misunderstanding. "I don't know. I guess I just don't like being the center of attention."

Ah! He had heard that one before. He cast his eyes down, feigning shyness. "I know exactly how you feel."

———

With just a few hours left before her keynote address, Gracie sat alone in a dark conference room. An abyss yawned open beneath her. She had turned the lights off after the hint of a migraine announced itself behind her eyes—a menacing pain that was somehow both sharp and dull, like an old kitchen knife worn down from years of use. The windows facing the hall, half covered by cheap Venetian blinds, let blocks of light break up the room's blue darkness and reach across the long conference table. An awkward black plastic circle with holes for cords dominated the center of the table, being, she guessed, the place where one of those special conference call doohickeys would usually go. On the wall opposite her, a large framed print of some geometrically inclined Native American art: a killer whale in sharp, curved red and black shapes.

She was afraid. She swiveled in her chair.

It made no difference that she had addressed the public many times before. Fear walked where it would, and there was no use pretending it away. The best course of action, as she had related to her readers in *The Golden Road*, was to "name fear, acknowledge fear, look fear in the eyes and say, 'Hello, fear. I see you there.'" This she had borrowed from a short instructional guide on Buddhist meditation and adapted for her own purposes. In times like these, however, it could be difficult to recall what she had ever felt her own purposes to be. Because she considered herself a card-carrying member of the "do something, anything" school, she took pen to yellow legal pad, pleased that in the darkness she could only just barely make out her own writing, and submitted to one of her own list-making exercises.

Acknowledging Fear

1. *I'm afraid that my speech will bomb.*
2. *I'm afraid that I didn't prepare enough.*
3. *I'm afraid that it will be a lot of work to be with M. I'm afraid he'll hurt me.*
4. *I'm afraid that everyone will think I'm a fraud.*
5. *I'm afraid of what comes after my speech.*
6. *I'm afraid that I'll embarrass myself in front of my friends and intimates.*
7. *I'm afraid to let go.*

8. *I'm afraid that if I do let go, I'll say something offensive or inappropriate.*

9. *I'm afraid of God's plan for me.*

10. *I'm afraid that God doesn't have a plan for me.*

Right away she returned to the third item on her list. It nagged at her. She and Marvelous were walking in the mystery now, that was for sure. After calming down a bit and collecting his thoughts the other day, he had confessed to being intimidated by her, and said that this fear had mingled with his attraction, creating—what else?—confusion. In his confusion, he had been unsure how to proceed, and had kept putting off telling her the truth until it had felt too late. "I take full responsibility for my own confusion," he had said, wiping forehead sweat away with his arm. (Actually, he had said "my own conclusion" first—a slip of the tongue—which left them both laughing.) He had owned, too, that there might have been some subconscious motive at work, a cloaked desire to gain power over her by keeping his knowledge of her to himself. "Can I change this instinct in myself?" he said. "I'm not sure. I do believe that I can learn to recognize it, and to work with that energy in a more productive, less secretive way."

That had impressed her. It frightened her, too. She hadn't been sure how to proceed, but felt that, whatever else might be happening, the two of them were learning new things about themselves in each other's presence. They ended up having a lively and stimulating conversation about the mysteries of human desire: the at times alarming mixture of fear, lust, affection, distrust, kindness, vulnerability, regression, violent urges, absurdity, excitement, and so on and so on that comprised the whole endeavor of two people coming together. Marvelous, she had to admit, was a good listener. (All that sharing and witnessing in AA must have helped.) He had listened when she told him how *she* felt: angry, deceived, unsure of his intentions. "Between the sobriety slip-up and this," she said, "it doesn't paint the most trustworthy picture." She did give him credit for making himself vulnerable and stepping that much further into uncertainty.

"So where does this leave us?" Marvelous had asked.

A good question. She could not discount the magnetic pull between them, the natural affection. "Let's leave that question open," she said. They would see how things unfolded; they would proceed with caution and see what happened. "We're both adults here."

These words echoed in her head as she sat there in the dark conference room, biting the end of her pen. She needed to put Marvelous out of her mind now; she had other work to do. The very act of acting—of writing that list—provided a little relief from her preperformance jitters. She exhaled and set her pen down on the yellow pad, letting it roll at an odd angle. Then the last two named fears stared back at her from the page—*I'm afraid of God's plan for me; I'm afraid that God doesn't have a plan for me*—as though together they formed two eyes capable of a soul-searing gaze. Her brain felt wonky, not quite capable of switching into an analytical mode, and she found herself confronted with a physical sensation of un-knowing. A chasm within her widened and widened, creating a vast emptiness.

She must be of service, she knew that much. And *of course*, God, or what she called for convenience's sake God, had a plan for her—her faith in a nondenominational, order-making higher power was too strong to break beneath the glare of her fear. It was almost Christian. The real trouble, and the real fear, lay in the possibility that God-or-whatever's plan for her led to a life quite unlike the one she pictured for herself, the one she actively manifested through collage, visualization exercises, and long walks steeped in positive reinforcement. There were times when she wanted to be a rock unmoving, and the Artist Formerly Known as God (a little zinger she had come up with in a freewrite one morning years ago; she laughed under her breath to think of it now) called upon her to be responsive and flexible. In this she occasionally wondered if she would lose herself in flexibility—how could she know exactly when to stand firm, exactly when to bend? It was all so confusing. Thinking about it didn't help at all, but surrender had its own challenges.

Her cell phone came out then, and the light from its little square display beamed up at her. She had done what she could to embrace the flood of new technology that had defined the last couple of decades, integrating a few electronic bells and whistles into her way of life. To this end her phone was filled with calming meditational songs; she could pull her device out anywhere, and thereby make of her surroundings a kind of holy shrine, a spontaneous cloister. And though with *The Habit of Wildness* she aimed to provide alternatives to the present over-reliance on quick technological solutions, at present she succumbed to the temptation to call up a Gregorian chant track. As the phone groaned with monastic voices, vibrating when the levels dropped too low, she moved from her seat to the head of the conference table; she pushed the chair out of the way and dropped to her knees, hands folded in prayer. Fear may be a fact of life, she reasoned, but one could still ask for help, for divine intervention. This, in her own way, she did, reciting a made-up prayer to God or the universe, who or which she thanked for guiding her through the remainder of what she could see might be another all too human day.

———

"While I was in India, my perspective on human suffering underwent a completely radical shift. We think that we know poverty, or that we know pain here in America, but I'm here to tell you that if you think you have it bad, think again. Now I don't mean to dismiss anybody's sense of being wronged, or to trample all over anybody's feeling that their circumstances could be improved—we're all gathered here today at a conference devoted, in part, to the ongoing journey of self-improvement that has brought us together in spiritual synchronicity. But what I would like to say to you is that we must be grateful for the very opportunity to improve ourselves. Spiritual growth and growth of the self are imperatives, but they are also luxuries. Do all of us here have food in our bellies? Yes. Do all of us have a roof over our heads? I would venture to say *yes*. And yet we feel a certain dissatisfaction gnawing at our cores—gnaw, gnaw, gnaw. Can you hear it? Can you feel it? I do feel, strongly, that part of our work, our great ongoing work as spiritual beings set on improving ourselves and thus making our contribution to a better, a more enlightened world, is to learn gratitude for what we have. To learn to be aware that, yes, perhaps things could *always* be better, but at the same time, things have never been as good as they are right here, right now. We have the opportunity to become spiritual leaders here, people, and part of that work as I see it is learning how to be content with what we have.

"Now, suffering is not a competition. But if it was, I'll tell you who would be winning: not you or me, no, not with our bellies full of food, rooves over our heads, and every opportunity to align ourselves with an abundant, giving universe. To return to India for a moment, I was in New Delhi this last year. City of millions. Very hot. In India you will have these profound, spiritually uplifting and sublime experiences one minute—the stillness and ceremony of a temple in the hills, the feast for the senses that is the marketplace with all of its colors, sounds, and enticing aromas—and then you will round the corner and encounter something so shocking, a spectacle of suffering so horrific, that it will shake your faith in the benevolence of the universe. That was just what happened to me when, one day, after feasting to my heart's content, after hours of sightseeing, illuminating conversations with my guide, and the glimmer of a kind of spiritual equilibrium, I rounded the corner. And do you know what I saw? A boy without a face."

The speaker, a middle-aged man with short, silver hair, a tan white man dressed in a white button-down and slacks, paused. A guilty paralysis afflicted the crowd. Even though the speech so far had gone some way toward moving Carol, she felt that the next and most obviously important thing for him to do was to describe for the audience just what it meant not to have a face. Instead, after letting them stew in discomfort for a moment, he repeated the words "a boy without a face" in a tone even more solemn than before, as though everyone knew what it meant not to have a face—as though it was somehow their responsibility, too, that things like these should happen in their day and age. Thanks to this, Carol only half absorbed the remainder of the talk, which seemed ultimately—and confusingly—concerned with both embracing the full range of opportunities available to them as Americans by working hard and allowing spiritual growth to happen naturally by challenging the American preoccupation with work. Instead, her imagination turned itself to the task (*did* she have ADD?) of visualizing what it meant, physically, not to have a face. She saw the boy first as deformed at birth, his features collapsed into one another, fused and retreating inward, leaving a kind of contorted tree-trunk whorl where his face should be. Then she pictured herself traveling along the same road in India and being approached by a young beggar with no eyes, eyebrows, nose, cheeks, mouth, or chin, only a featureless sheet of brown skin that absorbed her merciful gaze without returning it.

These images haunted her still as she wandered, dazed, from the panel and into the ladies' room. Her heart had thrilled at the initial mention of India, sensing that here, perhaps, was a sign as to where she was meant to go on her travels. But now so many faceless boys danced in her head, holding hands in a merry ring, and—but surely, they couldn't be merry! How could they be, living in the streets without even faces to their names. Awful, awful. No, she was thinking of the Matisse painting. But then she, Carol Widdicombe, had a face, as did all the other women in the ladies' room, who now stood with her in a row before the sinks and mirrors, washing their hands and checking their appearances. And how many of them could be said to be merry? Of course, one couldn't be merry all the time. If one was, it would cease to be special.

Deep in these thoughts (and the thought that when she got home she ought to get online and do some research into generalized anxiety disorder as well as the many varieties of depression; she was beginning, she felt, to show signs) she took a moment to regard her own face in the mirror before her, and, touching it delicately with her hand as though to make certain it belonged to her, felt a kind of glad shock.

———

Michelle sprinkled nutmeg on her latte. She had to admit that the meeting between Christopher and Jens was turning out differently than she had imagined. The two did not just *like* each other—no, that would not be enough for people like them, who never did anything halfway. They were like wind and fire, like the sun and the sea; it was as though without one another they had been mere isolated forces of nature. Now they formed a landscape together, came alive.

That was how she saw it, anyway. And she could not help but feel a little proud.

"—well, I'm not sure I would say that the concept of maritime law has, what did you call it?"

"A metaphysical aesthetic essence."

"Yes, a metaphysical, aes-thetic, essence. Ah, you're giving my mouth a serious workout."

Michelle rolled her eyes at this, joining them at a small, circular table. She had heard Jens try and trot out similarly clumsy flirtations before, and felt it rarely worked in his favor. Christopher, however, was in such a fervor that he failed to register either the suggestive nature of the comment or the sly grin that accompanied it. "How can you say that? Your entire vocation is devoted to imposing order on the wildest, deepest, most anarchic psychological territory on earth. The universal symbol of mystery, fathomless, chthonic female energy, the untamable subconscious, the unpredictable violence of Nature herself!"

A single, loud laugh burst from Michelle at the words "chthonic female energy." Christopher was rocketing off to dangerously conceptual heights. Jens's English was practically without flaw, but she felt that even a high percentage of native speakers often required a translator, or at least a lot of patience, when faced with Widdicombe the Younger. Her Danish friend was not known for his deep funds of the latter. Nevertheless, Jens carried on admirably, flicking his hand in a dismissive gesture and saying, "You're not wrong, you are just very abstract. My job simply asks that I prosecute on the behalf of men and women who injure themselves while at work aboard seafaring vessels."

Despite their apparent disagreement, both men smiled as they argued, as though stimulated in the utmost by a little sporting conflict. Michelle suffered from the sense that everything the two of them said was spoken in a special code that eluded her. It was not unlike the feeling she sometimes had when all the Widdicombes were in one room, united in antic chatter as though they were playing out scenes from an old screwball comedy. This was different somehow, though. What did it really mean when Christopher said, "untamable subconscious," or when Jens said, with bizarre formality, "seafaring vessels"? She had felt this particular strain of paranoia before when she found herself in conversation, or ancillary to conversation, with two or more gay men. How to shake the feeling that with the right turn of phrase, the right combination of special words, she would be allowed access to a shadow kingdom of subtextual meaning? The swirling shallows of this suspicion disguised a deeper, *20,000 Leagues Under the Sea* kind of terror: that soon, her matchmaking having succeeded, she would be left alone again. This, she thought, was what she got for being so *helpful* all the time. Not once, not *once* did anyone think to return the favor! Everyone thought her so infinitely capable, and though she had built up a sizable fund of goodwill that she supposed she could draw upon, she didn't want to have to be the one to demand it. Was it asking too much to be wanted and doted upon not because she was owed a favor, but because she deserved it inherently? Was it asking too much to be swept away?

Her phone vibrated.

I'm OK. I'm sorry. I'll call you after work.

"Oh my God," she said, "I just got a text from Bradford."

Jens, all-too familiar with the name at this point, wrinkled his brow. "Really now?"

"What does it say?" said Christopher, who had taken to running his fingers through his hair quite frequently over the last hour. Michelle interpreted this gesture as evidence of his carefully cultivated image—did not many geniuses have untamed hair through which they combed their fingers from time to time? "It says, 'I'm okay. I'm sorry. I'll call you after work.' How am I supposed to take that?" She was taking it, she neglected to mention, with a surge of hope, a desperate feeling that some prayer of hers had been answered.

"Work?" said Christopher, astonished. "*Work?*"

"This is all I get after a week of silence?"

Jens folded his arms, by all appearances unsurprised, making it clear by his posture just how he felt she should "take that." "A bit short," he said.

"But he's going to call you," countered Christopher—rushing, in a way that surprised and moved her, to provide comfort and hope, to hold up a kinder mirror. "That's good, right? And he did say he was sorry."

"I guess that's good," said Michelle.

"Your guess is as good as mine," said Jens, managing to be impertinent, idiomatic, and nasty all in one go. Michelle glared at him—a glare between friends, full of admiration and frustration. This was the thanks she got for setting him up.

Christopher turned on Jens. "Don't be such an asshole," he said. Michelle startled; her instinct was, of course, to apologize, say "It's okay," use every tired charm she could muster up to prevent conflict. Instead, she thanked Christopher (with more vehemence, perhaps, than she meant to), who then continued, "Michelle *likes* Bradford. Hello! Even if he can be a real dick sometimes. Okay, a lot of the time. I'm sure you can be as much of a dick as the next guy, too. And you should know that just because you're *beautiful* doesn't mean I'm not going to call you on your shit!"

Oh my God, thought Michelle. Was he defending her or hitting on him? Both, somehow—he *was* a genius!

Jens looked like he might close up, might sulk and seethe as Michelle knew him to do when confronted. He looked like he might be about to say, with grim finality, "I've known Michelle longer than you." Instead he sighed, then said, making a visible effort to be both contrite and lighthearted, "Well, which one is it, then? Am I a dick or an asshole?"

The way he said this made her start laughing. Christopher started laughing after a second, too, and then so did Jens, his haughtiness melting away. "Don't make me answer that," said Christopher. "I don't know you very well, and I'm tired of quips today."

———

In a spacious atrium where vendors had set up booths and tables to hawk their services and wares, light was shining through the irregularly angled panes of glass that made up the building's exterior. Whoever organized Green Dawn had secured weekend residence in a newish building designed by a famous and controversial Dutch architect. Marvelous recalled reading about the commission and ensuing controversy years ago in the *Seattle Times*, *Seattle Weekly*, and *The Stranger*. Though he was not persuaded as to the value of novels and short stories, Marvelous liked immersing himself in nonfiction, mostly by reading a great deal of news both online and off, and on occasion through a blockbuster *Times* bestseller. (A copy of *Helter Skelter* had been sitting on his nightstand for several years, elevating his ashtray. He had only read about half of it but had grown used to its unfinished presence in his life and kept it there with the professed intent of getting around to plowing through it eventually. A bookseller had recommended it to him one day when he popped into Elliott Bay Books while out on one of the "Serendipity Dates" demanded during each week of Gracie's *The Seven Directions of Positive Thinking*. The bookseller, a tall and scruffy man with salt-and-pepper hair who looked to be in his early thirties, had asked him, "What kinds of books do you like to read?" He was probably a writer getting by at his day job. Marvelous felt strange asking at all—especially since the guy had been flirting with another guy, a customer holding a gay-looking hardcover that the bookseller had described as a "pansexual fever dream," and Marvelous hadn't wanted to interrupt—but reminded himself of Ms. Sloane's mandate to follow one's instincts on a Serendipity Date. "I prefer nonfiction," he had said, surprising himself by adding, "I like to read about things that really happened." The bookseller raised his dark, heavy eyebrows; a look of impatience flashed across his face. But he collected himself and began to lead Marvelous around the store. "Are you interested in World War One?" he said, pulling a copy of *The Great War and Modern Memory* from a shelf labeled "Staff Picks." "This is excellent." Marvelous looked it over, and though it sounded fascinating, and he felt like he *should* read it, he didn't quite feel the "spark" that Gracie had described, and he was trying his best to simultaneously cut loose and follow instructions. *You will know the spark when you feel it*, read Gracie's text. *It will feel familiar, a thing remembered. It might bring you back to some simple joy you felt as a child: pretending you were a wizard in the yard, climbing trees, secretly reading under your covers with a flashlight past bedtime. When you find the spark, protect it. Follow it. Keep it alive as if your life depended on it. It does.* "This looks great," said Marvelous, "but I'm not sure it's what I'm in the mood for." The bookseller nodded. "Fair enough," he said, then hummed to himself as he drifted to another section nearby. "Are you interested in art history?" he asked. "I loved this book *The Banquet Years.*" Marvelous told the bookseller that he was, in theory, interested in art history, but that he was not in the mood to read a four-hundred-page book about the origins of the avant-garde in France. "Fair enough," the bookseller said again, though with growing disinterest. "You're going to have to give me a little more to go on." After a moment's contemplation, the spark came to him: he saw himself many years earlier, house- and dog-sitting for a friend with a place in the University District, terrified and rapt reading about Ted Bundy, whose grisly trail of serial murders had passed through that very neighborhood. "Do you have any true crime?" The bookseller's eyes lit up. "Have you read *Helter Skelter*?" he said. Marvelous felt a little guilty when, holding the book in his hands, his pulse quickened with fear and excitement. Should his Serendipity Date have led him to an interest so lurid? *Beware of* should *on your Serendipity Dates*, Gracie had written. Later, when she lay beside him in his bed, he was tempted to tell her he had read the whole thing. Instead, intent on starting to tell the truth, he repeated this whole anecdote to Gracie, and the two had a good laugh. "You should tell the truth more often," she had said then, and kissed him sweetly.)

Now he wandered the aisles of the Green Dawn Marketplace, fascinated by the space he was in—though he liked the feeling of bouncing around between opposing viewpoints, he usually came out on the more progressive side of local issues, including the legalization of marijuana, gay marriage, and futuristic architecture—and curious to see what people were selling. There was no shortage of handmade jewelry, from rough-hewn and twisty bracelets made of metal to gemstones set in necklaces and rings said to have unique energetic properties. The woman working there, lithe, tattooed, bespectacled, recommended a fetching necklace with a cluster of translucent, glossy orange carnelian stones when asked about a gift for someone very creative. "This would be perfect," she said. "They call it the 'Singer's Stone.'" Marvelous wished he could present it to Gracie before her speech but thought it would still be well received after. It wouldn't be the last time she performed. The jewelry maker put it in a simple paper bag for him and stuffed the bag with tissue paper to make the presentation more gift-like.

His thoughts had been drifting from his immediate surroundings all day. Maybe there was something astrological going on—was Mercury in retrograde? Chiron flipping out? He ordered a hibiscus lemongrass iced tea from another booth and took a seat in a green plastic chair. He admired the curving surface of the ceiling, which put him in mind of the firmament, the dome of heaven; he wondered who cleaned all those windows, and, as he often did while moving about a city, began to contemplate the elements of construction, the built environment—steel, glass, electricity, plumbing, etc. While doing so, some work on the Gracie question, he felt, was clearly taking place in the back of his mind. It was like he could faintly hear it, like he was standing outside of a workshop of some kind without knowing exactly what was being made there. Better than an analysis paralysis, he told himself. He had felt like a fool the other day, in the moment; now he felt vaguely proud that the two of them had managed to talk it out, to arrive, at least, at a mutual understanding of the role being hugely flawed might play in a connection such as theirs. "I'm no saint, either," Gracie had said. "So don't try and make me into one. I'm not here to be worshiped. I'm human!" She had persuaded him that they didn't need to *solve* whatever this was right now. "This is not a problem, or a riddle," she said. "This isn't math." He knew he did have this tendency; even now, though he was doing his best to muster patience, it drove him a little crazy, that workshop in the back of his mind where something he didn't understand was taking place. Letting himself feel frustrated, he took a deep breath and then swore aloud. That turned a few heads.

He wondered what love was. He thought he had been in love a few times. It angered him to feel that every time something that might be love came around, it made whatever loves had come before seem like they might not have been love at all. He knew, though, that this kind of thinking—of degree, of primacy—was another desperate attempt to categorize and control. He guessed that maybe love could look like different things at different points in your life, and that all of those could still be love. Then he felt not so sure about that. Every time his thoughts tried to blaze a trail through love, it seemed more impossible to understand. Every time he turned around he felt that his mind was attempting to construct some new metaphor or analogy that prevented him from really seeing or understanding love. There was the Ocean of Love, out of which he had crawled onto the Shores of Love, only to walk along the Road of Love and into the Forest of Love. And now he felt as though he couldn't even see that forest for the trees, and by the time he had finished drinking his iced tea, he felt dulled and angry about it all.

There were things about Gracie that amused and thrilled him—her creativity, her drive, her skill at facing each new situation as it arose, her radiant eyes. There was a pure connection of heart and body between them that had shaken them awake. Other things, he knew, annoyed him: her tone could be condescending, and there was something about the way she seemed to take success for granted that could grate on him. Love brought out his controlling side, and he had, if he was being honest, avoided it for a while for that very reason. He couldn't figure out how to let things be. His own obsessiveness could be exhausting and frightening. He felt good, at least, that he had started to talk about these things with Gracie. He might need to get some help if it was going to work between them. His need for control needed outlets, etc.

Marvelous decided to get up and go for a stroll to try to stop himself thinking so much. He would think himself all the way to a pub—maybe he would call Mitch, check in. Yes, that's what he'd do. Just then, however, the young woman from the jewelry booth came walking over toward him, smiling—yes, and with the express intent of approaching him. She waved as she grew closer, then called out, "Hi!" She sat down in the green plastic chair beside him.

"Hi," said Marvelous. "Did I forget something?"

The young woman shook her head. She was very attractive. Was she coming up to him to . . . ah, no way. Some nonverbal part of him experienced a flash of possibility, though, enjoyed a vision of noncommittal pleasure that eased his aching mind. "This might sound a little strange," she said, "but I think you need this." She held her closed right hand out. Marvelous, surprised, put his open hand out beneath it after a moment—a moment in which he subtly felt as though he was being called upon to make an important decision. Whatever was happening right now, he was not sure it had ever happened to him before. The young woman placed a smooth, opaque stone in his hand, a banded, many-hued green thing, a funny little shape with rounded corners.

"Goodness," he said. "What is it?"

"Malachite," she said. "Are you thinking about someone?"

Marvelous cocked his head. Most people were, he thought. Did he look like an easy mark? Had she noticed his billfold when he bought the necklace? "I was indeed," he said.

The young woman nodded. Inexplicably, he felt a kind of warmth toward her all of a sudden. "I thought so. I sense things like that sometimes. I feel things. I have a kind of empathic gift. It's hard to explain."

Don't be so hard on yourself, he thought. Well, if she was going to hit him up for a reading, he felt it would do no harm to give her a little extra cash and come to it with an open mind. "Okay," he said. "So, what do you see?"

"When you left with that necklace, I started to feel that you were very confused about something to do with love. There's a kind of block there. You've come up against something new. Malachite is said to help men with love in particular. It'll open your heart chakra. Like, if you're waiting for something to change . . . it helps you do something yourself. Or if you're waiting for perfection, it can help you, um, get over that."

Marvelous sat dumbfounded. He looked at her in a way that he could tell communicated how right on she had been; there was a powerful moment of wordless exchange between them. He would later regret that he broke this spell by asking her how much he owed her for the stone.

"I won't accept anything for it," she said. "It's not just for you. It's for her, too—do you understand what I'm saying?"

Marvelous nodded.

The young woman folded her hands over his, serious but smiling, too. "The world needs more love. Let yourself be transformed."

Marvelous held her gaze. He was moved, and frightened. "Thank you," he said.

She wished him luck. When she had disappeared from view, Marvelous sat turning the stone over in his hand. It's hard to account for the things that give us hope. A little while later, walking outside with the stone in his pocket, he called Mitch. "The strangest thing just happened," he said. "I mean, really strange."

————

The main auditorium at the conference center had plenty of seating. Even still, the six of them were lucky to have returned in time to secure a row, for the crowd had swelled to the point of forcing some latecomers to settle for standing room. Carol, antsier than usual after her truly disquieting encounter with the idea of a boy without a face, craned around in her seat to better scrutinize the bulging audience.

"This must fly in the face of some kind of fire code," she said to Jens, from whom she was separated by Michelle. She thought the Dane handsome, with his golden scruff, his stuffy white button-down and slate-grey trousers—why did so many men think that shorts were appropriate for any occasion come summer? Yes, she liked the figure Jens cut with her son. *And* she liked his accent. He possessed a certain gravitas, an appealing European dignity.

"Too bad for us," Jens said.

"Especially since Gracie's gonna be *on fire* today," said Christopher.

Michelle groaned.

"Hey, you guys," said Marvelous, leaning over Carol (who thought he seemed different somehow—radiant, excitable; she felt proud that he and Gracie had come together at Willowbrook), "don't forget to turn off your cell phones."

Backstage, Gracie stood with her eyes closed, lips drawn into a tight circle to shape a slow, whistling exhale. She had thrown on a black suit for the occasion; the wide collar of her shirt spread over the lapels as though it might, at any moment, take flight. She knew she looked good today: professional, imposing. She tried to remind herself that however terrified she might feel on the inside, she projected a strong image of confidence and authority. So much depended on perception. Even still, as this gulf between inner fear and outer calm widened, her sense of a troubling abyss at the center of it all became ever more acute. What she really wanted to do was to walk out on stage, throw herself down on the lectern, and weep before the gathered audience. No, what she really wanted to do was to blind them all with the white-hot light of her oratorical brilliance, move *them* to tears, leave them on their knees, wailing, clinging to their theater seats as though begging for mercy in the midst of a massacre. No, no—what she really wanted to do was go home, back to Berkeley, and never lay eyes on another human being again. What she really wanted to do was to disappear.

She took another deep breath and clasped her hands together. She could hear her heart pounding, and the wide, simmering sound of the auditorium full of people. What she really *had* to do, if this was going to be what it was meant to be, was to fling herself into that gaping, hungry abyss. The source of all fear, and of all miraculous light; the abyss was what people had paid to see. Not her, really—they had paid to hear a voice call up to them from somewhere in the pit, to say to them, "The water's fine!" She laughed at herself, and then heard herself being introduced, described. Her mind went gloriously blank.

When she walked out onto the stage to a wave of applause, she went through her usual routine. These first concrete gestures she could, at least, count on every time: she moved the lectern, which felt as light as air, to the side of the stage (she used to have someone else do it, but now insisted that she be the one—it signaled to her audience a rebellious informality, and they liked that); she then slipped her flats off and stepped barefoot onto the Persian rug that had been placed, at her instruction, center stage; finally, standing tall, looking out on the tense, expectant crowd, she spoke the two words that communicated, every time, that something extraordinary was about to happen.

"Hello," she said loudly, in a tone of half surprise, as though she had not quite expected such a large and eager showing. She smiled, and then she said, "Good-bye," giving the word firm finality. Closing her eyes, she took three long, deep breaths, feeling as she did so the malleable energetic material of the audience before her. The time had come. She flung herself into the void.

As if she had a choice.

From where Marvelous sat, things seemed to be going well

so far. Gracie looked beautiful—vulnerable and brave before this pack of strangers. Unruly anticipation scratched at him from the inside, an animal trapped behind a door. There was this electrified feeling in the crowd—whatever energy she was putting off, damn: it was strong—but then he felt especially receptive and porous.

Gracie's eyes opened again, and her face struck him as changed: more relaxed, more playful, less mediated by a frenzied backstage crew of thought and intention. For a brief moment fear seized him, and he felt like a child who witnesses some too-convincing transformation of a playmate, a switch from their known personality into a make-believe character so fully formed it seems they might never change back. Some primal instinct reared at the possibility that the collection of qualities he had known as Gracie had just disintegrated and re-formed into an entirely new and unknown entity, and that he would never again be allowed to touch the original.

"Hello!" said Gracie, her voice changed, too. She threw her head back and gave a startling howl, and then, having done so, took in every swath and corner of the approving audience. "It's a blessing, not to mention a treat, to be here with you today." This new way of speaking, this "giving a performance" way, popped with energy and vivacity even as something about it made him recoil. Each word had a bright gloss to it, as though it had been shined with oil.

"It is good to come together for the purpose of reconnecting with our wildness. Do you agree?"

The crowd assented with a forceful "Yes!" It was clear that Gracie had groupies, and that some of them were there today.

"Oh yes, we are *very* pleased," she said. "Pleased to be in each other's energy. You come here today not only as knowable individuals, as a dazzling display of biodiversity, thrilling to the naked eye—I see you there, in all your splendor!" Here the crowd murmured with laughter. "Not only as knowable individuals, but as mysteries. You, *you* are a deep, deep ocean; we are fishermen, floating on the surface with our flimsy rods, our buckets of bait. *You* are a dark, dangerous forest; we are walkers, hesitating at the edge, wondering just how many wolves you contain, and whether or not we might make a satisfying meal. *You*, my friends, are like a library in a dream, full of books that at first glance promise all the knowledge of the world, every secret revealed. Only when we pull one of these dream-books from the shelf, and only when we crack it open, do we see that the text slides off the page before our eyes. Ladies and gentlemen: today you are unreadable."

Christopher dug the nails of his good hand into Jens's leg. It was shaping up to be a bizarre speech, and good grist for the mill. Already he wanted to paint a series of abstract watercolors that served as a visual legend to its fulsome, fatuous come-ons.

"You are unreadable because: before you learned to speak and to please, you were written in a language older than the one on your tongue. You are unreadable because: before you learned to name every movement and sound, you were, like it or not, dancers in an ancient, an unnamable dance. You are unreadable because: no matter how much you have done to wash your hands of that untamable heritage, a trace of the mystery that marks it remains." Here she paused, spreading her arms as if to embrace every man, woman, and child. "*So*. This is the secret we have been keeping from ourselves.

"We have all been taught, or have learned, different ways of keeping this secret. But by far the most common, and by far the most revealing of our era, is to turn away from it. And what do we do when we turn away from it? We go in search of answers, information, knowledge, road maps, solutions. No one *wanders* away from the mystery—*oh* no. We only run. Now, what if I told you that I had no idea what I was going to talk about today?" She smiled as the crowd joined in laughter once more. "What if I told you that if you ran into a friend tomorrow and your friend asked you, 'What was Gracie Sloane's speech about?' that you wouldn't know what to say? Would you be angry? Intrigued? Annoyed? Would you feel cheated? Would you feel like I had wasted your time? 'Well, it wasn't *really* about *anything.*' I want to talk about that word, *about*. When we turn away from that wild essence that is our birthright, it is often because someone has turned the spotlight on it and asked us, nervously, what it's all about. Answers, my friends, are the currency of our time, even if a little seed of doubt in the pit of our stomach is planted every time money changes hands.

"Answers and explanations. 'Oh, a new movie came out today? What's it about?' 'Oh, I see you're reading a book. What's it about?' 'My spouse is mad at me—what's *that* all about?' What's it about? What's it about? What's this about? What's that about? *What's it all about, Alfie?* Well, wouldn't *you* like to know." Laughter. "What I would like to say to you today, you beautiful creatures, is that knowing things is all good and well—our curiosity, after all, is to be cherished. But knowledge, as you probably know, is not the whole story. We may be anxious to jump up at each question, to cry, 'I know the answer! I know!' But there is a part of us that sits back, wild, serene, majestic, and lets out a big old boisterous laugh: HAW-HAW-HAW!" She paused to take a deep breath, letting the surprise of the big old boisterous laugh sink in. "For that part of us understands: there is no joy in knowledge. Knowledge is the carrot on the string, my friends; it makes donkeys of us all. There is no light that lays the whole world bare."

While Gracie retreated momentarily to a side table for a sip of water, a soft commotion sounded from the audience. It quieted as she returned to the center of the stage.

"This we have learned from the time we live in," she continued. "The time that we live in is hungry for knowledge. 'Knowledge, knowledge—mmmm, yummy yummy yummy, eat it up.' 'What are you doing? When are you doing it? Where are we going? How did we get here? What's the weather like outside? What time is the movie playing? What's it about? How can I get from my house to the movie theater? How can I get from point A to point B to point C to point D? How many miles will it be? How much gas will I need? How much does gas cost these days? What happened to my old friend? What are my new friends doing? What's happening in China? How can I be more successful? Who died today? How should I make love to my spouse? Where should we go on vacation? Where should we eat dinner? How much will it cost? Will there be a line? What do other people think of it? Am I even hungry? How will I know? What should I bring? Am I sick?' I say to you now: *ENOUGH!*" A pause. "And in answer to your last question: *yes*. The time that we live in is a sick time. The time that we live in is making us sick."

Christopher observed as the audience responded with shudders of relief and recognition, nods of eager agreement. An audience like this wanted always to be told that it was sick. Next up: the remedy. He imagined an all-sisters doo-wop group called the Remedies rushing out onto the stage in sequined gowns and towering bouffants, the hysterical cries of their fans and the steady thwap of a snare drum.

"This is not to say we aren't grateful for technology. We are grateful for the human effort that has been made to provide the physical world with easy access to information—that easy access that lies in wait in many of the pockets in this very room. But you know and I know that this is not the solution to the so-called *problem* of being alive. There comes a point when that effort to explain, to answer, to map is driven not by curiosity, but by fear. The so-called *problem* of being alive only feels like a *problem* when we have rejected that part of us that doesn't want to argue but wants to scream; that part of us that would rather roam than know, would rather tear life off at the teeth than cut it into manageable little cubes with a fork and knife. This part of us serves a purpose, folks, and when we are not in alignment with that inner wilderness, when we are *trapped* in this feed-back loop of, 'Oh, something doesn't feel right, what do I need to know to shift this emotion? Great, I know it now—wait, I don't feel better. Okay, something definitely still doesn't feel right, what do I need to know to shift this emotion?' The hunt for knowledge leaves a lot out of the picture when it becomes an addiction. We all know what addictions do sooner or later. Sooner or later, our addictions make us sick."

Marvelous, though on the edge of his seat, receptive and enthused in a way only those truly wracked with guilt can be, felt a sharp little stab in his gut when Gracie said "addiction." The sound of the word alone was prickly and discouraging, the shape of it like one of those spiked shells around the chestnuts that fell from the tree outside the post office on the island, a menacing, urchin-looking thing.

"I can hear you wondering: 'And the cure for this addiction?' The cure for this addiction is that which we have thrown away. In this case, not knowing. In this case, faith. In this case, risk. In this case, wildness. And the secret—to return to the subject of secrets—is that there is no secret. We are already accompanied everywhere by our wildness. We have only to turn around to see that it has been following us all this time, dog-like. A dog made scrawny from neglect, perhaps, but a tougher little bugger there has never been. Never a thing more hell-bent on survival, more capable of waiting out its own hunger. Let me say this: when that dog dies, so do you. What I'm going to do, what my next book aims to do, is to teach you how to turn around. What I'm here to do is to teach you how to turn around, kneel down, and feed that dog again. Yes, you may scoff—you may recoil, you may roll your eyes or wrinkle your entire face in disgust. But when you're climbing into bed tonight, pulling the covers up and reaching for that bedside light, I want you to think about this: when you're feeding that dog, there is no word for *risk*, no word for *faith*, no word for *knowing*. When you're feeding that dog, there is joy, but there is no word for joy—enlightenment, but no word for enlightenment. And when you turn that light off, friend, remember this: you are already wild, whether you like it or not. Thank you."

The place erupted with noisy applause. Some people even stood, and though Christopher would have never felt compelled to do so on his own, once all the others had joined in the standing ovation, it was only natural for him to follow suit. As he did so, however, he made the face of a man who has just swallowed vinegar. Since he couldn't clap his hands together, he slapped his thigh.

———

That evening, Christopher and Michelle returned with Jens to his room at the Hotel Max downtown. By the time they had, in a quorum of temporary misanthropy, renounced any further bar-hopping in favor of a private afterparty at the hotel, they were plenty drunk, united too in a frenzy of parody that took as its target Gracie Sloane's speech.

"For when you are aligned with inner wildness," Christopher screeched, staggering through the doorway and into the *modernische* little room, gripping a bottle of whiskey in his good hand, "vibe-self is at peace, *ree-cep-tive* to vibratory vibes."

Jens, though enjoying himself thoroughly, was a less effusive drunk. He entered the room with purpose, hefting first a suitcase and then a black leather duffel bag off the bed so they could all have more space. "Sooner or later," he said, fetching a few glasses, "our addictions make us sick."

While he poured whiskey and ginger ale over ice, Michelle threw her arms around his neck from behind, burying her face in his back. She had already cried once that evening, after excusing herself from a bar booth for the third time to try to call Bradford. He must have gotten a new phone, because every time the call went through to voicemail, she was greeted— *insulted*—by that eternally foreboding saying:

You've reached the voice mailbox of—

—at which point she promptly hung up, before the bitch could spit out the seven-digit string of numbers that meant Bradford was an asshole, or dead, or just an asshole. Now she felt like she might cry again. "Where are we?" she said, parroting Gracie. "When did we get here? Where are we going? How much will it cost? Is it hot outside? Where's my purse? There it is. What's it all about?" She pressed her face harder into Jens's back and, sufficiently muzzled by his shirt and his flesh, screamed.

"As you can see," said Jens, gathering her up and handing her a drink, "we are already wild."

Christopher sat on the sill by the open window. He produced and lit a cigarette.

"You can't smoke in here," said Jens.

"Oh, stop," said Christopher. He leaned his head a little further out the window, peeking over the suicide guard and blowing smoke into the night. "As you can see, my head is not inside."

"Christopherwouldyounotsmokeinthehotelroom," Michelle said. It amazed her how quickly he could turn into a stubborn brat—if he kept this up, she feared that Jens would fall out of love as quickly as he had fallen into it. Yes, she had been *right* about the two of them! So right. Maybe she should be a goddamn matchmaker for a living. This was not a good turn for her thoughts to take: soon everybody in the world would be matched up by her matchmaking, and she would be alone, the sad, singular remainder in a world of happy couples and solved problems. Suddenly the whole picture of the hotel room before her, orange and white and mirrored and bright with Christopher and Jens in it, rushed at her in a single, horrid frame, slamming against her as though someone had stamped her with it on the forehead. If the party was over, why was it still happening?

Christopher, after tormenting them a moment longer, said, "Watch this." He blew all the air out of his body, then used the emptied-out, urgent hunger of his lungs to suck up, in one uninterrupted go, the entire remaining length of his cigarette. He felt himself swell like a poison balloon, tried not to laugh, flicked the wasted butt out the window, then collapsed forward in a fit of coughing while a huge cloud of smoke billowed from his mouth. "All done!" he cried hoarsely.

"All done," Michelle said, leaning back against the head-board of the bed.

Jens, who had stepped into the bathroom, returned with a large white towel. He held it by one of the short ends and began to flap it in long, angry gestures, trying to move the hanging smoke out the window.

"I surrender!" said Christopher, who had settled into a rest-ful position stretched out on the floor. "Just kidding."

"God, you are such a . . . *I don't know what!*" said Jens. Mi-chelle noted that, as before, their little quarrels were laced with desire. How great, she thought a little bitterly, taking a big drink from her glass. It would probably be better if she disappeared so that the two of them could get down to business; she was alone, they were on the brink of love or at least a wild bout of lovemaking—why the hell did she hang around? Christopher had been downright gallant, it was true. But then something had been swelling in her chest with each new contemptuous thought, and now, too full of fear and hate and injustice to fit any more, she broke down. It took a half minute of tears and twitching before Jens came to lie by her side, pulling her head to his shoulder and stroking her hair. The room fell silent, almost reverently so. She didn't feel like talking anymore. She didn't feel like asking for help with words, especially now that it had become, in an instant of collapse, so very evident that she needed some. Christopher, prone on the floor at the end of the bed, probably sensed every detail of the pain she felt passing through her, probably saw it on the back of his eyelids as an intricate embroidery, a paintable vision. Jens, at her side, had become unspoken understanding made flesh. And even as she poured these last waves of sorrow into her friend, with her nose running and her cheek damp against his fancy shirt, a warm darkness crept up on her, tucking her into the heavy bedding of oblivion. She must remember, when she pulled herself together again, to tell him about the book she had been reading: *A Clean and Simple Line: The Triumph of Scandinavian Design*.

Many minutes had passed, with all audible sniffles long since ceased, by the time a great idea occurred to Christopher. He knew that Bradford had done Michelle wrong; he knew she was about to be unmoored, lost for a day-to-day thread of purpose. And in the back of his mind the landscape of his own exciting plight loomed, sunny and mountainous, a backdrop to the gloomy, barren plain of her prospects. It might be just the right moment to suggest something adventurous.

The thought of going back to Rhode Island, to the sterile halls of art school, had sickened him for some time. He had learned so much more in the last two days than he would in another semester of lectures and critiques. Jens was an absolute dreamboat, even if he had an insensitive streak. Though they hardly knew each other yet, the coming week would undoubt-edly confirm for Christopher what he had already started to suspect: that love required he go ahead and take a risk. He saw himself, clear as day, overseas, further from his family than ever before, the tie that bound them snapped at last by the sheer undeniability of distance. Even school remained too close to them; it was as good as a playpen in the other room. Didn't some ancient tradition exist, in some culture somewhere in history—some buried, strong-boned culture he intended now to exhume—that demanded every son walk away from his mother and his father and their home, not just temporarily or as an experiment, but *irrevocably*? Something in him longed for those barbarian days, that feral era, its fur matted with blood, when one only heard word of one's son if by ignominy, infamy, or glory his deeds became part of oral legend—an echo or cry, the only mercy carried across the merciless gulf of the world. Not a quick email or call just to *check in*. Gross! It was this train of thought that drove him to announce, above the wave of nauseated stimulation brought on by his bombshell dose of nicotine, "I'm moving to Berlin. Michelle, you're coming with me."

When no response came, he managed, with the help of the edge of the bed, to pull himself up to his knees. Jens and Michelle had fallen asleep. They lay half wrapped in a pose of sorrow and succor, half splayed. Jens's mouth had dropped open just slightly, and if Christopher was not mistaken, he could detect a gem-like glint of drool forming at the corner of his mouth. He looked, for the first time that day, positively vulnerable, and for this he liked him all the more. He lurched over to a seat at the little table in the corner. It would be such fun to move to Berlin. "After all," he said aloud, imitating the words his mother had spoken earlier that summer, "I've come to believe we've been put on this planet to have as much fun as possible. And Berlin is known to be very fun these days for people like us." Neither of the sleepers showed any signs of hearing him.

The sketchbook came out of his bag, and though the angle was an odd one, he began to draw, in his still psychotic-looking left-handed scrawl, a portrait of his hapless models. As usual, it took only a minute or so for time to start disintegrating; urgency, which had been on its deathbed, died, sheer emergence replacing it, just as a charming host succeeds by sweeping into a room, beguiling her guests with the impression that they need never leave, indeed that leaving and arriving belonged to a separate, more vulgar reality. In this manner each shaky, unpredictable line he drew looked finally as though it had always been there. Michelle's hair, made from shadow and light, had always been there, just as it was in this moment that wasn't. The surprised crease between Jens's eyebrows, on paper a mere faint furrow of darkness, had always been there, as had the fluted arc of the lampshade beside them.

———

A few days later, Frank woke after a long sleep. Carol was not in bed beside him. The book about Genghis Khan that he had been reading before bed lay open facedown on his nightstand. The light glowing around the edge of the window shades alerted him to its already being somewhere in the neighborhood of 10:00 a.m.—late for him. During his unusual bout of illness—psychosomatic, perhaps, maybe even prophetic, arriving as it did just in time for him to ignore everybody else and consider *The Widdicombe Way*'s potential eventual publication—he had managed to sleep in every morning. He made a mental note to write an essay titled "On Sleeping In." Yes, his thoughts had regained their spry, sporting spirit. Vim and vigor beckoned to him like those twins in *The Shining*: "Come play with us." Soon, he thought, soon. Reveling in the glory that his strength would return after all, he rose from bed and made for the shower.

What a swell job Carol had done fixing up that bathroom. Tiles of a somethingish shade of mint or sage, marble sinks of a marbley hue. Truth be told, called upon to describe the room when he was not standing in it, he would probably have butchered the details. However, the *feeling* it all created—of cleanliness, confidence, luxury, a feeling that his life was somehow a natural life—made him happy to start his days there. "On the General Feeling of a Room"—yes. It came as no surprise that this idea popped into his head while he stood in the pressurized spray of water, scrubbing himself with a soapy sea sponge and turning this way and that; he had already written a short chapter on the importance of showering for generating ideas. In fact, he would expand upon it later, starting a new paragraph with the words: *Many of the best ideas in this book came to me in the shower.*

A damn good idea took hold of him just then—one nothing to do with the book.

After toweling off and dressing, he jotted down some notes, then set out toward the faint sounds of life issuing from downstairs. The green circular sofa, the potted palms, the leather chairs, the splendid ottomans: all of it looked like home now, in that peculiar way that anything can once you've returned to it enough times. His wife sat on the dark grey loveseat, looking regal with her hair in an updo, a pair of pearl earrings on. A certain actress came to mind, though he could not say who; in any case, he resolved to tell her the things he had noticed about her.

"Hi!" she called, and then, "Don't move!" She held her phone out to take his picture. "Actually, move a little to the left. What great light."

"Like so?" said Frank, who did as she said but also struck a thoughtful pose, holding his chin between thumb and forefinger, surveying a stack of decorating magazines on a table in the middle distance.

"Oh, you goof," she said. "Come look."

He crossed to her, sat by her side. "You've changed your hair."

"Do you like it?"

He did and said so as she patted it with her free hand. With the other she showed him a photo in which he looked a bit like landed gentry casually dressed. He chuckled, which set her off laughing, too. His fondest moments with Carol had always been full of laughter: hers, a kind of elegant collapse; his, a loud braying at its most unguarded. He wrapped his arm around her and kissed her forehead.

262 EVAN JAMES

"Somebody's happy today," she said. "You seem so much better."

"I feel that life will soon be mine to live again," he said, affecting a soft English accent.

"Oh, darling," said she, doing the same. "How delightful."

A French press of probably lukewarm coffee stood on the table before them. Frank got up to grab a cup for himself; returning, he announced, "I've had a damn good idea, Carol. Damn good."

"Damn me once, shame on you; damn me twice . . . color me intrigued!" Carol set her phone aside—she could multitask with the best of them but had picked up from Gracie a habit of trying to give her full attention to friends or loved ones. "Does it have to do with chickens?"

"You never did get those chickens, did you?" he said.

"*We*, Frank," she said. "*We* never got those chickens. And it's never too late, you know."

He feared opening this subject again after the chickens discussed what seemed like more than just a few months ago had miraculously failed to appear. He attributed this to his habit of buying very good eggs at the farmers market in town. "*Oui, mais oui*," he said. "But no—it's about France."

Carol's eyes darkened. For an instant it was as though he had brought up an ex-girlfriend, or some imagined Continental interloper who had once threatened to destroy their marriage. *France*. That bitch. "I'm all ears," she said.

"What if next summer, instead of going to Auvergne, I invite Channing and the others to come stay here for a spell?"

Carol looked at Frank, who, after disturbing her earlier in the summer with his erratic moods and behavior, now appeared so relaxed and sane as to cause another kind of suspicion entirely. While confirming her original intention that Willow-brook become a place where they could refresh their senses and reclaim their sanity in a chaotic world, she felt in some respect that the success of her project somehow amplified just how chaotic the world remained. "I think that's a wonderful idea!" she said.

The two began, like old times, to riff together, what Carol knew Gracie would call to "cocreate": to imagine what the future could be like. "Think of all the cooking you could do, Frank." "I have a whole year to bulk up the wine cellar." "Are any of them allergic to cats?" Carol threw in that she might invite a few people from her own network as well, and that they could build the Midsummer Feast into an annual tradition—something a little different each year, with a mix of people from different corners of their lives. "We should warn them, though," said Frank, "that Cupid has been known to strike at the famous Widdicombe Midsummer Feast. Who would've guessed: the gardener and the guru?"

They chatted on these pleasant topics a little longer before beginning to putter their separate ways: Frank to the kitchen to fix himself a fortifying late-summer breakfast, Carol to her office to perish on the chaise a while before everyone returned for afternoon tea. She called it "afternoon tea" though had never obeyed the rules and regulations of the English teatime tradition; she simply liked tea and snacks and people, and therefore would call it "tea" whenever she could manage to bring these things together. She turned on the radio in her office, a sleek model given to her by Frank as a birthday gift, and turned the volume low; she preferred her dozing set to a barely audible background noise of classical music, ideally something with some Baroque formal grandeur like Vivaldi's *La stravaganza*, at any rate not upsetting Beethoven or one of Erik Satie's *Gnossiennes*, which made her feel as though she were floating in an unreasonable and ill-formed netherworld. They were playing some kind of concertante for clarinets—fine, she would live. Curling up beside the reliably lazy Princess Magdalena, whose grey tail twitched in a contented rhythm, she closed her eyes.

Sleep had eluded her the night before. While Frank had sunk ever deeper into an apparently nourishing slumber, she had turned this way and that, convinced that each new rotation would bring sweet oblivion. With a lifetime of occasional insomnia under her belt, however, she knew eventually to give up the fight and do something else. She knew that she needed a new project to shape her days—she had slept well during the redecoration of Willowbrook, the completion of which had afflicted her with a kind of creative postpartum. Having sent out feelers and inquiries, a possible lineup of visiting artists and writers who were either friends or friends of friends was taking shape for the coming months: a Colombian American painter whose work had been featured in *Inside Places*, and whose canvases reflected her interest in "lowbrow North American cultural toxicity pitted against a chaotic and sacred feminine"; an unaffiliated scholar of civilizations and languages, the eccentric son of a San Francisco family she knew who wanted to spend a month quietly perfecting his literary Persian (before Jens came on the scene, she had wondered about him as a match for Christopher but ended up thinking they might be too much alike); a poet who wanted to use Willowbrook as a base of operations from which to conduct "a necromantic investigation into the literary madness of Theodore Roethke." Still, this left *her*. She had read an interview somewhere in which an artist or musician said that he always worked at three in the morning, since that was the hour that God talked to him. With this in mind, she did her hair and dressed up a little bit—it couldn't hurt to look one's best before the Divine!—and decided to give herself a tarot reading.

The cards came out, as did the little book that suggested interpretations. She had been playing around with these things over the summer, now and then reading Gracie's fortune—just a bit of fun. She shuffled the deck for a minute or so, pouring her intention into it. *What's next for me?* Then she cut it and laid out for herself a simple three-card reading. Out came the Three of Wands, the Eight of Cups, the Two of Cups.

She stared at this spread a moment. She preferred the Major Arcana cards like the Magician or Death—to be faced with these puny ones always seemed like such an insult, suggesting as they did that her fate could be summed up without the inclusion of any truly significant or dramatic figures. Almost without conscious awareness, she found she had flipped another card from the deck—the Page of Wands—and then another—the Hanged Man. "Now we're getting somewhere," she muttered, pulling another—the King of Cups. Carried away by a kind of rebellious glee, the pace of her new generous mode of fortune-telling quickened, and one after another the cards came down on the table face up, her interest piqued only when some major card appeared, rising above the static of cups and pentacles and swords and wands. There went the World! There went the Fool! And look, who was that? Why, it was the Empress, followed closely by the Devil, the Sun, the Chariot, and the Tower.

Before too long, she had exhausted the deck. As she looked down at the full range of possibilities in a heap, she felt clever and subversive. Then, however, she began to wish that Gracie were awake so that she could share this joke, and her sleeplessness, with her friend. And that was the crux of it: it wasn't God she needed, but friendship. She suspected that if you did friendship right, they might amount to the same thing, though she wasn't sure exactly how that worked. Some things keep their power by remaining unexamined. In any case, even though she and Gracie had had their ups and downs over the summer—the creative temperament, she thought, must account for some of this—Gracie's imminent departure now filled her with sadness. With whom would she take shelter from the men (even the gay ones, who could be every bit as, well, *male* as their hetero counterparts)? To whom could she turn for deep understanding, for the feeling that she might be seen and affirmed for her true and whole self? Who the hell would she *talk to*?

A grand idea took hold of her. She hastened to her laptop and began to write an email:

Dearest Gracie,

I'm writing this in a fit of inspiration and during a bout of insomnia. I know I've said it to you in person several times by now, but I want to say it again. Your presence at Willowbrook this summer was a breath of fresh air. Your wisdom, your humor, your kindness, your vision. All of this means so much to me. I would have gone INSANE here without you. You know as well as I do that life can be so lonely, even when it's full of family and activity. I am still thinking about some of the conversations we've had on this topic.

I am absolutely thrilled for you that you found love this summer, and that our little house on the Puget Sound provided a productive atmosphere for you to CREATE. Selfishly, might I add that your friendship kept me stable during a time of strange transition? I'm going to miss you terribly!

Which brings me to an idea I've just had. Gracie, if anyone has taught me to listen to the voice inside, and to trust that my own ideas have value, it's you. Here's what I'm thinking: this winter, I want to have a retreat here just for women. I want us to dream it up together. I'll send Frank packing to play tennis in San Diego or Miami for a couple of weeks. Imagine it: creative gals gathered here just to get away from it all for a while. Inspiring one another. Uplifting one another. Healing, for God's sake. Oh, I know it's gloomy here in the winter, but that's nothing a blazing fire and a whole lot of Beaujolais can't fix!

Am I crazy, or does this sound like it might just work?

Warmly,
Carol

Carol knew she was not crazy, and that it would work if, as Marvelous might say, they *worked it*. And after she had saved this email as a draft—she would send it after Gracie left, so as not to put on too much immediate pressure—she walked into the *salon* feeling excited and hopeful. The sun had just started to come up then, and the sky was beginning to lighten. If Gracie was willing to climb aboard, if she was willing to take a chance and play, well, then her own hope might take on a greater meaning. She could throw its doors open and welcome friends in. They could share this world. Maybe then she might start to feel at home in it again.

———

Marvelous and Gracie returned to Willowbrook around three, when the clear day outside had grown uncomfortably hot. The intrepid couple had been celebrating together after Green Dawn. They had gone out to a high-end Vietnamese restaurant that Gracie adored and visited any time she came to Seattle. There Marvelous had presented her with the carnelian necklace; she had gasped, shouted "The Singer's Stone!" and, after admiring it for a minute, put it on with his help. Then, still riding a stage high, she had sung a few bars of "Too Darn Hot," which made him both blush for her and laugh. ("*I'd like to sup . . . with my baby tonight . . .*," Ann Miller? *Kiss Me, Kate*? No? Cole Porter?") The story about the malachite stone had moved her: his openness to the extraordinary, to divine interventions and serendipity, boded well. During a hike in the Grand Forest, when he began to fret a little about her returning to Berkeley, she took him aside, said, "There are these things called planes," and kissed him by a short wooden bridge. She added, then, "You'll like it there. Even though it's changed a lot since the last time you saw it. Nature there is still beautiful. Glorious, actually. We'll walk up in the hills." Yes, they had decided to pursue the complex love between them, little by little, "one day at a time," to give their thing a go long-distance. Though she trusted her own gut, Gracie had also called a psychic she consulted on occasion to talk about it. "Give it time," he had said, "see what develops. In the meantime, enjoy each other." "How banal!" she had cried, both seized by angst and amused by her own impatience. The psychic and his querent had laughed together. Then he said, "I don't know what else to tell you. That's what I see."

Now she and Marvelous sat side by side in the *salon*. Frank, in one of his fits of cutting-through-the-bullshit that she so admired, was amusing himself by detailing all of the ways in which he would keep Marvelous busy and out of trouble while Gracie was by herself in Berkeley. "I'll be feeding him grapes and fine artisanal cheeses while you're down there finishing your book. I know which *I'd* rather be doing. We'll take long, romantic walks around the island, play couples tennis, plant vegetables. Yes, that's it, we'll be thick as thieves, just a couple of very close friends, that's all . . ."

"Friends who go to the movies together," volunteered Marvelous.

"Friends who keep fit together," said Frank. "And gossip about their loved ones."

Marvelous laughed. "Foot rubs!" he cried.

"Of course," said Frank, "you can rub my feet while I finish *my* book. That's what friends are for."

Marvelous turned his head between Gracie and Frank. "Wait a minute. Am I the only person in this house who isn't writing a book?"

"Hey, you should start one, buddy!" said Frank. "It's fantastically easy. You'll wonder why you didn't start years ago."

Gracie groaned. "What have I gotten myself into?"

"You can call it . . ." Frank pondered a moment. "I know: *My Years with Frank: A Foot-Rubber's Story*. Yes sir, we'll just be a couple of close male friends writing books together, clucking away like little darlings."

"Carol!" cried Gracie, craning her neck to look toward the kitchen. "Help me!"

"That reminds me," said Marvelous, "weren't you going to start keeping chickens?"

Frank narrowed his eyes at his friend. He held up a menacing forefinger. "Don't you say another goddamn word."

Carol, her regal hair slightly mussed from her nap, came in to say they should help themselves to tea and things in the kitchen, which they did, returning with cups of Assam variously whitened, and plates of triangular sandwiches—egg and watercress, cucumber. "The children were supposed to pick up some sweet things," she said, settling in. She had taken to calling Christopher, Michelle, and Jens "the children." "God knows where they've run off to."

"We'll let them be young," said Gracie. She blew on her tea.

"There will be hell to pay if I don't taste a scone today," said Frank.

Fortunately for the younger generation, they arrived mere minutes later. Christopher led the charge, entering the room with a long-suffering look on his face. "They simply refuse to speak English!" he cried.

"Christopher!" said Carol, holding a sandwich triangle in the air. "That's not a very nice thing to say about anyone."

"Michelle and Jens have been intentionally excluding and alienating me all day by speaking Danish," said Christopher, throwing himself onto the grey sofa with a growl. The polyglots in question entered the room then, performing a private conversation with wide, sparkling eyes. They held brown bakery bags in their hands. "You *see*?" said Christopher. He cast his gaze upon the tea snacks. "My demoralization is complete."

"You had better start learning now," said Frank, nodding in Jens's general direction, "or your husband will forever have the upper hand. As I've told you before, marriage is a state of never-ending psychological warfare."

Carol scoffed. She threw a piece of bread at her husband.

"Don't mind him," she said to Jens, who looked somewhat uncomfortable. His relatively reserved manner stood out among the Widdicombes and their friends. Michelle said something to him in Danish, and then they both laughed. "I for one find it refreshing to have a foreign tongue in the house," Carol continued.

"Thank you," said Jens.

"I'm writing that down," said Christopher. "Then burning it."

Carol sighed. "We are so blinkered here in America."

"Is marijuana legal in Denmark, Jens?" Frank asked.

"Marijuana?" said Jens, who was being pulled by Michelle toward the kitchen. "No. Though it is tolerated."

"Here it's legal, for medicinal purposes," said Frank. He looked around the room at those gathered. "I think it may be high time I got a prescription."

Christopher gave his father a sad look. "It might help with *your* pain," he said, "but what about ours?"

Michelle and Jens poured tea for themselves and for Christopher in the kitchen, and arranged scones and cakes on a platter. They had, it was true, been tormenting Christopher all day by speaking to each other in Danish—Michelle's was rusty but still serviceable enough to sustain this game. It only seemed fair to take Christopher down a notch every now and again, given how well he had it. Oh, sure, he could tell them that their exclusion of him compounded his "already profound sense of otherness," he could respond to them with a dramatic monologue about how their "flaunting" of their friendship only reminded him how "truly friendless" his own life had been, and how, under the circumstances, *he* should not be the one "feeling like a faggoty third wheel for the umpteenth time." She felt for him, she really did. At the same time, she wished he would cheer up a little. He complained a lot for someone who appeared to be surrounded by so much good, and who had gone some way toward creating an already remarkable life for himself. Even thinking this, she imagined how he might take issue with the word *remarkable*, break it down into a curse somehow, turn being merely remarked upon into evidence of an inescapably sorrowful fate. It's funny, she thought, the way we internalize one another, become, for a time at least, the means through which we think about life. This must be part of what it meant to know someone.

And then there would be the part that relied not on thinking, but on seeing, on hearing. Returning to the others, she saw that Jens had taken a seat next to Christopher. There was room for her, too, but at the edge of the gathered group she paused, arrested by a feeling of absence. In comparable moments that summer, Bradford had often sat among them, gesturing as he matched wits with the Widdicombes, seducing them with his charm. Startling, but she had briefly forgotten him. What had it been like to be him, sitting there that morning months ago, watching her, saying the words *most dolphinately*? Why should it cause her a jolt of fear now, standing by the circular green sofa, to feel that she would never really be sure?

"Everything okay over there?" That was Carol speaking to her.

"Yes," she said. "I was just admiring the room. I've said it before, but I love this room so much."

"It really is the perfect room," said Gracie.

Carol beamed. "Thank you."

Michelle took a seat then. The many-named cat appeared, rubbing itself against her legs, and afternoon tea continued without a hitch; nobody mentioned or even alluded to the young man who had come through Willowbrook earlier that summer, the well-dressed family friend with his lust for life, his screenplay, his jokes. Michelle settled into a quiet, watchful mood. People never ceased to amaze her. Just when you thought you knew them, they went and did something surprising. But what really killed her—and what she felt she had only begun, in a small way, to understand—was the extent to which a person could surprise themselves. What had she really been doing, working for the Widdicombes? Had it all been preparing her for *this*? It seemed absurd that any one thing should lead to another, or that anyone could look back—even just over the course of a season—and see causes, effects. A warm feeling filled her as she entertained, for the moment, the possibility that the Widdicombes, whose mouths were now moving as they carried on in their own language, and whose gazes were swinging first to this person and now that, drawing them into their world, had seen something in her that she couldn't, or wouldn't see—at any rate, that she didn't. Perhaps it was all unconscious, she mused. Perhaps all this time they had been, in their weird way, loving her, steering her—knowing, too, that she would leave them. Perhaps they were about to break a bottle of champagne against her bow.

Jens nudged her then, and asked her, in Danish, what she was thinking about. ("Monster!" whispered Christopher.) She smiled at him. Later that evening, she would take him to see the phosphorescence at Hidden Cove. She would show him how you could fan your foot across the wet sand and glittering light would follow in its wake like a comet's tail before disappearing. She would throw a rock into the glowing bluish-green water, show him how the splash lit up into a burst of sparkling stars. Later still she would check her bank balance online, just to be sure that it hadn't all been a dream, and that the Widdicombes had really been paying her with a wild generosity that, whatever its hidden motivation, she profoundly appreciated in that moment. Then she would start looking up flights to Berlin; sublets, neighborhoods; German language schools. Someone had to tend to the details, after all.

But to Jens's question: what was she thinking about?

"Nothing," she said. She sipped her tea.

"Finally," said Christopher, "a word we can *all* understand."

Acknowledgments

I would like to express my gratitude to the Corporation of Yaddo, the Carson McCullers Center for Writers and Musicians, and the Virginia Center for the Creative Arts, all of which granted me time and space to work on this novel. Thank you also to the University of Iowa and the La Hart-Van Bortels for their support.

I am indebted to Rakesh Satyal for his concise and pragmatic editorial guidance, his kindness, and his good humor. I have been grateful every step of the way to work with the wonderfully skilled and upbeat team at Atria. Thanks are due to Loan Le for all of her editorial assistance. Robert Grom came up with the clever and colorful cover. Kyoko Watanabe created the elegant interior design. Thanks to Patricia Romanowski and Laura Tatham for their eagle-eyed copy edits.

My deepest gratitude to Jin Auh and Jessica Friedman at the Wylie Agency, who have worked for years helping to place my work and who found this book a fantastic home.

Thank you to Beowulf Sheehan for the author photo, and to Rizwan Alvi for his assistance.

I learned so much from my time at the Iowa Writers' Workshop and have many people to thank who I met there. First and foremost, thank you to Lan Samantha Chang, who called me while I was at work one day to talk about my novel, and whose guidance, support, and example have been crucial to me for nine years since. Thank you to Michelle Huneven, whose generous readings of this book in earlier forms were invaluable and whose mentorship and friendship have sustained me for many years. I would also like to thank Andrew Sean Greer, Allan Gurganus, James Alan MacPherson, and Wells Tower, all of whom encouraged my work and offered recommendations. I would be remiss not to thank Connie Brothers, Jan Zenisek, and Deb West for their extensive support. Thank you to Tai Chang for occasionally building ant civilizations with me and for drawing and discussing ants, penguins, and other fascinating creatures.

I owe a debt of gratitude to many other writers I met in Iowa for their encouragement, their openness, their perspectives, their productive arguments, their distinct varieties of humor, and the many hours spent hanging out and talking about books, movies, ideas, music, ourselves, other people, art, and life. While the list is long, I would like to thank especially those with whom I have continued these conversations, either in my head or elsewhere: Emma Borges-Scott, Ellie Catton, Ossian Foley, Angela Flournoy, Gerardo Herrera, Carmen Maria Machado, Kannan Mahadevan, Kyle McCarthy, Ayana Mathis, Ben Mauk, Andrew Nance, Amy Parker, Yuly Restrepo, Rebecca Rukeyser, Bennett Sims, Justin Torres, Steve Toussaint, and Tony Tulathimutte.

I spent a number of the years it took to write this book working in bookstores, where good humor, intelligence, and the clash of ideas kept me sane (but not *too* sane), and I want to express my gratitude to those who hired me and with whom I had the privilege of working. A special thank-you to Jan Weismiller, Terry Cain, Kathleen Johnson, and Paul Ingram at Prairie Lights. And another special thank-you to the crew at Three

Lives & Co.: Toby Cox, Troy Chatteron, Joyce McNamara, Carol Wald, Miriam Chotiner-Gardner, Ryan Murphy, Jo Stewart, Nora Shychuck, and Ruby Smith.

Thank you to everyone at Pierrepont School: you have helped make juggling teaching and writing rewarding and fun.

Love and gratitude to my family, who have been endlessly supportive. A special thank-you to my mother, whose philosophical sense of humor, love of stories, and quick wit have shaped and inspired me. Thank you to my brother Tad Mitsui and to Tifani Mitsui, and to my nieces and nephews, Mariko, Ryota, and Koji, who have brought so much joy into all of our lives. Thank you to Jim-Dad Macpherson, and to my younger siblings, Mike and Mary Macpherson.

Lastly, thank you, Hilton: your patience, partnership, love, and laughter brighten my days.

About the Author

Evan James was born and raised in the Pacific Northwest and is a graduate of the Iowa Writers' Workshop. His work has appeared in *The New York Times*, *Travel + Leisure*, *Oxford American*, *The Iowa Review*, and many other publications. He has received awards and fellowships from Yaddo, Virginia Center for the Creative Arts, Lambda Literary, the Elizabeth Kostova Foundation, and Arteles Creative Center. He lives in New York.